Crumpled

First printed April 2003. Re-Printed July 2011.

Published by: Fortunediablo Productions Ltd
www.fortunediablo.com

Contents

ACKNOWLEDGMENTS

To Roger for a lifetime of laughter and your belief that I could do this. To James for your faith and unwavering support - I couldn't have done it without you. To Mom and Dad - a constant source of joyous material. To Jack Rosenthal for telling me that I could write! To Simon Cutler and Andi Carless - your laughter rang inside my head while I worked on this book. To Sybil Ruth at the Midlands Arts Centre and Cynthia Rogerson at The Literary Consultancy for giving me the confidence to show my work to the world. To David Pearman for your kindness and technical advice. To Phil and Dill at Laughing Gravy for the superb front cover and all the lads at A.D.S for your help. And finally - to Levy - my shadow - always by my side - a constant companion and an inspiration for this book. Thankyou.

Tilly my therapist sat opposite me in the counselling suite. She was asking me to sum up my feelings in just one word and I was struggling to respond. Disorientated, exhausted, barking mad with a tendency to wander around with my pants on my head. Whatever, I was falling apart and she held the glue to put Humpty back together again. After what seemed like forever, I remembered the word, crumpled. That was me. Completely crumpled. Celebrities check into the Priory, I was about to be carted off to the nearest Crumple Clinic.

CHAPTER ONE

Remember Your Breathing

I'm running late again. Well, I'm late anyway but not running. I'm not built for speed. More of a sauntering pace. I'm late because I no longer wear a watch. Since I joined the ranks of the unemployed and gave up clock-watching as a career, I don't see the point. I no longer have to be anywhere at any given time so why carry an appliance on your wrist to remind you of the fact? The Health Centre is just across the main road so if I put a spurt on I'll be there in a few minutes. Group Therapy today. Six of us Trifle Heads all coming together to share our sponge experiences, and Tilly of course. Tilly the therapist. Tilly the Top Banana. However she puts up with us droning on, week after week, I'll never know. If she's on medication herself I'd like some please. Never yawns, never shows the slightest sign of boredom or sheer despair. Like I say, Top Banana. I wonder if therapist's have their own therapist's for when things get on top of them?

Right, think that's everything, keys, fags, lighter, Giant Size Mars Bar, that should do it. Off we go. Rather I should say, off I go. This is one venue where donkey-sized dogs are not allowed. Levy will have to entertain himself for an hour while I'm out. He's got a half hundred-weight of Winalot Shapes and the remote control for the telly so he should be okay.

I'm just dashing past number 17 when Mary hammers on the window with a cucumber. She normally hammers on the window with a walking stick but she's obviously in the middle of preparing a salad.

"Cassie, can you give us a hand?" she pleads.

"Course. What's up Mary?"

"I've dropped my teeth down the back of the kitchen table. Buggering things!" I resist the temptation to laugh and head up the path instead.

"No problem. Can you open the door?"

Mary is ninety-three and a martyr to all sorts of problems. Arthritis, crumbling hips, poor eyesight and now trampolining teeth apparently. It takes several concerted efforts and the help of the cucumber before the door finally creaks open. She is obviously distressed. I can tell by her flushed cheeks and the fact that she's wearing a tea-cosy on her head.

"Everything alright Mary?"

"Our Geoffrey's popping in later with his young lady and I've gone and dropped my best set behind the table." I try to remain calm in a crisis and reassure her.

"Not to worry. We'll soon get you sorted."

She shuffles off slowly in the direction of the kitchen and I follow at a snails pace. You can't really hurry an ancient invalid along can you? It's not decent. Even if you do have an appointment and are already late. Hey ho. Three hours later we finally reach the kitchen, both of us exhausted from the effort.

"Down there, I tried poking them out with this but no joy," she quivers, waving the cucumber under my nose.

"I see them, let's have a go eh?" The teeth are sitting grinning at us both. Wedged behind the far leg of the formica kitchen table. I crouch down on my knees and slither along on my belly to get to them. They put up a helluva fight but I'm well hard and they eventually give up and come quietly.

"There you go, all sorted," I grin, handing her the gnashers.

"Bless you. I couldn't face our Geoffrey with my old set in. His young lady's an accountant, what on earth would she think?"

"Never mind. Would you like me to rinse them off for you?"

"If you could. There's a bit of buggering broccoli stuck in the front. Can you get it out?" The buggering broccoli turns out to be a slither of green carpet and it takes me about ten minutes to dislodge it. I can only assume that Mary had taken a tumble in the past and chewed on the axminster until help arrived.

"There you go. All done."

"Thank you. What would I do without you," she grins, flashing me a huge gummy smile.

"I have to dash Mary, sorry."

"I'll see you to the door."

"NO... honest, I'll find my own way out thanks." As I turn to leave, she shoves something into my hand. I try to decline but she insists. As I reach the front door I find it's a black jelly baby... minus the head.

Now I'm forced to break into a slight jog, while trying not to break into a sweat. I feel it's most unattractive to arrive anywhere dripping in perspiration don't you? The room we have our sessions in has very little ventilation and I don't want to be labelled as Stinky. I have enough problems without adding that one to the list. The rest of the group already think I'm retarded. This is because on my first visit I got lost in the maze of corridors and ended up in the wrong room. I waited for ages and was getting quite panicky when an assortment of odd people began to drift in. I was wearing one of Jack's gardening jumpers and a pair of old Levi's and was shocked to see the rest of the group were in an assortment of lurex halter-necks and high heeled shoes. It was only when their instructor arrived that I realised I was in the Salsa Class.

They rent out the room apparently. Every third Thursday in the month. I stayed for a while, not wanting to appear rude. I even had a bash at the gyrating groin section but it wasn't for me. Some people are born to dance. I am not one of them. My breasts take on a life of their own on the dance floor and could prove fatal during a disco version of Y. M. C. A.

The rest of the group are already seated. Shit! I hate waltzing in late. It makes it look as if I don't really care and believe me I do.

"Sorry, got held up on the way," I waffle, making my way to the only empty seat.

"That's fine Cassie. We were only just about to begin," Tilly whispers kindly. My throat is terribly dry now after all that exertion. I have a Callard & Bowser Creamline Toffee in my pocket and slip it into my mouth while the others are not looking. Just as it begins to dissolve and wrap itself around my jaw, Tilly decides to ask me the first question.

"We are discussing assertiveness today Cassie. How do you feel about assertive people?" I am in deep shit here. Callard & Bowser's make magnificent toffee, mainly because it melts all over your tongue and takes ages to disappear. Swallowing one whole could prove fatal so I improvise.

"Tossee… schtuk… solly," I gurgle, while the rest of the group stare at me as if I'm insane…

"Tossee… in maarf… solly."

"Sorry?" Tilly tries again, convinced I am having a stroke. She waits but I'm unable to answer.

"Right, we'll move along shall we?" she finally giggles. Bless that woman, saved again. I think the group suspect I've been overdosing on my medication. I'll have you know I have never taken any of my medication so there! Christ, my brain is foggy enough without the aid of some prescribed drug thank you.

I prefer to do without and I'm coping... sort of. I have a naturally glazed expression. Just think what I'd be like on 75mg of Dothiepin a day. Heaven forbid! Tilly is directing her questions at Alicia. Alicia Afterbirth I call her. You know the sort. Stout, sensible Hush Puppies and a rucksack. I'm sure she has some good points but for the life of me I can't see any. I have to resist the temptation to slap her face at every session. She's a nightmare. Spouting on about her anxieties while making notes in a little pink book. The rest of us have given up trying to contribute when she's in full flow. Blah, blah, blah. Apparently, she's considering going off to live on some remote Scottish island to find herself. Several of the group have offered her a lift to the station. Here she goes...

"I am drained. I have nothing left to offer," she whimpers, rolling her eyeballs and coming over all Barbara Cartland, "I'm exhausted, I truly am," she spouts. Oh get a grip woman. If you were a one-legged bus-driver in Beirut I'd probably have some sympathy for you, but really! There's an Alicia in every road in the country. Never married, never worked, never known the joy of just belting up and listening to other people. I just know she buys all her food at Marks & Spencer's and goes on walking holidays in the Lake District. If she has any nieces and nephews I bet she gives them a pound coin each at Christmas and tells them to invest it wisely. This is not very charitable of me I know, taking a dislike to another human being but I've done my bit for charity. Alicia can go forth and multiply as far as I'm concerned. Off she goes again...

"I just cannot say no to people," she moans. I'd like to think this means she is a slut who cannot resist the advances of the entire male choir at her local church but I doubt it. I suspect she can't say no to the Women's Institute when they have a marmalade making bash. "It's just impossible to drag myself out of bed some days," she trills.

Oh fuck off you madwoman! Try living in a high-rise block with five kids to feed and clothe. Then tell me you can't drag yourself out of your ever so comfortable Silentnight bed. Blah, blah, blah and on and on and on. Most of the group appear to have lost the will to live now. Little Alan has tiny beads of sweat forming on his upper lip again. Alan is a particular source of concern to me. We have been meeting for these sessions for months and I don't think he's said more than half a dozen words. Every Thursday, he arrives in his nylon kagool and hand knitted scarf, nods to everyone, sits down and remains silent for the rest of the session. What is going on inside that head? I know it's none of my business but I worry all the same

I could adopt Alan but I daren't. Jack has warned me in no uncertain terms not to bring him home for tea. I do have a tendency to collect strays and sad people. Alan has frayed shirt collars and plastic trainers. Where is his Mother? I need to know. It's something that keeps me awake at night. I have visions of him returning home to his maisonette alone, sharing a tin of pilchards with his cat and listening to the radio. Because his television is broke. And he can't afford a new one, and he has damp in his bathroom which is affecting his chronic chest problems, stop it!

I am seated opposite Alicia Afterbirth and for some unknown reason she gives me one of her glares. You know, the sort of expression that you have when you've just trodden in some dog shit. I glare back. A few short months ago I might have been intimidated by her but not anymore. Becoming a resident of Trifletown makes you tough. Tilly, bless her, senses that the vibes are not good and reins us in. She has the knack of stopping Alicia in full flow.

"Time for some relaxation I think," she sings in that lovely soothing tone.

"Time to stab Alicia in the head," I mutter to myself.

"If you could push back your chairs and assume the position."

We are nothing if not pliable and in seconds, all six of us are flat out on the floor, eyes closed, listening to Tilly's soothing voice.

"Breathe deeply… remember the rhythm… just relax." We do exactly as we are told, her velvet voice wafting over us like a tranquil sea. I don't know how she does it. Always calm, always in control, a true professional. She must be because she never cracked her face when Alan farted. Poor diet you see, living on baked beans and fried eggs I bet.

"It's important to remember your breathing techniques," Tilly continues. Alan is breathing so deeply it sounds like a snore. I squint my eyes and realise he is snoring. He has a nasty shaving cut on his chin and the strip of toilet paper he's stuck to it wobbles as he exhales. Bless him. Probably doesn't sleep very well in that maisonette. What with the mice scratching at the floorboards all night long… and the rain dripping through the hole in the roof.

"That's it, focus on your inner calm," Tilly urges.

I can't find my inner calm. Not here with Alicia lying in such close proximity. I just keep getting this overwhelming urge to dive on top of her and choke her to death. I can find my inner calm at home. Lying on the back lawn gazing up at the cloud formations. Or romping in the woods with Levy. That's my inner calm. This place is not conducive to inner calm. It's a hive of noise and activity. You can do sketches, arrange dried flowers or just snooze in the sunroom if you want. I'd like to arrange an outing for the group but I'm not sure they'd like the idea. Tilly would love it, she'd be first on the coach with several hundred egg sandwiches I bet. But as for the rest…

See, even after all these months, we are still strangers really. We bare our souls in front of each other week after week and yet still avoid eye contact. It's that good old British reserve again. I will tell you all my deepest darkest secrets but I won't look you in the eye. Odd. Tilly tries her best. Time after time she leads us along the path of awareness in an attempt to show us all how to love ourselves. Self esteem is the first thing to go when you visit Trifletown apparently. That, and the ability to dress yourself properly in the mornings.

And this therapy does work. In as much as it makes you take time out and think about what went wrong in your life. How to focus on rebuilding yourself. How to say 'no' to people when they make demands on you. How to find time just for you.

"That's super, if you could all be seated again please." We sit, apart from Alan who is still snoring. Tilly coughs discreetly and he jumps up looking quite startled. Bad nerves you see. Probably been on Valium for most of his adult life. After leaving the orphanage… And the abuse.

"We are going to try a new exercise now. I want you all to take a few seconds to think. Think of the two little words… I CAN… now take your time, you can what? Think about it, when you have we'll go round in a circle and you can give me your thoughts." Mmm, I can, oh dear, that's a hard one. I can… eat a Mars Bar sideways… drink vast quantities of Jack Daniels and remain upright… no, that won't do… I can cross the road on my own, oh shit!

"Alan would you care to go first?" Tilly asks.

The entire group hold their breath waiting for this one and it's a long time coming. After what seems like a week he swallows hard and says…

"I can name all the characters in every series of Star Trek." The boy is positively beaming now. I knew it! He's a Trekkie! Go for it lad!

"Marvellous!" Tilly grins… "Now Alicia, how about you?" Look at her silly cow… all puffed up like a rampant rooster.

"I can quite honestly say that I excel in most things. When I decide to indulge in a hobby I never do things by halves. I'm committed…"

"Okay Alicia that's lovely, can we move on," Tilly snaps, cutting her off. She should be bloody committed. To an asylum of some sort. In the maximum security wing.

"Cassie, your turn." In situations like this I tend to wing it. Basically I just lie to get it over with.

"I can knit Arran jumpers," I boast.

"Excellent!" Tilly beams. The rest of the group seem impressed and I am basking in their glory when the timer goes off on Tilly's desk. How time flies when you're having fun.

Arran jumpers! What nonsense, I can't knit at all. When my son, Tom, was a toddler, he begged me to knit some clothes for his Action Man. Jack is still wearing the jumper. Knitting and I are just not compatible but it worked see. One quick fib and it's all over.

We file out like penguins on Prozac, muttering our goodbyes without really meaning it. Alicia is first out of the doors, barging her way past Alan and almost knocking him over in a rush to get back to her cottage in the country. How rude! Try that with me missus and I'll punch your lights out. I might be only three feet six at the moment but I'm up for a rumble if you carry on like that.

It's pouring down now and I don't have a coat. Sod it! Not much chance of a lift off this lot. Alan comes by bus and Alicia flies here on her broomstick. The others just sort of melt into the distance as I trudge along the driveway onto the main road. It's at times like this that I wish I could drive. I never learnt. Mainly because I have no sense of direction whatsoever. I'd start out for Asda and end up in Aberdeen. Mention any of the points of the compass and I lose the will to live. It's a cerebral thing I think. The part of my brain that's supposed to deal with direction just doesn't work.

Last year we went to Yorkshire for a week. We stopped at the services and I came out of the ladies, turned right and followed the hordes of people going towards the car park. The fact that I had crossed over the motorway and onto the other side escaped me totally. I ended up in the lorry park with several hundred truckers. A very kindly driver offered me a lift to Glasgow and a bite of his Yorkie bar but I declined. Suffice to say, when we travel now I am securely fastened to Jack's wrist with a piece of long elastic. For my own safety of course.

Better get a move on. Levy will be glaring at his watch and wondering where I am. He frets when I'm out of the house for too long. He worries. Mainly about who will feed him and buy his vast supply of chocolate buttons. Stuff like that.

CHAPTER TWO

First Tram to Trifletown

I'm dressing very carefully today for a change. I have a date with the doctor. Well, not so much a date as an appointment. Since becoming a patient at the Crumple Clinic I feel as if he is scrutinising me for signs of deterioration. Considering I arrived for my first appointment wearing my pants on my head, his concern is quite justified. Doctor's appointments make me nervous and it shows. I'm normally the patient being restrained in the waiting room by several hefty receptionists. My phobia regarding anything medical is ingrained. I'm the hysterical sort who suspects a malignant brain tumour when in reality the elastic on my pants is too tight.

A slight cough means consumption to me and God forbid that a rash should appear on my body overnight. This can only mean I have been struck down by that deadly flesh eating disease found only in the lower regions of the Umkoko river. See what I mean? This irrational fear leaves me very confused. Surely hypochondriac's spend every waking hour at the surgery driving their poor G. P insane? I don't fall into that category. I have to by physically dragged to the chemist since pharmacists started wearing white coats. There's probably a correct medical term for my fears but I'm too scared to ask. I think it may be a severe case of Cowardy, Cowardy, Custardness.

Smart casual I think today. Well, casual anyway. My black trousers appear to be relatively snot free. Those will do. I have a jumper somewhere without a gravy stain on the front. Now where did I put that? Here it is, oh, it's custard not gravy. Crikey, can't remember the last time we had custard. Is it custard? Could be banana yoghurt, oh sod it! He'll never notice. I daresay he's seen much worse. A sceptic boil perhaps or some poor devil's puss ridden abscess. My boots could do with a clean but it's pointless really. I am a veritable magnet for shite of every description. Squirrel, fox, you name it and it will end up on the bottom of my boots. If I pass a puddle on the way I'll have a splosh in it to wash them off. There you go. That will have to do. I don't have time for a complete makeover. I'm running late as it is, mainly due to the fact that Levy ate the laces in my walking boots and now they are held together with bits of orange washing line.

Attractive eh? Must try to co-ordinate. Where's that black scarf with the orange flowers on? Never let it be said that I don't accessorise. At my age and in my present state of mind, I have to be perfectly honest and say I don't give a shit. Time was, not so very long ago, when I couldn't dress myself at all without the help of someone from Social Services, so at least I'm improving. My pants appear to be underneath my trousers so that's a bonus.

The surgery windows are all steamed up. That can only mean one thing. The place is heaving as usual. Just finish my fag before I venture into the lion's den. I can just about make out Rasputin the receptionist's head through the condensation. She's on overdrive again. Her neck is revolving violently as the queue of people at the desk grows by the second. Steam is billowing out of her ears. I seriously expect a priest to arrive at any minute with his exorcism kit.

"Doctor is on call. You'll have to see the locum!" she yells at some poor bloke in a neck brace.

"Lend her your brace mate before her head blows off," I volunteer. This little gem serves to reduce the queue to a tittering mass. I'm not sure if it's the witty repartee or just nerves. We are all just a tad nervous of being eaten alive by she of the revolving neck.

"Watkins! I won't call you again. Doctor is waiting!" she bawls, shattering several light bulbs in the process. Watkins, a tiny old man with two sticks, hauls himself up off one of the vinyl chairs and painfully drags his weary body towards the surgery door.

"Come along! There are sick people waiting to go in!" she screams at him. This barrage of abuse proves too much for old Watkins who drops both his sticks and collapses onto the floor in a heap. He has obviously decided it would be easier for everyone if he just died instead of bothering the doctor. Several concerned faces rush to his aid and I breathe a sigh of relief as they get him to his feet and carry him into the doctor.

"Tranter for the nurse. Don't forget your specimen!" she booms. I just know that Tranter is now wishing the floor would open up and swallow him. I know this because as he runs past the queue he has a

Tesco carrier bag over his head and a specimen jar in his sweaty little hand. We all crane our necks to try to identify the contents of the jar but his grip is like iron and he refuses to let us see.

"Looks like sperm," volunteers an obese woman in a nylon rain hat behind me.

"Really?" I say admiringly, amazed at her powers of deduction.

"Either that or it's an amoebic bowel," she crows, showing off.

I have no idea what an amoebic bowel is and suspect she just made it up. Nobby Knowall.

My turn now and I approach the desk with an inane grin on my face, Rasputin hates it when you grin.

"You'll be with the locum. There will be quite a wait!" she snaps.

"That's okay. I have a packed lunch," I grin back, doing my famous impression of The Joker. This attempt to lighten the mood is lost on her. She may have a flip-top head and green ectoplasm spewing from her mouth but she is definitely lacking in the laughter stakes. I have been with this practice for years and have never seen her smile. Scream, yes. Slam doors, yes. Smile, no.

Yet another case of mistaken profession. Why do these people choose a career that they so obviously hate? Why not go into the army and take your aggression out on somebody else? Come to think of it, I suspect Rasputin may be ex-army. She has the voice of a sergeant major and the face of someone who's experienced germ warfare. Maybe she was in the services. Maybe she got kicked out for being too violent. Lost her army pension and all that. Methinks I have it sussed. I should tell her they're looking for car park attendants at Safeway. She could do that job.

"Bowers! Your swabs back. Go to the hatch now!" she bellows. Bowers, a young lad with the look of a sexually transmitted disease about him, shuffles to the hatch. He is obviously in some discomfort and holds onto his crotch as he walks. Maybe if he didn't hold on it would walk off on it's own. Crabs, as they say at the seaside. It has to be. Poor lad, I trust he'll be more selective about his sexual partners in the future.

"Piles, strangulated I'd say," old Fatso whispers across to me from her seat opposite. She is beginning to piss me off now, with her Readers Digest Diagnostics. I say nothing and just smile sweetly, convinced I am right and she is wrong. The only sure way to solve this would be to ask Bowers but he's already on his way out of the door, clutching his crotch in one hand and a prescription in the other.

I could follow him to the chemist but he's walking so slowly it would take forever. Besides which, the buzzer interrupts my train of thought as the next patient is called in… me.

"Ryder! First on the left," she roars, "And your smear's overdue!" Talk about mortified! Why not just pass my notes round for everyone to read you old bitch. For god's sake is nothing sacred? Fatso is nodding knowingly now at the woman sitting next to her. She'll have me down for a hysterectomy in five seconds. I try to rise above it and simply waft past them all, still grinning inanely at Rasputin because I know it drives her mad.

"Thank you your highness," I trill, heading for the safety of the surgery.

The locum appears to have had a busy morning. He is sitting in his chair fast asleep with his head lolling back against the wall. I'm reluctant to disturb him but will only have to face the wrath of Rasputin to make another appointment. I'll just have to sit it out for a while. Maybe read a copy of the Lancet while I wait. I sit down, very quietly and take a closer look at his face. He appears to be very old and sort of crinkled. His glasses are lying at a funny angle across the bridge of his nose and his dentures have slipped forward making his jaw seem deformed. He could be dead and I have no idea how to take a pulse. I wonder if there's a medical book in here somewhere? You'd think so, wouldn't you, in a surgery?

Small beads of sweat are beginning to form on my upper lip at the prospect of spending the rest of my life with this corpse. If rigour mortis sets in they'll have a job to get him out of that chair. Have to break his legs I should think.

I shall have to cough. Politely of course. Don't want to bring on a cardiac arrest. Perhaps a gentle fart would be better. More delicate. Trouble is which one will surface first. Cough or trouser cough, so to speak. My dilemma is solved when the phone rings. Loudly enough to jolt him out of his semi-comatose state and back into the surgery. He looks quite startled at first, then smiles sweetly as if waking from a pleasant dream.

"Yes, lovely, two sugars please," he yawns into the mouthpiece.

Poor bloke. Obviously in need of some refreshment I'd say. And perhaps a gentle shove towards retirement. He's obviously been dragged out of the embalming suite to cover in an emergency. Bless him. He should be taking it easy at his age. Resting at home with a ventilator on standby just in case. Still, it's good of him to volunteer.

"Now, let's see, just get you up on the screen," he nods, tapping away at the keyboard in front of him.

I'm impressed. Barely breathing and computer literate. Can't be bad eh? I watch fascinated as the screen rolls and yards of information spew forth about yours truly. I had no idea I had so much data. I can't read a word as the screen flickers faster than my brain. When it finally stops, he scans the information in front of him then takes off his glasses.

"How is the new kidney?" he asks, still tapping away at the keyboard.

"Sorry?" I gasp, unaware I'd even had a transplant.

"Marvellous how you bounce back, eh? You look well!" he smiles.

"Should give you a whole new lease of life!" he chuckles. Indeed it is marvellous. Miraculous in fact! It would appear I have undergone a major organ transplant without even leaving the house. Who's kidney did I get? I feel I have a right to know.

"I think you have me er…" I try to explain but he's in full flow now and impossible to stop.

"Amazing organ, the kidney. Manufactures gallons of urine a day. Amazing don't you think?"

"Yes amazing but," I try again.

"Well you look fine and dandy to me. Any problems passing water?" he asks.

"Not that I've noticed," I concede.

"Off you pop then, Dr Green will do the follow up."

In my capacity as the worst patient in the world, I meekly stand and allow myself to be ushered out of the consulting room. Protesting will only prove to be embarrassing for both of us so I simply smile like your average village idiot and close the door behind me. Well, at least my new kidney has shown no signs of rejection. Phew, that's a relief! I can't even remember what I came in for now. It seems irrelevant. There is obviously some poor soul in the waiting room who needs help far more than I do. Somebody with renal problems which outweighs my visits to the Crumple Clinic.

Rasputin is gnawing her way into a baguette as I make my way out. Obviously chicken and mayo as a dribble of it plops onto her chin. I just can't face trying to explain that fiasco to her. Like I say, she's got no sense of humour and would no doubt insist that doctor was right. If doctor say's you've had a transplant, you've had a transplant! That sort of thing. I'll make another appointment by phone. Wait for Dr Green to come back. He doesn't bother with computers. He relies on the old fashioned methods. Just looks you right in the eye and says..

"Who the hell are you and why are you bothering me?"

It's a much more effective method don't you think? No pussyfooting around. I prefer my doctor to be direct. It saves a lot of confusion. I'm confused enough already without any added problems. It's quite frightening really I suppose. You pitch up at the surgery with a sore throat and end up having your cervix removed. Computers see. This is how a lot of medical mistakes occur I should think. Press the wrong button and bang, you've amputated a perfectly healthy leg. They should revert back to the old methods. Writing on patient's with one of those huge marker pens. "Cut this off," or "Whip this out," was a much more foolproof method. Although if your surgeon happens to be dyslexic it could prove to be a problem.

Rasputin has the whole baguette in her gob now. How unattractive is that? Leaning over reception with a gaping gob full of chicken and mayo. No manners some people. Although I expect as a Marine in the jungles of Borneo, she didn't have much time for etiquette.

The noticeboard looks full today. Lots of interesting titbits for me to mull over. I have to say, I think the noticeboard was an innovation on Rasputin's part. It gives people something to read while they wait and saves her having to bring in tattered copies of SAS Monthly. I love noticeboards. They tell you such a lot about people don't they? The world appears to be full of people with electric blankets to sell. Electric blankets and formica coffee tables. Funny that. I need my glasses for this. Where the hell did I put them? Oh here they are, tucked inside my sock. Now what delights do we have today?

"BANGKOK BRENDA… UNHURRIED MASSAGE… WILL TRAVEL" I bet! She must have travelled a fair distance to get to Birmingham. She can't really be from the far East with a name like that surely? Doesn't quite ring true does it? Brenda from Balsall Heath more like. Really!

"ANIMAL WATER TROUGH… GALVANIZED… BUYER COLLECT… £20." Sounds like a bargain for twenty squid but how would you acquire an animal water trough living in central Birmingham? Some displaced farmer perhaps forced to sell off all his belongings. Shame. Just one sad little card in the lost and found section. I hate this half of the board. It's so depressing.

"MANSELL ARTHUR: 17/4/1904: FORMERLY OF NETTLEFOLD & SON: LAST HEARD OF IN THIS AREA: PLEASE CONTACT OLIVE ON 0121-423-6642: FAMILY CRISIS." Oh Arthur! Wherever you are please phone Olive! I shall have no sleep if you don't. He's a bit old to be getting himself lost isn't he? Let me see, must be ninety-nine! That's awful. He could be anywhere. Lying dead in a ditch or huddled under a tree in the park. Arthur! You have a crisis. Olive needs you! How on earth do you lose someone of that age? It's not like a teenager who runs off to London searching for excitement and decent nightclubs. Unless Arthur's a goer of course. I suppose he could be. It's very ageist of me to suggest otherwise really. Arthur could be in Stringfellow's right now strutting his stuff with some Page 3 model.

"Brown anorak, hearing aid, walks with a limp." They should have added a photo or at the very least a description. Something similar anyway. Arthur could be anywhere and it bothers me I have to say. I wish I hadn't seen that card. I shall be scrutinising every old man I see now. If Olive would care to give me a scrap of his clothing, Levy could find him no problem. Still, I expect the police have thought of that already.

Enough of this. I cannot allow myself to get involved. The Ryder household would be positively awash with strays if I had my way. The four-legged and two-legged variety. I try to distance myself but the heart invariably rules the head and I end up knee deep in other people's problems and pets.

All week I have been following the progress of a dog called Minnie on Central News. Minnie is a stray with an adorable face and eyes you could easily swim in. Minnie is also deaf! I ask you, what more grief could you inflict on a dumb animal? Minnie needed a home and if I knew where Tunbridge Wells was I'd have willingly walked there to collect her. Thankfully, on last night's update, some kind soul offered to give her a home. A home along with another dog called Moose. And guess what? Moose is deaf as well! See, ying and yang. They were obviously meant to be together. I'm a believer, as the Monkees used to say.

I don't suppose Rasputin has any pets. Well, not the soft, furry adorable kind anyway. She looks more like a ferret person to me. Ferrets or a Pitbull. Probably the Pitbull. He'll be called Gnasher and wear one of those ridiculous studded leather collars. I can see them now terrorising the kids in the park.

Well I can't stand here all day fretting about ferrets. Tom and Hannah are trekking along the Brecon Beacons this weekend and I feel obliged, in my capacity as the Worst Worrywart of a mother in the world, to get them some supplies from Safeway. They are both intelligent, articulate adults and have been married for five years but I fear the worst as ever. Mention hill walking to me and I get the over-whelming urge to strap on my crampons and safety helmet and hang around in case they get into difficulties. Levy is poised with his brandy barrel as we speak. He tends to fret as well when members of the family indulge in weekends in the mountains.

We both lie awake at night, waiting for the emergency services to contact us to join in the search party. It's a Mom sort of thing. You have to have been there and done that to even begin to understand. If only they'd have left the umbilical cord attached at the hospital, I could have reeled him back in should he slip down the sheer face of a cliff.

I live in mortal dread of the day when their treks in this country will become too tame and they'll suddenly announce that they are off to scale the north face of the Eiger. I am already in training for this exercise. I do this by crawling up the stairs on all fours attached to the banister by a guide rope. I am also well practised in secreting Mars Bars and glucose tablets about my person. I like to be prepared.

I have no idea where my son gets his daredevil streak from. Certainly not me. Perhaps it's the result of being suspended in one of those baby-sling contraptions as a child. Daring and I are not really compatible, due largely to the bright yellow streak down my back. And of course my age. Should I fall off a cliff now, no doubt I would have to wait at least a year for a hip replacement. Young bones are more pliable and prone to bounce. Of course it's the Pepsi thing. You know, live life to the Max and all that. I have the utmost admiration for this generation. They grab life by the bollocks and go for it. You have to give them credit for that. The word CAN'T is not in their vocabulary and I'm envious of that. I truly am. It's an age thing again. My schooldays were spent being beaten with a slipper and reading Janet and John. Today's infant school kids are surfing the net and dabbling in the stock market at six.

We did have plus points though. Sooty and those delicious Smiths crisps with little blue bags of salt in. Not that we are allowed to eat salt now. Just add it to the list of deadly poisons scientists tell us will clog our arteries and lead to an early death. Tell that to my Grandad Finnemore pal! He lived to be roughly a hundred and five and sprinkled salt on everything. Porridge, mashed potatoes, even the ulcers on his legs.

Is there anything we are still allowed to enjoy? Salt's out, so is butter, full fat milk, red wine, the list is endless. It would appear we are condemned to roam this planet chewing on a stick of celery with the odd sultana thrown in for a treat. Not really worth getting up for in the morning is it? We are allowed to eat muesli of course. What's all that about then? Is somebody having a laugh at our expense? I think so. If I really wanted to start the day with a bowl of sawdust and wood-shavings, I'd be a lop-eared rabbit called Bertie living in a garden in Cheltenham.

These lunchtime queue's are a nightmare. Just two checkouts open as usual and talking of rabbits, the irate looking woman in front of me now, resembles a rabbit. Her eyes are protruding quite badly and her front teeth look just like a row of tombstones in Quinton cemetery. It could be a thyroid problem I suppose or just plain ugly. Whatever, she's giving off some very hostile vibes. I back off with my trolley in case she snaps and bites off my nose. Supermarket rage is becoming the norm and she looks like a rabbit who could rage. Any minute now she'll start thumping her hind leg as a show of aggression. Steady girl, get a grip, it's only a bit of shopping. This place is heaving. The lunchtime rush of stressed out parents and office girls searching for a suitable fat-free sandwich to go with their diet Coke. Go on be a devil! Buy a chocolate donut and a bag of chips instead.

I have a nice juicy Kos lettuce in my trolley and feel tempted to offer the Bunny Lady a bite in an effort to calm her down. She really is in a fury about something. Perhaps the price of carrots has tripled. The poor kid serving her looks terrified. Stuff is flying all over the place. Look! There goes a jar of beetroot skidding off the end of the belt. This accident is obviously the straw that broke the bunny's back. Here we go. It's kicking off.

"Get me security now!" thunders Thumper, slamming her bag onto the belt, her face contorted with rage. I can sense a checkout crisis coming on. The assistant is only a kid and obviously wet behind the ears where rabid rabbits are concerned. I can see tears forming and wish I'd gone to Tesco's now.

"Sorry?" she quakes, unsure of what's going on. Thumper presses her ugly face dangerously close to the girl's, almost taking an eye out with those bloody teeth.

"Security now!" she rants, leaving a trail of spit on the conveyor belt. I manage to grab my bakery bags just in time before they get soaked. I can tolerate most things but not other people's saliva on my Cinnamon bagels. I give her one of my looks. She has been warned.

As if in sheer panic, the assistant hits a button under the cash drawer and within seconds the till is surrounded by two hefty security guards and an elderly German Shepherd. I don't think the dog is part of the team. He looks quite friendly and isn't wearing the obligatory army surplus jumper.

These guys, Bernard and Brian according to their security tags, are primed for action and even I start to panic in all the confusion. Perhaps it's me! Maybe I have inadvertently shoved a Bernard Matthews turkey up my jumper in my rush to get home. These things happen. You read about it all the time. Hormonal woman arrested for shoplifting. Oh my life! Is that a turkey or my left breast? I am just about to give myself up when Thumper booms,

"I came in here to do some shopping, not to be sexually harassed by some pervert. It's totally disgusting. Look at him, leering… over there!" By now, the entire store has ground to a halt to watch this farce. We all turn as if in unison to get a look at the pervert. Bernard and Brian follow her gaze to a perfectly ordinary looking guy in the opposite queue. Well, he probably does look normal on a normal day but I have to say, with several hundred pairs of accusing eyes focused on him he looks quite mortified. I'm on his side poor sod. I think Thumper's been overdosing on the raw cabbage.

"What exactly has he done madam?" Bernard asks diplomatically.

"Winking!, he's been winking at me non-stop for ages!" she snarls. Did she say winking? For God's sake woman, if you'd said wanking I could understand your distress but what's a wink for Christ's sake? Not exactly sexual harassment is it, you sad git. Methinks Thumper is an attention seeking rabbit. Probably lives alone and relies on cheap thrills like this for excitement. Come to think of it, with a face like that it's odds on that she does live alone. And always will.

Bernard and Brian are bemused and I expect they've seen it all in their line of work. The German Shepherd has lost interest altogether and has his nose shoved up some man's crotch in the lottery queue now.

"Could we calm things down a bit madam?" Brian suggests quite assertively. He's hoping to clear this up and get back to his crossword. Thumper is having none of it and looks as if she's about to lose it.

"Yes that's right. Let him get away with it. He's a man after all!" she shrieks to anyone who will listen, "Typical male!"

"Now madam let's not get this out of proportion," Bernard pleads. Small trickles of sweat are forming on his forehead and I suspect he hasn't been called upon to deal with a crisis for a while. He may be trained in martial arts and truncheon wielding but dealing with a psychotic woman is another ball game altogether.

"Screw the lot of you!" Thumper roars, and with this last vicious remark slams her shopping bag over her shoulder and strides off towards the exit. I think I'm the only one to notice that she hasn't actually paid for her groceries. I'm tempted to alert Bernard and Brian but decide against it. They probably have wives and children at home. It's not really worth risking life and limb over a few items of grocery is it?

The poor winker is still rooted to the spot and my heart goes out to the man. He probably has a nervous tic. Either that or he's partially sighted. I can't see any man willingly wanting to wink at a woman like Thumper. Poor sod. I bet he'll never shop in this store again. Several other shoppers obviously feel the same way and try to jolly him along the queue. The general consensus seems to be that Thumper is barking mad and I agree. Crazy isn't it? Where do you draw the line on all this political correctness? Is it really such a crime to wink at a woman? Nobody ever died from a wink did they? Or a smile or a friendly nod? If things carry on at this rate men will be terrified to leave the house. Which would probably suit Thumper. I feel the problem lies within her head, not in the Winker's eye.

"Never a dull moment eh?" I giggle to the girl on the till.

"I'll be glad when I'm back on cheese," she sighs. Bless her. I don't suppose they get many punch-ups on the cheese counter. You can rely on cheese to remain calm in a crisis.

"Six-fifty-nine please." It's hard to know what to do in situations like this. The poor kid's in a right state and there are no suitable words to say really. I offer her a fun-size Twix as a gesture.

"Thanks. I'll have it with my coffee later."

"You're welcome pet. Keep smiling!" This is turning into an eventful morning. What with an organ transplant and a case of sexual winking. Will the excitement never end? Little did I suspect when I joined the ranks of the unemployed, that I'd be spending my days like this.

When I first lost my job, I was so full of guilt and downright shame, I thought I'd never be accepted in society again. I'm over that now. It was but a brief period in my Trifletown days. A trip to the shops like this was a nightmare as I dithered over whether or not I should go for that extra donut. After a lifetime spent working and paying my own way, it came as a shock to suddenly become financially dependent on Jack. It came as a bit of a shock to him too but he's recovering slowly.

It was Maureen Lipman who once said "This hump on my back is guilt," and boy did I have a hump! I was a veritable camel and it has taken me a while to adjust to the fact that when you are without a salary you become a nonentity in some people's eyes. Banks, credit card companies, even the milkman look at you in a different light..

"You sure you want an extra yoghurt today?" He'd say while adding up the bill for the week, as if I were about to do a runner with his rhubarb crunch.

Other people's perceptions of you alter as well. It's a guaranteed conversation stopper at parties.

"And what do you do for a living?"

"Nothing, absolutely diddly-squat."

"Oh sorry, I see Gemima over there, must dash!" See what I mean? I did consider lying just to avoid embarrassment but why should I? I worked for years, got sick, got the sack, end of story.

Thumper is at the bus stop as I stroll past with my bags. Regaling the people in the queue with tales of her trauma. Silly mare! Go home and get a life! Correction, get a personality first, then some dental work, then a life.

I think I'd be pleasantly surprised if some guy winked at me in Safeway. Well, anywhere really. It doesn't have to be Safeway. Some of us are grateful for small mercies. I would have smiled back and walked home with a spring in my step. No harm done. No need to bring in the heavy mob and a legal team.

A lawyer friend of Jack's suggested I sue when my employer let me go, so to speak. We live in a culture of compensation claims. It's mad! I took the job on. It was my decision and my mistake so you just live with it and move on. I can't be doing with this "Sue-Society." It's ridiculous. Somebody bursts into tears in an office after a bollocking and suddenly a six-figure sum is being discussed. Completely mad!

I may be crumpled but I remain optimistic. I have a giant pack of fun-size Twix in my bag.

CHAPTER THREE

Surgical Stockings and Sensible Pants

It's just after six in the morning and I am wide awake contemplating my decline. A downhill slide into the basement where they sell surgical stockings and sensible pants. Whereas in reality I long to be up in the lingerie department buying lycra thongs and black uplift bras. Sadly, the lift doors keep closing and I can't make the stairs. It creeps up on you, you see. The decline. Without warning.

This is not just simply a case of mind over matter. I truly do not mind being over forty. It's just another number after all. What I do object to is the fact that since achieving this milestone my body has decided it's all over and refuses to play ball. Or any other sort of sport for that matter. I have long since given up hope of ever representing Great Britain at the Olympics. My idea of exercise is jogging around Thornton's on a Saturday afternoon searching for the Cappuccino truffles.

Mother never warned me to expect full blown fossilisation at forty. I can distinctly remember her going through the 'hot flush' phase. As children, we would gather round and warm our hands on her face during cold winter nights. We thought it was hilarious. That laughter has come back to haunt me since I can tell you.

This flush phase does have it's plus side. After years of sleeping in several layers of flannelette nightie I now sleep naked. I have to, otherwise my boiling blood would exceed temperatures of possibly two thousand degrees and my head could blow off. This is one aspect of ageing that Jack is enjoying. Although, I have to say, his eyesight's not what it used to be.

And the height thing of course. That's a bummer. According to my passport, I used to be five feet two. Now I'm barely touching the five feet mark.

If it's true that women diminish in height with age, I shall be roughly seven inches tall at sixty. A veritable midget with osteo-arthritis and attitude. My grandchildren will be able to dress me up and push me around in a dolls pram. I expected to lose a few brain cells along the way of course. That's nothing unusual as you approach Senile City but these awful memory lapses are something else. On Friday I put the hedge trimmers in the freezer and a lovely leg of lamb in the garage.

This rugged face on the pillow beside me now. Know it well but I'll be buggered if I can put a name to it. Whoever it is, he's awake …

"Do I know you?"

"Mr Ryder, we met twenty-eight years ago in a pub?"

"Was I drunk?"

"No, I was, it helped." I suppose a sense of humour is essential. He's watching me now. Probably for further signs of deterioration.

"Why are you awake at this hour?" he frowns.

"Just considering my options. You know, career wise and that."

"Go back to sleep. It's Sunday." We make spoons and I feel myself drifting off again snuggled against his warm body.

"You could do adverts… for those lady things," he purrs into my neck.

"What lady things?"

"You know, those panty liners, for women who dribble."

"Charming! Thanks a lot pal!"

You see! His perceptions of me have changed as well. Just a few short years ago I was his strumpet and now all I'm fit for is advertising incontinence pants. Nice!

"They're all the rage for women of a… certain age," he stutters.

"What, as in over sixteen you mean?"

"No, just mature, you know."

"As in a good Stilton?"

"Oh shit. Have I said the wrong thing?"

"Absolutely! Keep your ideas to yourself."

"Sorry, just trying to be helpful." He's dying to laugh. I can tell by the way his shoulders are shaking under the duvet. It's a dead giveaway.

"Anyway, I don't," I bite back.

"Don't what?"

"Dribble, well not down below anyway." He's losing it. His whole body consumed with mirth.

"Are you sure Cass? You can talk to me you know. It's good to share."

"Fuck off!"

"Yes dear." and with that he explodes. Great big bellowing roars of laughter echoing around the room. If the neighbours were asleep before they certainly won't be now. Idiot!

"You are SO not funny!" I tell him but to no avail. He's lost the plot and will go on forever. Levy's awake now. Bounding up the stairs like a small bull elephant. Wondering what all the fuss is about. Revenge is sweet as he charges through the bedroom door and hurls himself on top of the hysterical hyena, landing with full force on it's naked testicles. I can think of better ways to start the day than to have your genitals crushed by an enormous black Labrador,

"Christ!" he splutters, his face contorted with pain. It's my turn to laugh now and I do, long and hard. The three of us rolling about on the bed. One helpless with laughter, one writhing in agony, and the dog simply enjoying the game.

"I'll take him out for a stroll," I offer by way of compensation. It could be a while before the swelling goes down and he can walk properly again.

"Cheers," he groans from under the covers. As I close the door behind me, he can't resist one last quip.

"Do you need the toilet before you go?" I shall rise above it. It's a beautiful morning and I don't want to waste a minute of it. Besides which, Levy has a firm grip on my left ankle and is dragging me gently down the stairs. When this boy wants to go out, we go out.

My beloved boy. Ninety pounds of solid muscle. Built like a solid brick wall with shoulders quite capable of pulling a double decker bus. Apparently, he has the equivalent body mass of a small Shetland pony. So Mr Orchard our vet informed me on our last visit. He pointed this out as I was dragged headfirst through the waiting room. Levy was in hot pursuit of a sassy golden retriever at the time. Much to the horror of her owners. No harm done. Just a few ruffled dog hairs and profuse apologies. I have told him time and time again that he can't expect these bitches to come across without at least an invite to dinner or a phone call.

The Black Labrador! Heaven! I am besotted and never more so than with this latest addition to our family. By the way, the Levy is as in biblical and not the jeans! Thank you. If you are not into dogs then you'll have no idea whatsoever. If you are, then you'll understand the sheer joy of owning one of these magnificent animals. My entire wardrobe is covered in dog-snot and black hair but I wouldn't have it any other way. I spend a vast amount of my time being dragged through bushes and bracken as he searches for treasure to carry home and my body is covered in huge purple bruises from our nightly romps on the lounge floor. Like I say, heaven!

He's just disappeared into the Spinney on the trail of a Cyril, or squirrel to you. Chasing Cyril's is one of his favourite pastimes. Thankfully, they are very nimble and fleet of foot so he hasn't actually caught one yet. He's come close a few times but not quite. They have a habit of disappearing up trees out of his reach where they sit grinning down at him. Laughing their furry little socks off and giving him the finger. He lives for the day when he'll encounter one in a barren desert and it will have nowhere to go.

"Come on lad let's go see Gertie and Gilbert." His face peers out of the hawthorn, a bicycle saddle firmly wedged between his jaws. Yet another piece of treasure to take home. Soft mouthed dogs see. They have to carry something at all times. It's in his blood. Retrieving and all that. Gun dog stock. He can't help it. Over the years, he has carried home an assortment of finds. Traffic cones, litter bins, milk crates. Even a small child once from the play park. Although, in his defence, I have to say I feel the child's mother should have been paying more attention. Suffice to say, they are collectors.

"Clever lad finding a saddle." He struts his stuff towards the duck pond, showing off his latest find to any passing person. I feel the need to check on Gertie and Gilbert every morning just in case. They pitched up a few weeks ago as they do every Spring and I feel sure that any day now they'll be out on the water displaying yet another brood of gorgeous goslings. Every year they come and every year they breed and every year I cry at the sight. Wonderful!

Gertie and Gilbert are Canadian. I feel honoured that they choose to visit us every year and spend a lot of my time during Spring keeping a watchful eye over them and their offspring. Last year they had five goslings and they all survived. I breathed a huge sigh of relief when they took off back to Ontario. What with cats and foxes and an assortment of other predators it's a miracle they made it.

"We'll cut through Paul's back passageway." I'm not sure how Paul feels about people using his passageway as a shortcut through to the pond but it's the quickest route and cuts out the main road. As we round the bend by the trees all hell breaks loose. The passage is quite narrow and overgrown with beech trees and we suddenly find ourselves confronted by a snarling Corgi. All fangs and froth, lunging at us without any provocation whatsoever. My first instinct is to protect Levy but since I cannot lift him up without the aid of a crane, we are forced to stand our ground. It's one of those 'fight or flight' moments in your life, if you know what I mean.

"Steady lad... steady!" The sound of my voice appears to enrage the Corgi even more, and in a flash he sinks his teeth into my right arm. I respond by grabbing his testicles with my left, which funnily enough seems to annoy him even more. He is dragging me downwards by the jumper and I fear is about to go for my throat.

Now, I don't scare easily, but the prospect of bleeding to death on a remote wooded path ruffles me somewhat, so I scream. A scream that can probably be heard in Nottingham. A streetlamp shatters in the distance and I fear pregnant women in the area may go into premature labour. The scream has the desired effect as Levy, who up until now had been in his corner polishing his gumshield, flies into the ring and demolishes the demon dog in five seconds flat. As the bell rings for seconds out, the Corgi is carried off on a stretcher. His career in shreds. Ditto his fur, his tail and most of his street cred. My hero! He's busy trying on his Lonsdale Belt while I'm left shaking and bruised and partially deaf from my own screams. Somebody in the distance seems to be playing the bagpipes. No, sorry... that's just my breathing.

A few short years ago I would have seen off that bloody dog in two seconds flat. A size five Dr Marten applied to the cobblers would have done the trick. Today, with my ever so comfortable walking shoes and a dodgy hip, I feel quite pathetic. Reduced to a quivering wreck by a dog no bigger than your average hamster. Sad eh? Even sadder is the ruddy owner. Finally, he now decides to crawl out of his pit and investigate the fracas. His string vest has seen better days and he apparently has a tattoo on both of his heads.

"Is that your bloody dog!?" I bawl.

"So what?"

"Well, would you mind keeping it under control?"

"Can't do that. He likes to go off by himself," he sneers, scratching his crotch.

"Oh, self sufficient is he, walks himself?"

"Pretty much yeah," he yawns. Enough already! I can take so much but conversing with cretins is beyond me.

"Look moron, if the complexities of a collar and lead are too much for you, there are books in the library!"

"Uh?"

"Library, big building, lots of books in it?"

"Eh?"

"Oh never mind? You are quite obviously the product of inter-breeding yourself, like your dog." This last little gem rattles his cage somewhat.

"Silly bitch!" he snarls at me.

"Ugly bastard!" I yell back.

And on that parting shot, I leg it towards home as fast as my wobbly little legs will carry me. With Levy hurling insults over his shoulder as we go. Of course the moral of this tale is, if you are not at your physical peak don't take on savage dogs. My chest is pounding, my legs ache and my throat is sore from screaming. I am a wreck.

What is it with these canines with street cred anyway? And their moronic owners? My gentle giant is quite content to lie in the sun listening to Radio 2 while chewing on the carcass of a passing wildebeest. These Rambo Rovers are only happy when they're roaming the streets terrorising some innocent passer-by. The difference between them and Levy is, he HAS the power and the build to be aggressive but chooses not to. He uses his strength in other ways like bouncing off my belly at night and running amok with the lawnmower in his mouth. All just good clean fun.

We arrive home panting and both wearing a startled expression after our ordeal. His Lordship has readjusted his gonads and is waiting in the porch.

"That was a quick stroll," he ventures.

"Corgi… fight… tattoo," I gasp.

"What sort of a tattoo?"

"Eh?"

"You said a Corgi with a tattoo. I was just curious." This conversation is going nowhere. He's got his stupid head on this morning.

"Tea, three sugars please," I groan.

"That'll be for the shock then?"

"Mm.."

"Well it would be, fighting a tattooed Corgi." I refuse to get into this and flop down on the sofa instead. Levy clambers on top of me and we lie there together recovering from our trauma. I stroke his humungous head and try to disentangle the wool the Corgi has shredded from the arm of my jumper. Bloody good job that dog didn't mark my boy. He's determined to enter Cruft's this year. I've tried to break it to him gently that his chances are zilch but he won't have it. I even showed him last year's winner on the television. Immaculate and trained to perfection.

He, on the other hand is caked in mud and dog snot and resorts to selective deafness whenever I ask him to do something.

If they had a Giant Genitals Group he'd walk it. I swear this boy is deformed in that department. Grown men stop and stare admiringly in the street. Add to that the huge head and size fifteen paws and you're getting the picture. Of course the eyes have it. Deep, bottomless pools of ebony that melt your very soul. I distinctly remember gazing into those eyes a second before he broke my nose last Christmas.

It was an accident of course. I bent down to put his lead on and he got all excited as ever and jumped up, smashing that huge bucket head into my nose. The nose exploded all over the kitchen. I was mopping blood off the walls for days but the odd thing is, I felt very little pain. Just shock as the bone crunched under the force of the impact. And the realisation that my days as a model were over.

As I looked in the mirror it didn't seem too bad. The nose was swollen and roughly three inches further to the left hand side of my face than before, but I could cope with that. Just as the bleeding began to subside the phone rang. It was Jack.

"Might be late tonight. Things are crazy here today."

"Thhokayth."

"Sorry?"

"Ay thiad thhokayth."

"Cassie is that you?"

"Corth ith me thsupid!"

"What's wrong? Are you ill?"

"Lithen! Lethy bloke my dose."

"Christ! Shall I come home?"

"Ith notheen."

"Sounds terrible."

"Lookth worth."

"Oh shit!"

"Thankth."

"Luth you."

"Bollokth!"

"Bye." And so this witty banter went on, for days. There was a major flu epidemic at the time and all the local hospitals were struggling to cope with an influx of people lying around on trolleys in corridors. This gave me the perfect excuse to avoid treatment. Every now and then I'd slap a bag of frozen peas on it to ease the swelling. It's healed up nicely now thank you and with subtle lighting you can hardly see the bend in it.

Battle scars come with age anyway. Jack knows every blemish on this weary bod and regularly records them in his filofax of faults. I suspect he is gathering evidence for a divorce.

"And what reasons are you citing for this divorce?"

"Saggy tits and facial hair, your honour."

"Divorce granted!"

"Thank you your worshipfulness." I mean, if we all packed our bags and buggered off every time we noticed an imperfection in our partner, nobody would stay married would they? At this point Jack would like me to point out that he is indeed perfection personified.

"Would you like a Gypsy Cream with your tea?" he asks, poking his head around the door.

"Please… and some Bonios for Levy." He makes a cracking pot of tea that man. Brewed to perfection and a comfort in times of stress. Levy is snoring now. Right into my left earhole. A deep, pulsating snore that reverberates around the inside of my head. His eyelids are flickering as well. No doubt he's replaying the battle earlier in slow motion. The bit where the Corgi bites the dust. I can hear Jack rooting around in the biscuit barrel searching for my Gypsy Creams. Bless him.

To be fair, he's in quite good nick for his age but then men have a lot less bodily baggage to carry don't they? No pre-menstrual or menopausal phases for them. They grow up expecting a moustache whereas we have one thrust upon us almost overnight. No cellulite either or the over-whelming urge to eat six Mars Bars sideways during a period. A doddle. I am jolted out of my daydreams by the phone. It's 7am so it must be Ma and Pa.

"Hello."

"Hello… hello." Two greetings. They are on the extensions again, talking at once.

"Hi Pa."

Ma suddenly chips in, "I doubt if that car will take the weight," she sniffs.

"Sorry?"

"The coffin, Dolly was a big woman," she whispers. Dolly died last week and she was indeed a big woman. The funeral is tomorrow.

"Not taking the coffin on your roof rack are you Pa?" I ask him. He giggles. A trait I seem to have inherited from him.

"The hearse silly!" Ma booms into my ear. Pardon me, I was losing track of the conversation for a moment. Concentrate girl.

"According to the Mail, Cadbury have profits of two hundred million," Pa pipes up.

"They've got our Cassie to thank for that," Ma spouts. Now I know I'm a self-confessed chocaholic, but two hundred million! Seems a tad excessive to me. Sometimes during our increasingly weird conversations I feel as if I'm in the middle of some surreal French film.

"Just wanted to check if seventy-two would be enough?" Ma asks.

"Seventy-two what?"

"Lemon fairy cakes of course."

"Plenty I should think Ma. More than enough."

"I'll hand you back to your Dad now. Lots to do, big day tomorrow."

"Okay. You still there Pa?"

"Where else would I be at this hour in the morning?"

"Have you had breakfast yet?"

"Mm... lemon fairy cakes on toast," he laughs.

"Stop it!"

"Better go, she's in a flap over her icing, bye."

"Bye Pa." They celebrated their Golden wedding last March. Fifty years. A record in itself these days and still in their dotage they go everywhere together. Mainly to funerals and hospital appointments but there you go. They're together. A vast proportion of their savings have been swallowed up buying wreaths for departing friends and family. Their florist, Mr Armitage, has just bought a retirement villa in Antigua. I think they paid for the pool... and the barbeque.

"Who was it?" Jack wants to know, finally arriving with the tea tray.

"Ma and pa. It's Dolly's funeral tomorrow. She's flapping over the fairy cakes."

"Lemon?"

"Of course."

"Wouldn't like to be carrying that coffin," he grimaces.

"Quite."

"Heart trouble wasn't it?"

"Mm, she went to Lourdes you know."

"Didn't know she liked cricket."

He's back in his comedy routine again.

"No miracles for Dolly, sad to say."

"Much the same as England then."

"Shouldn't you be buttering some croissants or something?" I ask.

"Consider it done," he laughs disappearing into the kitchen yet again.

My parents have quite unique qualities actually. Pa is the only person I know of in the whole world who actually CHEWS jelly. He does! Most people just let it slide down their throats but not Pa. He chews it for ages. Savouring every morsel.

And Ma. Well, where do I begin? I suppose it would have to be the shopping bag. She never goes anywhere without it. I suspect it was transplanted onto her hip instead of a kidney. It's a nice enough bag, quite dinky with a tapestry panel on the front and sturdy leather handles. It has a pouch on the side for her bus pass and another one at the top for a spare pair of pants and a bottle of Olbas Oil. I have no idea why so don't ask!

"Better open the curtains. The neighbours will think we're having a lie-in." Jack pauses at the bay window and peers out into the morning sunshine.

"Meg's on the front lawn again with her legs wide open."

"She'll toddle off home in a bit. She's on heat again poor thing."

"The word slapper springs to mind."

"Don't be hard on her. She's obsessed."

"I know but I haven't eaten yet," he laughs.

Meg is a delightful black Labrador cross who lives a few doors away. Meg is also the canine equivalent of a tart. She has no morals whatsoever and Levy is truly madly deeply in love with her. When she's hot to trot, nothing will stop her, he is like putty in her paws.

Her poor owners have tried everything to contain her and yet she still manages to escape. It's not a problem. She simply rolls around on our front lawn displaying her wares and teasing Levy into a frenzy. After a while, she will swagger off, wiggling her hips at him as he drools at the window. We did consider letting them mate but I could never choose just one pup out of a litter. Some bitches have litters as big as ten or eleven. Joy oh joy! Eleven snuffling little black bundles of fur. In my dreams I'm afraid. I have to be practical on the point of puppies.

Maybe I should look for a job working with animals. Then again maybe not. I cannot watch Animal Hospital without a pair of socks stuffed in my mouth and a box of Kleenex shoved down my pants. My face takes on mutant proportions when I cry. It really is horrendous. I'd be of no use whatsoever to some poor grieving pet owner. Cross that off my list of job prospects then.

Something will turn up. Any day now. I have a feeling in my water.

CHAPTER FOUR

Love Thy Neighbour

There appears to be a fire engine outside my house with several incredibly rugged firefighters in attendance. It's the rubber trousers I think. That make them look so ruddy horny. The rubber trousers and the tight black t-shirts. Enough! It's not just me. Ask any woman about her most common fantasy and the firefighter will be way up there on top of the list. Trust me, I know about these things. Somebody is obviously on fire and it's not me. Come to think of it, I did get a whiff of something burning earlier but assumed it was the remains of my charred granary toast. Oh heck! They seem to be moving at a fair pace. It must be quite serious. Pound to a penny it's Pete next door. Or Pickled Pete as he is affectionately known locally. This will be his third house fire in as many years. Copious amounts of alcohol and cigarette butts are a dangerous combination. Better go and see if I can be of any help. Not literally, I'm not trained in the art of handling hoses. Maybe I can make tea and pass round a plate of biscuits.

This does indeed look serious. Pete is flat out on his back on the front lawn and huge clouds of black smoke are billowing out of the upstairs window. Shit! He's finally gone and succeeded in burning the house down. My life! Please don't let him be dead. I know he's a pain in the arse but he's human underneath all that Famous Grouse and fag ash.

There's quite a crowd now. People milling around on the pavement, craning their necks for a better view. Rubberneckers! How morbid. Who are all these people for God's sake? A couple over there are setting up a picnic table on the grass verge. Clear off ghouls! Some poor soul is dying here and you're tucking into your Spam sandwiches. Really!

I grab a fireman as he hurtles past with an axe in his hand. Well, I assume he's a fireman. He could be an axe murderer on his way to a massacre.

"Is Pete alright?" I ask nervously.

"Fine, just pissed, he'll come round in a minute," he laughs. Thank God! I was just about to run in the house and fetch a blanket to cover him over. It's difficult to tell if he's alive when he's upright, so seeing him on the lawn on his back came as a bit of a shock. It's a tragic tale really and such a waste. He's a smashing guy. Well spoken, incredibly well educated but permanently pissed. I believe the correct medical term is chronic alcoholic. In his prime, he was on the lecture circuit in Dallas. Beautiful wife, two kids, house with a pool, then cheers! He hit the Bourbon bottle big time and ended up back in England, broke and living with his elderly uncle. He died years ago, leaving Pete to drink on his own.

He's coming round I think. Well, he's rolled over onto his side and is now grinning at us all. That big, sloppy grin he adopts when he's in trouble. The old soak smile that says..

"All's well with the world and would you care to join me for a drink?" Silly sod! One of these days he won't wake up and will find himself at the Pearly Gates grinning at Saint Peter.

One of the firemen is having a word with him now. It's the one with the white hat which I believe means he's the Chief Fire Officer. All the others have the customary yellow hats. Not that I've studied this subject at all. Just a quick observation on my part. Yes, he's the head honcho alright. He has the look of a man who has dealt with several towering inferno's. If this crowd would disperse, I could hear what's being said. Come on now folks, move along, there's nothing to see. The Spam Sisters are packing up their stuff so it should clear in a minute or two.

"Just to get you checked out sir..." They obviously want him to go to hospital for a check-up. He won't of course. Never does. Most of his vital organs have been shutting down for a while and his liver surrendered years ago. Yet he still refuses medical help. There are days when he's the colour of custard and others when he's a nice purply bruised shade from falling over a lot, but what can you do? Me personally, I worry. I have to fight the temptation to invite him around for Sunday lunch every week. I don't think our booze supply would suffice. Instead, I ease my guilt by cooking him the odd meal and feeding his dog, Budd, when he's comatose. Oh my God! Budd! Where is he?

"Make way please!" I bawl, thrusting myself to the front of the crowd. I can be quite assertive in an emergency and everything falls silent as I crash through the mob.

"Budd!" I scream at the nearest yellow hat, "The dog, where is he?"

"No idea love, I'm with the Gas Board, doing the mains up the road," a burly bloke grunts.

"Oh for Christ's sake! Get out of the way, dog in danger here, shift you pillock!"

"It's okay, he's out in the back garden," another voice reassures me, "He's fine."

I feel like a right prat now. Standing here in my slippers, screaming at a load of strangers. Still, Budd's okay so that's the main thing. In a second, I shall discreetly melt back into the crowd and nobody will be any the wiser. They'll just assume I've been let out of the asylum for a day. How embarrassing! And in front of all these emergency service men. The police are here now, and an ambulance crew. There's nothing like making a show of yourself big style is there? It's my own fault for getting involved again. After every episode with Pete, I swear I'll keep my distance next time but it's difficult. You can't just write somebody off because they keep falling off the wagon, so to speak.

In his case, it's more a question of falling... well... everywhere really. His body must be totally desensitised, because he falls over all the time and just bounces right back up again. He has a permanent plaster on his chin and that ruffled look that can only be achieved by sleeping in your clothes for a week.

Location has a lot to do with it. His falling I mean. We live on The Cedars, literally. A circle of houses with a set of tennis courts in the middle. It's delightful but a bugger to negotiate if you're hammered. Suffice to say, as he wobbles his way home from the Pig & Whistle, rounding the bend to his house inevitably means that he overcompensates for the roundness of the road and ends up face first in our privet. It's one of the first tasks I perform every morning. Checking the privet for the pisshead. It's habit now, a bit like brushing my teeth.

"He'll be fine love, don't worry," a guy in green overalls assures me. I take him to be a plumber or something but on closer inspection realise he's a paramedic. I shall have to remember to grab my glasses next time I fly out of the house in a crisis. Blind as a bat without them. Yet another aspect of joining the Factor Forty Club.

I can see Pete's alright. He's just invited the whole crowd into his smouldering house for drinks. Nothing changes. It looks as if the entire ground floor is gutted and he's up for mid-morning martini's. The mind boggles, it really does. It must be amazing to be so hammered that your house burning down is of so little consequence. His brain must be pickled to the size of a walnut I should think. In his world, the only thing that really matters is where his next drink is coming from. Tragic I know.

And yet strangely enough, out of this tragedy comes a lot of comedy. His latest venture is taking on a paper round of all things to supplement his booze fund. On a bad day he just shoves the first paper in the bag through the first letterbox in the road and legs it. Or he doesn't deliver them at all and just stacks them up in the porch at the side of the house. Hence the fireball we have just witnessed. He probably dropped a fag end somewhere. As if reading my thoughts, a woman behind me suddenly blurts out…

"It was a chicken."

"Sorry?"

"Silly sod left a chicken in a frying pan on the stove."

"Really?" I'm amazed.

"Been there all night, so that chap in the white hat told me," she continues, in full flow now.

"What, the Chief Fire Officer?"

"No, him from the fishmongers, brings cod round every Friday." I should have known. This hat thing is getting ridiculous. I can see she means Mr Jenkins from the wet-fish shop. He does deliver every Friday and very nice cod it is too. Bit pricey but you get what you pay for don't you? Only Pete would attempt to cook a whole chicken in a frying pan. Bet he never got that idea from Delia. That one obviously came from the little green Martians who fly into his bedroom at night. And other assorted creatures who crawl out of the woodwork when he's coming down from a bender.

"His trousers are wet," she suddenly whispers, as if afraid to embarrass him.

"Probably where the firemen hosed him down," I offer.

Or not as they say. Over the last few months, he has started to develop damp patches, so to speak. Could be pee I suppose but I prefer to think it's where he's spilled his drink. Give him the benefit of the doubt and all that. People around here are quick enough to condemn him at the best of times and I don't want to be a party to that. You see, behind that whisky soaked brain lies a gentle giant. He is truly. A hopeless, harmless giant with a heart of gold.

This is the man who made me a clock for my last birthday. It consists of an old metal plate and a battery and the bloody thing fascinates me. He actually sat down and took time to make it and I was touched by the gesture. It's never worked mind you. One of the hands, fell off as he handed it to me but there you go. It was a nice thought.

"He won't be doing much cooking in that kitchen nos," the woman ventures.

"I'll rustle something up for him," a voice says, and I suddenly realise it's me saying it.

Here we go again. With just a few words I have committed myself to preparing and cooking an extra three meals a day for the next month or so. And food for Budd. And no doubt the odd bit of laundry if his machine has gone into meltdown in that kitchen. It's at times like this, I wish I had a zip on my gob like that character off Rainbow. I could just zip it up and save myself a lot of hassle. Too late now, the deed is done. Just live with it girl. Either that or Social Services will get involved and he'll be carted off to some unit for winos. And they'll take Budd to the dog pound. No, I can't be living with that. I'd have to go and visit twice a day. Much simpler to shove a plate of egg and chips through the hedge.

"Does anybody own this dog?" a deep, husky voice enquires. I swirl around to see Levy sitting in the cab of the fire engine. He's in the driver's seat and has what looks like the remains of a pork pie sticking out of his mouth. I could deny all knowledge and walk away but true to form, I step forward.

"So sorry, I really am, is that your pork pie?"

"It was, not much left of it is there?" he laughs.

"Sorry, what can I say, Labrador… totally insane."

"No harm done love, if you could just get him out of the cab."

I open the cab door and Fireman Fuckwit leaps out and onto my head, dropping the crust of the pork pie at my slippered feet. He is soaking wet and I suspect he's been mooching around inside Pete's burnt out kitchen. Probably eating the remains of that pan fried chicken. Honestly, I swear this dog has the best of everything. Chicken, fish, steak, and an assortment of treats and chocolate buttons yet he's ALWAYS starving. A perpetually open mouth, devouring whatever he can beg, steal or borrow.

It's startling just how much food he can consume and still come back for more. It's not worms. He's wormed on a regular basis, trust me. It can't be comfort eating. He lives the life of Riley in our house. His own duvet, hundreds of squeaky toys, fresh milk every day. It can't be Bulimia either, I'd have noticed if he was sneaking off to puke on the quiet. I'm afraid it's a severe case of Greedy Gutsiness. If it's vaguely edible then he will eat it. To him, vaguely edible encompasses such delicious delights as old socks, tennis balls and squirrel shit. Disgusting! True to form, he's lying at my feet now, with those wonderful eyes fixed on my face. Butter would not melt I can tell you. I can forgive him anything and would defend him to the death should the need ever arise...

"Did your dog eat that hamster as charged?"

"Yes, your worship, but he's a victim of his breeding, retrievers you see."

The fire crew are leaving now, including the man minus his lunch. How awful! He may not get chance to eat again before his shift ends. Perhaps I should have offered him a sandwich. Too late now, they're pulling away, leaving just me and Levy and Mr Jenkins, the wet-fish man, standing on the pavement.

"Don't suppose he'll be wanting his cod fillets nos," he grumbles.

"No, I think he's got some chicken for tonight," I laugh. He is obviously miffed and chucks his wicker basket into the back of the van, scattering fish heads and parsley everywhere. Some people! Poor old Pete has lost most of his belongings and he's fretting about a cod fillet. That's business people for you. The pound is more important than the person. Tosser! That's the last crabstick I buy off you mate. How callous!

"Come on Levy you soft lad, let's get you dried off shall we?" He thinks I haven't spotted the halibut head he's hiding in his gob. He thinks wrong. I am an expert at sussing out his secrets. If I ignore it, he'll take it inside and bury it under the carpet and in a few weeks the whole house will reek of fish. I fell for that once before only then it was a horned toad which squelched every time we trod on the bump in the carpet.

"Drop it!" I bawl at the top of my voice and surprisingly enough he does. Must be full after that pork pie. Pork pie and the three Shredded Wheat he ate for breakfast. And two of Jack's Cumberland sausages. I wish I had access to one of those body scanner things. Lord knows what we would find inside his stomach. A retired postman or a Vespa scooter probably.

"Go on, straight home please. That's enough excitement for one morning."

I follow him up the drive, watching his wonderful gait as he lolls along, his chest solid and puffed up with pride. I can imagine him later on, in the woods, exaggerating the tale to his mates..

"Honest, I leapt into the flames and dragged him out..." which is all well and good if you can back it up but should anybody sneeze within a five mile radius of this lad, you won't see his arse for dust. He is absolutely petrified of sneezes. Honest! It's weird, it really is. This is the lad who will take on vicious dogs and whistling window cleaners but sneeze and he dissolves into a quivering jelly. I have no idea why. It's yet another mystery as yet unsolved. A bit like Chinese builders. Well, there are none are there? Have you ever seen one? Nor me. Something else that keeps me awake at night.

We discovered the sneezing thing one December when Tom came down with a heavy cold. Every time the poor kid sneezed, Levy legged it and hid under the dining room table. I live in fear that we will be burgled by some villain with hay fever, in which case he'll just run and hide while all our worldly goods are loaded onto the van.

Pete will be sleeping it off now in what remains of his bedroom. With the amount of water the fire crew used it should be safe for a while. He can discard his fag ends willy-nilly and they won't catch light. I bet it will take weeks to dry that lot out. Wouldn't be surprised if Gertie and Gilbert take up residence in his sitting room. Waddling around amongst all the debris. He wouldn't notice. He'd think it was another of his delusions. Martians and mallards, it's all the same to him. Levy is sitting patiently on the front step. It's fast approaching lunchtime and he's keen to have a look in the freezer. Could prove to be a bit of a problem though as I appear to have locked myself out. In my rush to see what was going on, I've gone and left my keys on the hall table. Shit! This morning is turning into a right farce.

Jack's in Gloucester all day and Tom and Hannah are in London. Excellent. This should be fun. The guy at number thirteen is a doctor but he's at work and besides, unless he specialises in gynaecology, I don't think he'll be able to slide his arm through the letterbox and reach my keys.

Think woman! Keep calm! Remember your breathing as Tilly would say. Stepladder, that's what I need. One of the small windows is open at the front, so if I can climb up and thread something through onto the main window catch. Stepladder, now where can I get one of those from, with no money and only a pair of wet Winnie The Pooh slippers on? Could prove to be a problem. We have ordinary ladders. Out the back. Great big industrial things which Jack uses to climb onto the roof when necessary. I'd need the help of four hefty men to lift those. Maybe I could reach by standing on a chair. Chair, chair, never one around when you need one is there?

Aha! I know where I've seen a stepladder. In Pete's back garden. I'll have to sneak round and nick it. He'll never notice, not today of all days.

Right, problem solved, just change into my stripy jumper and black mask. Let's pray the Neighbourhood Watch team are all indoors. Getting arrested is the last thing I need. I warn the dog to "STAY," in no uncertain terms. I can do without him crashing around in the undergrowth. As I reach Pete's door I turn to find Levy behind me, his wet nose pressed firmly up against my arse, his face a picture of intense concentration as he wonders what this new game is.

"Lie down," I whisper "Keep a look out." He ignores me and picks up one of Pete's garden gnomes. It's one of those sitting on a toadstool and he has the whole thing in his gaping jaws. What a time to pick to play games, silly sod! I have my hand on the door knob when it suddenly flies open and we are caught, like rabbits in the headlights of a car. Both looking as guilty as hell, although he is guiltier than I, as he has already robbed a garden ornament.

"Pete! You okay?" I cry.

"Fine my dear, panic over. What can I do for you?"

"I've gone and locked myself out. Can I borrow your stepladders?"

"Sure, I'll bring them round," he slurs.

"Thanks, you've saved my life."

An hour later, we are still waiting on the front lawn. Lunchtime has come and gone and Levy is beginning to stare hungrily at my left leg. Just as I am about to give up, Pete finally appears, complete with his breaking and entering kit. This consists of a coat hanger, a copy of the Daily Mail and a can of Fosters. I can only assume that after breaking in, he sits reading the paper and drinking lager.

"Oh Pete, at last!"

"No problem, I'll soon have you inside."

"Great, I have every confidence in you," I lie. I say this without any conviction, convinced he will only fall and break his neck in the process. As if sensing my despair, he straightens up and starts to unravel the wire coat hanger. He even manages a few bars of Nessun Dorma while he works.

"What about the ladder Pete?"

"No need, I'll manage." I don't have the strength to argue and watch in amazement as he clambers up onto the windowsill, drapes the wire down onto the latch inside, and with a sharp crack, the main window flies open. Amazing! Before I can stop him, he leaps through the open window and is at the front door. I'm impressed. If he can manage that while drunk, what could he achieve sober? Levy is first through the door and on his way to the fridge, looking for food.

"Brilliant Pete, thanks a lot."

"All part of the service," he blushes. And with this, he leaps up onto the windowsill and jumps straight back out of the window, taking two of my hanging baskets with him as he falls. I am left standing with my hand on the open front door. Like I say, lovely man, just a bit fuddled. I'm afraid to look outside in case he's lying on the slabs with a broken collarbone but I needn't have worried, he's up on his feet and heading back down the drive, swigging his Foster's as he goes.

"Thanks again!" he waves, disappearing round the bend, back to his still smouldering house. The fridge must have remained intact as he still has cold beer in the house. Unless he grabbed it as he fled the flames. Priorities I suppose. In my case, assuming everybody was safe, I'd grab my photo's. You can never replace those precious memories can you after a fire? A whole lifetime caught on camera never to be seen again. Wedding photos, snaps taken at the seaside in 1978, baby pictures, a puppy paddling in a puddle. Priceless. It's a very valid question actually. What would you grab in the event of a fire? Alicia would grab a mirror so she could still marvel at her beauty every day. Alan would go for his back issues of Star Trek Monthly.

Ma would grab Pa. That's a certainty. And her lemon fairy cake recipe, a secret handed down through our family for generations. She hasn't entrusted it to me yet, I'm still at the burnt toast stage. Jack would grab his golf clubs. All three sets of them and the trolleys as well. Then he'd come back for me I'm sure. With Tom it would be his new Mac computer. State of the art contraption that weighs next to nothing and cost him roughly a thousand squid! It's an amazing invention and one which I am not allowed to touch for obvious reasons. And Hannah, bless her, it would have to be her Nike sports bag. She never goes anywhere without it. The girl is toned and honed to perfection. Probably due to the fact that she swims, plays tennis, cycles, works out at the gym and generally leads a disgustingly healthy lifestyle. Fair play to the girl. Ten to one she won't be wrestling with an orange peel arse at forty. They have been married for five years now and it's flown by. What a day that was. You see, I'd have all their wedding photos to save as well.

The empty-nest syndrome hit me particularly hard. Which is why I probably arrived at the church carrying a tin of rice pudding and a large box of Kleenex. During the run-up to the big day, I tried really hard to psych myself up not to cry and I thought I'd cracked it. Until I heard Ma sniffling behind me and I lost it. The organist had to pump up the volume to drown out my sobs.

On the aforementioned photographs, I have piggy eyes and a swollen nose. Nothing new there then. I got away with it on the video by pulling my hat down over my face and walking backwards. I stopped crying three weeks later when they got back from the Caribbean. It's a Mom thing.

It was a wonderful day and I feel truly blessed to have gained such a delightful daughter-in-law. It was three in the morning before we waved them off to the airport and we were exhausted. Jack was so 'exhausted', he sort of slid down the bedroom wall at the hotel and slept where he landed. Must have been the shock of paying the bill I should think. Now, we have all those memories on film and in albums. That's what I'd have shoved up my nightie if fire broke out.

I must crack on. A whole morning wasted and nothing to show for it, except a broken garden gnome and two hanging baskets. Ma says I lead a charmed life and she's quite right. If anything remotely bizarre is going to happen, then it will happen to me. You know that huge finger thing that points at people about to win the lottery? Well, I have one of those except it's got nothing to do with the lottery. It just says, "IT'S YOU!", and things happen. I'm not complaining. Life would be terribly dull without these little dramas.

I feel quite exhausted now. Think I'll go and sit out on the patio for a while. Get my breath back and take in a few rays while it's shining. Where's the local paper? I'm sure it plopped onto the doormat earlier. Nice glass of cold orange juice and a Benson & Hedges. Does it get much better than this I ask myself? Bit of a whiff of burning furniture from next door but it should disperse when the North Easterly blows up from the sea. I hope he's insured, but I doubt it. He forgets to wear trousers some days, so I don't suppose paying insurance premiums is high on his list of priorities. Right then, job section, what wonderful offers do we have this week? SWIMMING POOL ATTENDANT: I could do that. I can swim, badly, but I can swim. I can stay afloat anyway with my breasts. I could rescue a drowning person, no problem. If I'd been on the Titanic, thousands would have survived simply by clinging to my nipples. FUNERAL SERVICE STAFF:MUST BE RESPECTFUL AND WELL-DRESSED: That's me out then. I can do respectful but not the well dressed bit. And there's no way I could prepare the body. They make noises you know, corpses. They do! Someone in the trade told me. Pockets of trapped wind sort of escape and the stiff can even sit up and belch! Wouldn't you just keel over and die yourself? I would. SHOPLIFTERS REQUIRED:IMMEDIATE

START: Eh? Must be a spelling mistake. They mean shop fitters surely? Unless it's an organised ring recruiting staff. BAR STAFF AT CITY CENTRE CLUB: I don't think so. I wouldn't be able to see over the bar in my current diminishing state. Can you imagine… "Here's your bottle of Bud mate, can you lift me up to get the peanuts?" That's about it. Position closed as they say at the TSB. Well, that took me all of four minutes. A veritable wealth of opportunities in this area then.

I wish I could do something with my hands. I really envy people who have the gift of making those arty, farty craft things. My hands were designed for hammering in nails and concreting the drive. Anyway, you need to have a name like Octavia to be arty. It's compulsory. Your husband will be a Sebastian and you'll spend your weekends together stencilling the dining room and making your own beeswax candles. Your children have to be called Joshua and Jacinta and they both excel at playing chess and the violin. We are none of these things, so a career as a candle maker is crushed.

I can live with that. I'm useful when it's time to lay slabs on the patio and personally I think the violin is a vastly over rated instrument. I have so many joys in my life, I can't complain. I have Levy, who at this very minute is swinging on my Wonderbra on the washing line. Look at him, think's it's a hammock, silly sod.

CHAPTER FIVE

The Men in White Coats

I'm in casualty at Selly Oak Hospital. Nothing terminal, just a hugely inflated foot and ankle, as the result of an insect bite of some description. I didn't want to come but the foot in question was so swollen this morning when I got up, I couldn't get my shoe on. I couldn't even get one of Jack's shoes on and he takes a size eleven. And yes, it is true what they say! How ridiculous, to be forced to visit a hospital by an insect bite. Tiny little midget bugs that sink their fangs into you and make you swell up and go all toxic. Like I say, I wouldn't have bothered but he just reminded me that people have been known to lose limbs through blood poisoning. I thanked him for pointing this out as he dropped me at the hospital gates. Could be a long wait I suppose. I imagine cardiac arrests and ruptured appendix take priority over gnat bites. Not to worry, I have a Penguin biscuit and a copy of War & Peace.

I've been here an hour already. A nurse came along, looked at my foot and fainted so I guess I'm in for a bumpy ride. I have no idea what it was that bit me. It was days ago, in the garden, and I sploshed some TCP on it and assumed it would go away. It didn't and now I'm here, in a hospital, with an elephant foot and no clean underwear. I shall refuse an amputation. I'm stumpy enough without losing one of my feet.

This place is heaving! A positive mass of the dying and the drunk. I wish I were one of the latter. A nice, cold Jack Daniels would go down a treat now in my time of trauma. I'm not sure if I should drink though, anything I mean. Even a hot chocolate out of the machine. What if I require urgent surgery and I've just had a drink? Bit late really since I've just eaten my Penguin. I can feel it sloshing round in my stomach. No anaesthetic for me today.

I'm in a cubicle, with the offending foot elevated on a chair. Not my idea I should say. Some woman in a turban just wafted past and insisted

I elevate it. I don't think she was a nurse, just some well-meaning soul on her way back from the canteen. Nice turban though, one of those silk jobbies with a brooch at the front. I couldn't wear one but she had the face for it. I have pulled the curtain back a bit so I can see what's going on. If anything gory comes in, I shall close it again. I draw the line at watching head impact cases and stab wounds.

There's an old guy in the cubicle opposite, with stomach pains. Poor old thing. He's very old and very pale and has a woman with him in a beige overall. She's not a cleaner, I think she's one of those care assistants from a retirement home. She has a name badge on and sensible shoes. Dead giveaway. He appears to have lost his teeth. Perhaps Mrs Overall has them in her pocket in case he's sick. Is there no dignity in growing old? Sadly, I think not. No teeth and just his pyjama bottoms on. If that were Pa, I'd be livid. Cover him over you cretin. Put his teeth back in and stop talking to him in that ridiculous slow tone, as if he's retarded.

"They're getting you a commode Samuel," she drawls "and a s. u. p. p. o. s. i. t. o. r. y." My life... poor bugger must be constipated! No wonder he's in pain. I'm not surprised he's constipated, if they keep taking his teeth away. How can he ever eat anything? Except mashed banana and semolina. Give him his dentures back you bitch! Go buy him a double portion of cod and chips and mushy peas. That would get him moving.

I could never see Ma or Pa go into a home. I know it's difficult and you have to know all the circumstances, but I couldn't. Matron would nag Pa about him chewing his jelly and Ma would be up to her elbows in lemon fairy cake mix with all the residents dying. No, I couldn't.

The commode has arrived, along with a burly male charge nurse who I assume will administer the suppository. Please be gentle with him. I can't bear to think about it. Oh, they're pulling the curtains, thank goodness for that. Let the poor bloke poo in peace for God's sake. Mrs Overall is off to the canteen for a coffee, and a slice of fruit pie no doubt. Bet she doesn't bring old Samuel a slice back.

I have no desire to grow extremely old and frail. I have instructed Tom that when the time comes he can shoot me. Old is fine, but frail and alone is not. Samuel is destined to spend the rest of his days being shunted around from place to place with only Mrs Overall for company no doubt. It's so sad but what's the answer? How depressing. I shall have to draw the curtain and distance myself or Samuel could end up living on the Cedars with Levy and I.

It's getting on for nine-o-clock now. I wonder what everybody at home is doing? Levy will be up at the window, waiting for me, and Jack will be practising his golf swing in the garden. I'm to ring him when I'm ready to leave. Shan't hold my breath on that one.

There's a splatter of dried blood on the wall. Congealed and blobby. Nice! Apart from that, this cubicle is very clean. Nice new curtains and a poster about drugs. Oh, and a trolley with the usual bits and bobs on. Plasters and rubber gloves and scalpels. I'm just about to have a poke around, when a head pops around the curtain. A doctor at last! At least, I assume he's a doctor, he's wearing a white coat and a stethoscope so it's a fair assumption. He also bears a striking resemblance to Saddam Hussein. He steps inside and summing up his vast medical knowledge says, "Dat nasty!". I agree and grit my teeth as he pokes and prods the mutant foot. We reach a mutual agreement, whereby he agrees not to hurt me and I agree to let go of his scrotum.

"Is poison," he exclaims in a frightened voice.

"Wonderful!" I reply, in an even more frightened one. At this point, he sits down and stares me right in the eye. I prepare myself for the worst, all those quips about amputation coming back to haunt me.

"I cut it," he offers.

"I faint," I gulp. He grins. An enormous, toothy grin, exposing several gold fillings in the process.

I laugh too, but mine is more of an hysterical laugh than a jolly one.

"Be fine," he promises, gathering up instruments of torture as he speaks. I brace myself for the sound of flesh ripping but it doesn't come. It's all over in a flash, but then it takes him three minutes to release my vice-like grip from around his neck. Problem solved and strangely enough, with the pressure released, the fluid inside is now free to ooze out and the foot feels a lot more comfortable. He swabs it and bandages it and within no time at all I'm feeling a whole lot better. God Bless the NHS I say! If I were living in Botswana, they would have cut the foot off.

"Antibiotics. Take all the tablets. Good as nes," he smiles.

"I will, thank you doctor."

"Take this to the hatch on your way out," he tells me, pointing to the main doors.

"Thanks again." And with that, he disappears. Marvellous! You have to hand it to these medics. All that studying certainly pays off. Imagine being confronted with a thousand different cases every week and being expected to know all the answers. Amazing, I'm impressed.

As I draw back the curtain, Samuel decides it's time and let's rip with the most astounding barrage of wind I have ever heard in my entire life. And don't forget, I live with a Labrador and it doesn't get much worse than that. Tremendous, earth shattering farts ricochet around the walls for what seems like forever. The entire unit comes to a standstill, with nurses and patients alike, standing in awe at the outburst. When it's over, I quite expect people to applaud but instead Samuel let's out a long, satisfied sigh. The sigh of a man who has suffered and is now relieved. I'm so glad. He can have his teeth back now.

I hand my prescription into the hatch and wait. It's very dark outside and I shall be glad to get home. The clock on the wall says it's 7.32 but it also says it's the third of November 1987. My watch says 11.15pm, so not too bad. Should be home by midnight. The glass partition slides back and a bored looking individual pokes her head out...

"Ryder... Cassie?"

"Yes, that's me."

"That'll be twenty-four pounds please."

"Excuse me?"

"Twenty-four pounds," she snaps.

"It's a swollen ankle, not a triple by-pass," I protest.

"Very droll. Twenty-four pounds please."

"For antibiotics?"

She sighs, obviously having been through this conversation a million times before.

"Look, four items... Amoxcil, antiseptic swabs and two clean dressings," she sneers. I am stunned and it shows. I had no idea you had to pay for things in hospital. Shows how often I pay a visit doesn't it? I just assumed you got treated for free. Silly me. I decide honesty is the best policy and tell her.

"I've only got thirty-nine pence on me."

"You'll have to sign then."

"Sign what?"

"A legal agreement to say you'll pay later." This is ridiculous. I would pay if I had my purse with me, but I truly had no idea. Now, I have to agree to hand over my house if I don't cough up. My foot is throbbing and I snap back.

"Fine! Give it here!"

"Just there, at the bottom," she smirks. I sign it... Mo Mowlam. She doesn't notice, silly bitch. Obviously spends her life trapped behind that partition, scaring people to death. Imagine if your kidneys failed and you needed urgent medication afterwards. On a daily basis... for the rest of your life...

"That'll be eight thousand pounds please... no cards." No wonder people collapse and die in hospital. I'm not surprised. Jack is waiting at the entrance as I stagger out of the double doors. I think he's been there for a while as a cobweb is forming on the end of his nose. Levy is in the passenger seat, fiddling with the seat belt.

"Everything okay. Did it hurt much?" he asks as I fall onto the back seat.

"All done. Just take these antibiotics and it'll be fine."

"Any stitches?"

"Just a few, about a dozen," I lie.

"Christ Cass!"

"Don't fuss, it's nothing."

"I'd have come in with you if I'd known."

"No, it's okay, really." I give him my pathetic look, just to rub it in. I'll let him wallow in guilt for a couple of hours then tell him the truth. Levy is very sympathetic and shows it by gnawing at my bandage.

Back home, I'm safely tucked up in bed with the foot elevated yet again. The throbbing has eased a little now that the dog has stopped chewing at my ankle. Jack is engrossed in his Golf Monthly, while I count the cobwebs on the bedroom ceiling. Samuel is still playing on my mind and I say a silent prayer that his bowels are now functioning properly.

Genetically speaking, I suppose I can look forward to reaching a ripe old age. My Gran, on my Ma's side, lived well into her nineties. Thankfully, she ended her days at home and not in some anonymous hospital ward, surrounded by strangers. Although, to be honest, towards the end even her close family were strangers to her. She took to calling Ma, Gerald and was convinced Pa was the insurance man. Gran never saw the inside of a hospital. All of her ELEVEN kids were born at home! Goodness me! I gave birth just the once and still have flashbacks twenty-six years later. I won't say it was painful, but Jack and I have only recently resumed a normal sex life. No wonder I have a phobia about hospitals. I was ten months pregnant when they decided to surgically remove my tights so that I could give birth. And from that moment on, things went downhill fast.

I was pregnant in the Summer of 1976. Remember the heatwave? Water was rationed and people were collapsing everywhere with sunstroke. I was with child and waddled around in seven yards of

Mothercare gingham with chronic wind and sore nipples. Once again, as now, with my hormones raging, I lost several fillings, most of my hair and on very hot days, the will to live.

On the labour ward, I was greeted warmly by the sister on duty, who shook my hand, while expertly inserting an enema with her free one. Charming! Inside my overnight bag, I had packed a dozen pairs of clean pants and two hundred cigarettes. My litre bottle of Jack Daniels was confisticated by the guards at the checkpoint. I also had a lovely new flannel. It was purple and I bought it especially for the birth. All the books said you needed a flannel. Jack was supposed to bathe my weary brow with it during labour. Except the midwife got in first and soaked it in very hot water, leaving it to rest on my forehead. When Tom was finally delivered, several days later, Jack was allowed in to see me.

"Cassie, he's beautiful. Are you okay?"

"Mm… thanks."

"Why are your eyebrows purple?"

"Sorry?"

"Your eyebrows. They're purple."

Still shattered and woozy from the gas and air, it took a while for his words to sink in.

"It's the flannel."

"Will it wash off?"

"What?"

"Will it come off?" he asks again.

"Does it matter?"

"No, course not."

"Well then!" I snap. There is an embarrassing silence while he continues to stare at my forehead.

"It's dyed your eyebrows as well."

"Oh for fuck's sake!"

"Sorry, I just thought… if it's permanent dye."

"Does this face care?"

"No… quite… sorry," he grovels.

"My vagina is probably a very similar shade at the moment all things considered," I yell. He knows when to back off and smiles sweetly.

"Right, just pop and ring Ma and Pa. Tell them they have a beautiful grandson."

"And a purple daughter."

"Fine, back in a jiff." I still giggle thinking about it now after all these years. It was weeks before the stains faded.

"What's funny?" he asks distractedly, sitting up in bed with his Nike golf cap on.

"Well, apart from that ridiculous cap, I was thinking about the purple flannel."

"Not getting broody are you?"

"Don't be ridiculous, at my age and with this body, perish the thought."

"We've never done it with your legs elevated," he leers.

"And we never will," I tell him quite firmly. You have to be clear about these things.

He goes back to his magazine, knowing defeat when he hears it. I have lost count of the cobwebs and anyway, they provide a home for valuable spiders, so I couldn't dust them off. Levy is hiding under the pine dresser. He thinks he's invisible under there but I can see his ebony eyes glinting in the light from the bedside lamp. It's one of his favourite hiding places. He lies in wait, watching your every move and just when you think it's safe to go to sleep, he'll leap out and dive on top of your head.

"We can't anyway, the dog's watching," I whisper.

"Better not then, he thought I was attacking you last time and bit my arse."

"Absolutely, protecting his Mommy."

I can feel my eyes closing, as exhaustion takes over. Jack meanwhile is wide awake and mentally playing a round of golf in Atlanta with Tiger Woods. He is way out in the lead and Tiger is getting stroppy. It's one of his favourite fantasies. That and anything that involves women with enormous breasts. I leave him to it and finally cave in to the waves of exhaustion washing over me.

I'm not sure if I have a slight fever with this foot, but I toss and turn for ages and seem to find it hard to wake up properly. Drifting from sleep to a semi-comatose state, then back again. Now I'm back in the hospital. Sitting on a plastic chair in some sort of waiting area. There's just me and a nurse behind the reception desk. She's reading a Mills & Boon and I am clutching Ma's shopping bag for some reason. What on earth is going on? This is extremely odd. My bladder is bursting and I look round anxiously for the loo. If I hurry, I'll make it back before they call me in. The nurse smiles knowingly at me as I run past her towards the ladies.

No toilet paper! Isn't it always the way? I'm here for some sort of examination and there's no toilet paper to wipe myself on. Oh pants!

Let's see if I have any tissues in Ma's bag. I know there'll be a spare pair of knickers and a bus pass but I need a tissue. Here we go, just a tiny scrap of Kleenex right at the bottom of the bag. That will have to do.

As I go back into the waiting room, they are calling my name over the tannoy...

"RYDER... CASSIE... CUBICLE THREE PLEASE!" Like a lamb to the slaughter, I meekly follow the nurse through to the cubicle. What the hell am I here for? I have no idea and nobody is saying anything.

"Undress and put this on please," the nurse says, handing me a butcher's apron? I don't like this at all. If this is a nightmare, I demand to wake up, immediately! Too late, the door opens and several doctors enter, followed by a cleaner in a beige overall.

"On the bed please Mrs Ryder," the cleaner snaps. I do as I am told and lie back on the bed. As I do so, my legs are strapped into stirrups. With my legs akimbo, the entire mass of medics, plus the cleaner, advance and appear to be scrutinising my nether regions. Well really! I shall go private in future if this is the sort of treatment you receive in the NHS. This is outrageous! Go poke your noses up somebody else's privates!

They appear to be puzzling over something. What is it for God's sake? A tumour? Massive and malignant I bet. Beyond treatment. Oh shit! Wake up Cassie, you dopey cow! They huddle in a corner and I can hear them whispering in sombre tones. The cleaner comes back for a second look and smiles at me sympathetically. That's it then! I'm a gonner. Serves me right for avoiding my smear test last year.

Finally, somebody speaks. It's the Jamaican doctor. The one wearing a straw boater.

"Interesting case Mrs Ryder, very interesting."

"Why?... what is it... tell me!" I bawl.

"You appear to have a first class stamp stuck to your clitoris," he grins. I must be hallucinating. The poison from my foot has reached my brain and I'm dying. Help!

"Bad dream?" asks Jack, still sitting up in bed wearing that ruddy cap. I am bathed in sweat and still shaking from the experience.

"Nightmare... it was awful... I was in hospital wearing a butcher's apron," I gasp.

"Shouldn't have had that Dairylea triangle. You know cheese disagrees with you."

"The doctor had a boater on and the cleaner had a look." I have his attention now. He's wide awake and interested.

"Look at what?"

"The stamp on my clitoris."

"What did the stamp say, KEEP OUT:NO GO ZONE?" he laughs.

"A postage stamp, first class. Must have been stuck to the tissue."

"Did they give you any injections in casualty? Painkillers, opiates?" he giggles.

"No."

"Told you, must be that Dairylea then." I'm too drained to argue, although he does have a point. Cheese does disagree with me. Just a tiny nibble of a Canadian Mature and I'm positively suicidal. Honest! Cheese depresses me terribly so I try to avoid it whenever possible. Cheese on toast signifies slashed wrists to me so I steer clear. I have no idea why. A friend of mine who's into holistic healing, thinks I may have a chemical intolerance to the stuff. I think she may be right.

"Think I'll go and make a cuppa, would you like one?" he asks.

"Does the Pope wear a funny hat?"

"Anything to nibble?"

"No, not for me thanks."

"I fancy some cheese and crackers, or cheese on toast, or maybe cheese and pineapple," he grins.

"Get stuffed!"

"Cheese and pickle, cheesecake, cottage cheese."

"Must be wonderful to be so funny," I growl.

His head, complete with Nike cap, disappears around the door, still muttering...

"Cheese and onion crisps... cheese straws." I can hear him still, all the way down the stairs, reciting his cheeseboard menu, prat! Levy seizes his chance and leaps into bed, splaying his legs out in all directions. Within seconds he is fast asleep and snoring loudly. I cuddle up to him for comfort. Much better than an electric blanket this lad. There will be no moving him now, he's out for the count. He of the Nike head will have to sleep in the fridge... with the cheese.

CHAPTER SIX

Fish & Chips and a Ferrari

We are driving through the Romsley Hills. A delightful wooded area on the outskirts of Birmingham. They say money talks, and if that's the case, this place is positively shouting. It's all part of my therapy program. Indulging myself. Taking time out to do the things that I want to do. And this is one of them. The quest to find a suitable playmate for Levy. A bitch whom I have already named Lyric, even though she is still a figment of my imagination. She's out there somewhere and today just might be the day that we find her.

Some of these properties must be worth millions of squids. They're enormous, set in hundreds of acres, right in the middle of rolling hills. Your nearest neighbour would be about three miles away I should think and a stroll to the shops for a pinta could take about a week. I'm impressed.

"This can't be the place," I squeak.

"Trust me, it is," Jack states quite confidently.

"Well, if the police arrive and arrest us, I shall deny everything." His face remains calm and confident. He's obviously not phased at all.

"You keep them talking and I'll grab some antiques," he laughs.

"Oh, very droll I'm sure."

"Look Cass, trust me. I know what I'm doing."

"You said that the night I conceived."

"I was probably drunk."

"Thanks!"

"Here we go, this is the one," he says, indicating to turn right onto a vast driveway. I sense a police helicopter hovering nearby, ready to arrest us for daring to enter the area in a clapped out Cavalier. I say nothing, mentally running through the statement I shall give to the police, as we crunch our way along the drive. As we approach the main house, I am gobsmacked by the sheer opulence of it all. The Georgian mansion in the distance. The stable block and ornamental lake complete with swans and a water feature! I half expect Jane Austen to come trotting towards us, riding a thoroughbred of course.

The word magnificent does not even begin to describe it. In the distance, an enormous black stallion is galloping around in the sun. Shafts of light reflecting off his glossy coat. If I wasn't so terrified of horses, I'd jump on his back and gallop off into the hills, facial hair blowing in the wind.

We're here to view a litter of pups. Black of course. Labradors. Would I be interested in any other breed? This particular litter are all spoken for, but the lady of the house very kindly invited us to have a look anyway, with a view to buying one from the next litter. I have been promising Levy a ladyfriend for ages and like I said, it's an indulgence for me too. He is at home, decorating the nursery and sorting out his old Bonio's ready for the new arrival. My heart is pounding and I'm not sure if it's excitement or the possibility of being arrested.

"Come on, let's take a look," Jack says, leaping out of the car.

I follow discreetly behind, praying that they don't have a Rottweiller on the loose in the grounds. As we get nearer to the main house, the heavy oak door flies open and a woman bounds over to greet us. Bounded being the operative word. Jodhpurs flapping in the breeze, she oozes the sort of confidence that having several million squid in the bank can bring. Jodhpurs and jewellery. An odd combination but quite the done thing in these social circles I should think. And the headscarf of course. I believe they are obligatory if you're stinking rich. Silk, Hermes no doubt, with a fine rose-petal pattern on it. It's hard to determine an age, probably mid-fifties or seventy with a skilled plastic surgeon. Who knows? Her solid leather riding boots crunch on the gravel as she heads towards us and I detect a faint whiff of Dior as she extends a hand in greeting.

"Sullivan… Hermione… come to see the pups have you?" she booms.

"Ryder, Cassie, yes we have."

"Marvellous… bloody marvellous… come through," she says, leading the way. I follow obediently, doffing my invisible cap in her wake, completely overawed by it all. Jack on the other hand wanders off to admire the sparkling red Ferrari parked outside the front door. I give him one of my looks, warning him not to even think about taking it for a test drive. She leads us through an archway and into the kitchen, an area that could quite easily rehouse the entire occupants of a city centre tower block. Everything is spotless, and new, and expensive, including the American style fridge-freezer which is bigger than your average bungalow. Hermione stands warming her ample arse on the Aga while I hover in the doorway, terrified my boots will scratch the parquet flooring. Jack meanwhile strides in as if he owns the place and wanders over to the window, admiring the magnificent view.

"Now, about these pups. If you do have one in the future, will you be at home with it?" she asks.

"Well, yes, except when I'm out of course," I stammer.

"And do you have a regular vet?"

"We have a vet, but I can't tell you what his bowel habits are," Jack pipes up. This is turning into an interrogation and he's not very good under pressure.

"Is money a problem?" she suddenly snaps, ignoring his last remark.

"Not if you have lots of it," he laughs. He's on a roll now, there'll be no stopping him. She obviously thinks he's a simpleton and directs her questions at me now instead.

"What about food?" she booms. This is ridiculous! I'm cracking under the pressure and my brain is turning to trifle yet again.

"We usually shop at Safeway."

"Right... follow me!" she barks.

I wobble off in her wake, stunned by the audacity of it all. I absolutely adore black labs. I would give my life if necessary to protect any puppy in my care, yet this woman seems to consider us unfit to be left in charge of a budgie. Jack senses my insecurities and grins at me. A great big sloppy grin that tells me to ignore her and just enjoy the moment. She meanwhile, is five strides ahead and we both have to run to catch up with her.

In the far corner of the courtyard is a horsebox and she suddenly vanishes inside with us hot on her heels. Inside, tucked up snuggly under the glare of a sun-lamp are the pups. Six in all, tiny little snuffling bundles of fur with eyes like saucers. I have to bite my lip hard to stop myself from bursting into tears. Joy oh joy! This surely must be what heaven is like.

Mum is nestled down in the middle of them, enjoying a snooze after her ordeal no doubt. Her curious eyes follow us as we approach her beautiful babies. She's a sloppy old thing and wags her tail as we kneel down beside them. The pups are all marked with a splodge of nail varnish in different colours to distinguish them from one another. Lilac, red, orange, pink, purple and gold.

"Smashing little buggers aren't they?" Hermione beams and I have to agree.

"Incredible." Jack is cradling the pup splodged with red nail polish in his arms and smiles as it buries it's tiny head under his armpit. I've seen that look in his eyes before. He's in love.

"Are they all spoken for?" he asks.

"Yes, afraid so. Four off to an estate in Aberdeen and the other two to Yorkshire."

I take it she means a shooting estate, not a council estate. Heaven forbid that these darlings should end up living in a council flat on some concrete jungle. These dogs are born to run and romp in the woods. To chase Cyril's and roll in mud. I can offer all of these things and much more. I shall lie if necessary. We may not live in a mansion with acres of land but we do have all the love in the world to give to a new addition. I shall lie if necessary, tell her we're lottery winners in the process of buying a pad in Oxfordshire.

"Have to get on," she warbles "Lunch party for twelve." We consider ourselves dismissed and reluctantly leave the horsebox but not before I grab a quick kiss with one of the babies. It's sweet smelling breath wafting across my face as I cling onto it for dear life. Back outside, Hermione is stroking the head of a grey filly tethered to a post in the courtyard.

"I can ring you, when the bitch is due to whelp," she gushes.

"Please, we really would love one of the next litter."

"Jot your number on this," she says, pushing a piece of paper and a pen into my hand.

"We'd appreciate it, thanks."

"You're talking round about the four-hundred mark," she tells us "Perfect pedigree you see."

"No problem," Jack tells her without even flinching. You have to admire his courage.

"Actually, you could do me a huge favour if you don't mind," she asks.

"Sure."

"I'm running late and as you have to drive past the grocers, could you get me some carrots?"

"Course, those little shops in the village?" I ask.

"Marvellous!" she booms and strides off into the house, leaving us to run her errands. Back in the car, Jack is laughing to himself. At me no doubt.

"Of course your ladyship, can I blacklead your grate as well."

"Stop it! I'll do anything to keep on her good side. Think of the pups," I whisper. We retrace our route to the shops and a few minutes later I'm struggling back to the car with the carrots.

"Cass, she said lunch for twelve." He's laughing at me, staggering under the weight of the sack of organic carrots on my back.

"I thought they were for the horses," I whimper.

"Silly sod!"

"Cost me fifteen quid this lot."

"We'll knock it off the price of the pup," he says "Tell her they cost twenty, she'll never know." With the carrots on my lap, we make our way back up the drive just as Hermione gallops off towards the hills on the black stallion. We can just about make out her bouncing bum as the horse vaults the gate. Perhaps she's expecting us to prepare the carrots as well. And do the washing up. My fears are unfounded, as we pull up outside, a guy in a white apron appears at the kitchen door. He's wearing a pair of those incredibly loud, black and white checked trousers that chef's wear, so I take it he's doing the cooking. Either that or he has no dress sense whatsoever.

"Carrots?" he drawls in a sort of mixed Mediterranean accent.

"Lots of them," I venture, handing him the sack. He takes it off me and disappears back into the house without even a thank you. Cheek! How the other half live eh? A brief insight into living in Nobland. Still, I'm not bitter as that Murphy's add says. Imagine having to mow all those acres of grass? And all that horse shit to clear up? Not that Hermione would do menial tasks like that. I bet she has a specially appointed shit-shoveller with his own gold-plated shovel. It's another planet isn't it?

We head home in silence, each of us wrapped up in our own thoughts. Me grieving over not returning with a pup and him daydreaming about that Ferrari. I missed my chance there. I could quite easily have secreted one of those pups inside my bra. Nobody would have noticed. Could have legged it down the drive before Hermione even realised. Better still, we could have loaded the entire litter into the Ferrari and driven off in that. Two fantasies fulfilled in one go.

"Would you care to join me for lunch old bean?" he asks, breaking into my thoughts.

"Absolutely, where does one go around here for luncheon?"

"Chip shop suit? I could run to a pickled egg."

"Spiffing!"

"And a battered sausage?"

I laugh. He laughs. I have my hand in his trouser pocket, checking to see if he really does have enough to run to a pickled egg.

"Steady girl, this fresh air's gone to your head."

"Just rifling your pockets."

"Nothing unusual there then."

"Talking of dosh, it's a lot of money… for the pup."

"Leave it with me, I'll sort something out," he smiles. I'm impressed by his confidence, especially since he only has four-pounds thirty in his pocket.

"You could sell your body," he finally says.

"Medical research or sex?"

"Medical research… definitely not sex," he laughs, turning onto the M6 "You could sell a kidney… to some rich Arab with renal failure."

"Thanks, I'll think about it."

"Or rent out your womb to a childless couple."

"Fine, enough now." He's on a roll again. This will be the tone for the rest of the journey I suspect.

"You could sell your sperm!" I bite back.

"Priceless that'd be… I'd be a millionaire."

"Yeah right!"

"Just imagine all those Baby Ryder's running around."

"Miraculous, considering you had a vasectomy three years ago."

"Oh right." He's deflated now, forgetting that he's been firing blanks for years. After the first few months of worrying, you sort of forget about it and just enjoy the obvious benefits, if you know what I mean.

"Best thing I ever did. Ten minutes and a lifetime of lust," he laughs.

"You told me it took an hour, and you were in agony, crippled in fact."

"I lied," he confesses "It was a doddle."

"You scumbag! All that fuss and propping you up on pillows."

"Well, you women have the fuss after childbirth, just redressing the balance."

I am trying not to laugh and turn my face away, pretending to look out of the car window.

"Besides, it was a much bigger op for me… if you get my drift."

"In what way?"

"Well, you know, the surgeon usually only has to operate on normal sized scrotum's."

"As opposed to…?"

"Enormous… I think that was the word he used."

"Liar!"

"Be fair Cass, you've only ever seen the one so how could you possibly judge?"

"Pardon?"

"The one… scrotum… whatever… how would you know. I'm considered humungous."

"Thanks for sharing that with me darling."

Silly sod! Humungous, really! I sometimes wonder what goes on in that head of his.

"How do you know anyway?" I ask.

"Know what?"

"That I've only seen the one."

"You told me."

"I lied!"

"Charming and I thought you were a virgin on our wedding night."

"No, I just kept my tights on."

And with that ringing in his ears, we finally arrive back in our own little driveway. No stallions galloping about, no acres of rolling hills, just Levy waiting at the window with a disgruntled look on his face and a rolling pin in his mouth.

"If he jumps up now, that window will be demolished," Jack observes.

"Not to worry, he'll have a playmate soon to toss around."

"As soon as you've sold your kidney."

We manage to get in the door and grab the rolling pin before he takes out the bay window.

"Lie down lad," Jack whispers and as ever Levy does exactly as he's told and retreats onto his favourite armchair.

"How do you do that?" I ask, trying not to sound too annoyed. It's so infuriating, one word from the Master and that dog turns to putty in his hands.

"It's a man thing," he sneers, winking at Levy in a conspiratory way.

Indeed it does appear to be a man thing. It was exactly the same when we invested in a month of dog-training sessions. What a complete waste of time and money that was! Well, from my point of view anyway. To this day, that dog will obey every single command that Jack utters, yet if I try it, he simply rolls onto his back and laughs hysterically. Infuriating!

He was only six months old at the time but still bigger and barmier than any of the other dogs in the group. Their respective owners would groan loudly as we pulled up in the car park every week. Any training their pets should have received, went out of the window when His Lordship arrived. Put it this way, if it had been a proper school, he'd have been labelled as disruptive and expelled.

The ironic thing is, he's an extremely intelligent dog. He has the ability to understand and respond to every word you say but gets bored very easily. At the first session, within minutes he was sitting and walking to heel and generally showing off to all the other dogs. Half an hour down the line and I could tell by his body language he was getting bored. He lay on his back in the middle of the arena, yawning. He ate several training manuals and as a finale he peed up Mr Morton's leg. Mr Morton was the trainer and he wasn't amused. The signs were not looking good and as I struggled to regain control, I could hear Jack laughing like a drain at the back of the hall.

Mr Morton had told us when we enrolled, that it was best if the person who did most of the dog walking took the classes. That was me obviously, so it was I who ended up in the arena, wrestling with half a hundredweight of excitable Labrador. It was I who showed the entire group my pants as my skirt flew over my head while trying to hold him down with my legs.

He was kindness itself, the trainer, a retired police-dog handler. I understand he retired for good shortly after we left the group. I actually have a theory on all this. If those training sessions had involved something more challenging, I'm sure Levy would have behaved a lot better. There's only so many times you can retrieve a ball without getting pissed off isn't there?

"Come on, this is kids stuff, fetch me some sheep to round up mate."

We did sitting, and walking to heel, and lying down and on-guard. He was good at that, passed with distinction in that category. Trouble was we did all those things over and over and over again, ad infinitum until he was fed up. Quick learner see.

There was a Bassett Hound in the group. With depression! I kid you not, it's owner was beside herself with worry over the poor thing. I felt sorry for Bertie and would have invited him round for tea but Levy was having none of it.

Anyway, the man-thing was proved to me at the final session. I had a heavy cold and was feeling dreadful, so Jack volunteered to go through the paces with him while I sat huddled up in a corner at the back. If I hadn't witnessed it myself, I'd never have believed it. That lad strutted his stuff like a champion, obeying every single command given, without any sign of tantrums.

He walked to heel, lay down on command and even waited until instructed to retrieve a Bonio! Little shit! He got his certificate and a rosette and lots of admiring looks from the crowd. I got a smug grin from Jack and a chest infection.

"I shall be firmer with Lyric, start as I mean to go on," I tell Jack. He's not listening but I can hear him laughing as he wanders off out into the garden. Probably looking for the wheelbarrow, to carry his enormous scrotum in.

CHAPTER SEVEN

Dumplings & Dreams

Tilly says I should take time out, recharge the batteries and be kind to myself. Stop pushing so hard and making impossible demands on the old bod. I think she is trying to tell me, in the kindest way possible, that I will never work again. Trouble is, I have always worked. Long and hard, with hours ranging from forty to seventy a week. And at times, done jobs that involved surgical masks and rubber gloves. I am a grafter and find it difficult to adjust to having time on my hands. When your whole life has revolved around deadlines and sales targets and meetings with morons, you sort of freefall into the unknown when you become unemployed. A bit like living in the Twilight Zone.

She is sitting opposite me in the counselling suite. She wants me to sum up how I am feeling in just one word and I'm struggling to respond. Disorientated, exhausted, barking mad with a tendency to walk around with my pants on my head. Whatever, I am falling apart and she holds the glue to put Humpty back together again. The only word that comes close is crumpled. I am completely crumpled. Celebrities check into the Priory. I have these weekly sessions at the Crumple Clinic.

"Let's approach it from a different angle. Tell me why you feel the need to push yourself so hard," she whispers "Why not allow yourself time to heal?"

I know exactly where she's coming from but still feel the need to fight it all the way. Without a salary, I feel like a second-class citizen. Tossed on the scrap heap before fifty. Destined to spend my days in the library, browsing through the situations vacant with the other saddo's. Eating fish paste sandwiches out of a Tupperware box.

This is a dreadful exaggeration of course. I have Jack, and know full well that he will support me whatever. I want for nothing really. I sleep in a warm bed every night with a full belly and have the love and support of a wonderful family, but way back in the corners of my fuddled brain, I still feel as if I'm letting them down. I used to contribute. I had a bank balance once. Now my bank manager sends me patronising letters every month along with vague threats to send round the heavy mob to kneecap me. I have told him in no uncertain terms, that if he persists in hassling me, I shall withdraw my sixty-nine pence and take my business elsewhere.

"I'd like to contribute," I waffle, playing for time.

"But you do, in lot's of ways," she smiles "Think of the things you do for your family. That's a valuable contribution don't you think?" I'm not sure they'd see it that way. Burning the Sunday roast, scorching shirts, forgetting their names.

"Tell me about your jobs in the past. What have you done before?" I smile just thinking about my illustrious career, "Have you got a week to spare?" She smiles back.

"Go on, we'll cover as much ground as we can." I take a deep breath and exhale. This could take a while.

"There was my last job, before I ended up here. You know, in the charity shop. I told you about it in our first session. The straw that broke the camel's back, so to speak."

"Why was that?"

"It was a complete nightmare, I ended up working twelve hours a day, six days a week, then I cracked. Went to bed one night exhausted and woke up with a head full of trifle."

"Go on."

"I was supposed to be the manager. You try managing a crew of twenty senile volunteers with an average age of ninety-six and health problems. They drove me insane, literally! The job was a doddle, it was the volunteers who drove me over the edge."

"Why?"

"Where do I start? They only turned up because the shop was warm and they got an endless supply of free tea and biscuits. Oh, and the odd piece of Wedgewood they could shove down their bloomers on the way out. Honest!"

"Really?" she blinks, looking startled.

"It's true! I spent a year trying to stop them fighting amongst themselves and picking them up when they fell over."

"Goodness!"

"Exactly, and the medical side. My life! It was like running a home for the chronically ill. You name it and they suffered from it. Bladder problems, dementia, strokes. Out of a workforce of twenty, I had just two women who were upright and mobile. It got to the stage where I had a paramedic on standby in case one of them keeled over."

"Oh dear." I'm on a roll now, there'll be no stopping me... the floodgates have opened.

"And baggage! God, do they carry some baggage. Arguing over who ate the last custard cream. Tantrums over who worked on the till and who sorted the donations out. I was forever wading in to break up fights."

"Sounds awful," she whispers sympathetically.

"It was."

"Were there no positive points. No aspects of the job that you enjoyed?" This stumps me momentarily. It's hard to recall one second when I didn't feel suicidal in that job.

"I suppose the Easter bunny thing was quite funny," I finally concede.

"What was that then?"

"It was Easter, and I had this promotion going. Trying to rake in some extra cash. I managed to talk a theatrical company into loaning me an Easter bunny suit. Trouble was, when it arrived it was way over the top. At least eight feet tall, with a head that weighed a ton. It was funny now that I think about it."

"Why?"

"Well, the poor woman who volunteered to get inside it was only tiny, so her line of vision came up to the bunny's navel. She staggered along the High Street, crashing into passers-by and knocking over display stands. Killed three pensioners," I laugh. Tilly is laughing too, "See, there were good days," she giggles.

"It get's better, honest. See, it started to snow of all things. A Good Friday and we had a freak snowstorm. Pouring down it was, like a blizzard. We legged it and ran for cover into the Blue Boy, that big pub on the High Street. Me, and an eight-foot rabbit, sitting in the bar, drinking Jack Daniels and smoking Marlboro Light's. What a farce!" Tilly is helpless with laughter now, tears are streaming down her face and she's crumbling.

"You're quite right, there are positive sides to everything."

"I told you," she splutters. It takes a few minutes before we can compose ourselves sufficiently to carry on. I am feeling much better already.

"Any other weird jobs?"

"God yes! I had a job ironing snooker tables once."

"You're kidding !"

"I did, honest. A friend of mine did it normally but she was going off to New Zealand for a month and asked me to cover. Little private snooker club, only six tables."

"And.?"

"I'm only tiny and I had to take a run at the tables to get a clear swipe at the cloth."

"You certainly pick them don't you?"

"I have a low boredom threshold see, like to try something different, bit of a challenge."

"Sounds like it."

"Then there was my wet-fish phase."

"Pardon?"

"Wet fish. I worked in a wet fish shop. Silly expression that, have you ever seen a dry fish?"

"Can't say I have."

"I liked that job. It was a scream. We laughed all day and went home followed by several hundred cats every night."

"I can imagine."

"Oh, and I washed up too, in a French bistro."

"Bet that was different."

"Mm... it was. When I applied for the job, I thought it would mean loading crystal wine glasses into the washing up machine."

"And it wasn't?"

"Hell no! I WAS the washing up machine. Great big mountains of greasy pots and pans. I could have rowed across the Atlantic in some of the industrial sized ones."

"Goodness!"

"That wasn't the half of it. The chef was French of course... and a bastard. He screamed at me during the entire shift, in French. I only lasted the one shift, that was enough."

"I'm not surprised."

"Besides which, the water was scalding! He kept filling up the sink when my back was turned. I had third degree burns up to my elbows when I finished."

She's laughing again now. Nice to know my illustrious career is such a source of amusement.

"Oh Cassie, why do you do these menial jobs, you're worth much more than that!"

"Like I said, I get bored easily, like to try new things. Bring in a few pennies."

"Maybe it's time you stopped and considered what YOU really want to do. A job that you can enjoy, take some pride in," she whispers, leaning forward in her chair. She's quite right of course, but admitting to yourself that you've wasted most of your life doing jobs nobody else will do is a bitter pill to swallow. Maybe it is time I came clean.

"I know exactly what I want to do but it's just a pipedream, it'll never happen." She leans forward again, her face lighting up with enthusiasm and curiosity.

"What, what will never happen?"

"Me, writing a bestseller. There, I said it!"

"Cassie! You never said, all these sessions and you never once said," she gushes.

"I couldn't. It's too embarrassing. It's a subject I never discuss with anyone. Except the dog and he's not a great one for books."

"Well you should! Do something about it now, go for it!" she yells excitedly. I'd love to get carried away on this tide of optimism, but past experience has taught me to be cautious where dreams are concerned.

"I have tried, years ago, sent my manuscript off to a publisher in London. Waste of time."

"You can't give up after one attempt!"

"I can do without the rejection slips thank you, it does nothing for your self-confidence."

"Bugger the rejection slips! Goodness, did I really say that, sorry!"

She makes me laugh this girl. So gentle and kind and almost prudish in her attitudes.

"Don't be daft! Buggers not a proper swear word... well hardly," I laugh.

"Cassie, you must try! If we all gave up on our dreams, life would be unbearable," she sighs. I detect a slight wistful tone to her voice and am shocked to see her eyes filling with tears. Oh God! what did I say to cause her this pain? What is it about our dreams that touches a raw nerve?

"Are you okay Tilly, you look upset?"

"Fine honest, this is very unprofessional of me, sorry."

"Don't be silly! You're allowed feelings too. Must be a bummer listening to other people's problems all day long."

"Yes, quite," she whispers, her voice quivering with emotion. Now I've gone and done it! I've made the therapist want to top herself! I'm a danger to society. I lean forward and gently touch her arm, hoping to offer just a fraction of the kindness she has shown me in the past. Goodness knows, she's picked me up off the floor enough times.

"Come on Tilly, it can't be that bad."

"But it is!" she wails "You have no idea."

"Tell me then, I'm a good listener." The air is heavy with silence, an oppressive silence that scares me somewhat I have to say. I'm not trained for this. What if she takes me hostage and tries to jump off the clinic roof? I wonder if there's a panic button in here? Keep smiling… reassure her.

"I hate this job," she suddenly blurts out "Hate and detest it!"

"Really?" I manage to say, while grinning like the proverbial Cheshire Cat.

"You have no idea, the whining and the despair," she sobs.

"Oh dear," I trill, exposing my gumline now in an effort to look chirpy.

"Day after day, week after week, the constant assault on my nerves."

"Fancy!" I beam, verging on the hysterical.

"I'm sick of going home at night and worrying about my case load."

"Goodness!" I grin, catching sight of my face in the glass on the coffee table. For some reason I bear a striking resemblance to Jack Nicholson in that film, The Shining.

"Sorry, I'm so sorry, this is unforgivable."

"Not at all, get it off your chest."

"I'm fine now, much better."

"See, things will work out," I smile, with my jaws beginning to ache.

"Yes, now where were we?" she sniffles. I hand her another tissue and glance at the clock on the timer.

"Goodness me… is that the time, better be off."

"Oh right, same time next week?"

"Yes, look forward to it."

"Bye Cassie, and thanks."

"No problem, anytime." I make a run for it before she insists on a group hug. Group hugs are for rugby players, not housewives and their therapists. What was all that about then? She always seems so together, totally in control and coping. Just goes to show, it can happen to the best of us. Life that is. Just jumps on your back and drags you down before you have chance to fight back.

I feel really guilty now, droning on about eight-foot rabbits while she's going through a crisis. I shall have to try and be a bit more upbeat next week. Tell a few jokes or something. Can't have her slitting her wrists while I'm waffling on about my brief trip to Trifletown.

I have to wait in reception for the dozy tart behind the glass partition to unlock the outside door. Why are women who have jobs involving glass partitions so obnoxious? Doctor's receptionists, bank cashiers, people who work in benefit offices, all hiding behind six inches of reinforced glass. I know this place has to adhere to certain security restrictions but she seems to take a delight in making you wait until she sees fit to unlock the gates to freedom. Bitch!

I pretend I don't give a shit and lounge around in the waiting area, casually sprawling on the sofa and flicking through outdated copies of Mental Health Monthly. Now there's a riveting read. She hates it when I finish the crossword. It's not exactly challenging, two down, person suffering from delusions… six letters… let me see… nutter!

Here we go, she's rattling her keys like an extra in Cell Block H. I wouldn't mind but the door is operated by an electronic lock. Silly cow. Ex-prison warder I should think. She has one of those spikey-dykey haircuts and flat shoes. Dead giveaway.

"I'm waiting!" she suddenly bawls at the top of her voice.

"What for, a frontal lobotomy?" I snap, giving her one of my looks. A look that says "Don't fuck with me, I'm mentally unbalanced at the moment." She get's the message and refuses to acknowledge me as I breeze through the door and out into the fresh air. What a morning! Poor old Tilly, I hope she'll be alright. Trust me to reduce my own therapist to tears. Should have kept quiet about the book. See what happens when you start dreaming dreams?

We are discussing my session over dinner. I say dinner in the loosest possible terms. It was meant to be a beef casserole with dumplings but the dumplings exploded all over the oven and I ended up having to bury them in the garden to get rid of the evidence. Must have put too much suet in the mixture. I could have thrown them in the dustbin but they were too big.

"How did it go today?" Jack asks, gnawing on a piece of burnt beef.

"Weird actually, Tilly just lost it and broke down."

"What, Tilly the therapist?"

"No, Tilly Trotter, who do you think?"

"Blimey, what's all that about then?"

"No idea, I was telling her about my previous jobs and she just burst into tears."

"Say no more," he gasps, choking on a piece of gristle.

"There's plenty left if you want seconds," I offer sarcastically.

"Thanks but no thanks."

"Levy will finish it off later."

At this point, Levy crawls under the fridge and refuses to come out. Daft dog.

"Did she say what it was all about?"

"Not really, just sobbed and kept going on about your dreams."

"What, my dreams?"

"No idiot… my dreams… her dreams."

"Does she have a first class stamp stuck to her clitoris then?"

"I have no idea I'm sure."

"Did you tell her about that?" he smiles.

"God no!"

"You should, dreams can be very significant."

"Give me a break, she already thinks I'm retarded."

"Sounds about right."

"Anyway, she had a good cry and seemed okay when I left."

"Poor girl, you should take her a little something to cheer her up."

"Good idea, I'll bake her a cake." He looks worried for a second, the lines on his forehead creasing into a frown.

"Maybe not, I'll pick her a nice one up from Druckers," he offers.

"Thanks."

He grins and I see he has a sliver of beef gristle stuck between his front teeth. The recipe said to bash the beef with a mallet but I don't own one so I used an old bicycle pump instead.

"Some woman in Essex is marketing a HRT cake you knos," I tell him "It was on the news."

"That should be a winner, women will be fighting over it in tea rooms all over the country."

"Two pots of Earl Grey and sixteen slices of that cake please." I laugh out loud at the thought.

"She'll be a millionaire."

"Why didn't I think of that?"

"Cos you don't do cakes, or beef casserole for that matter."

"Finish your dinner!"

He obeys and I can see he's struggling to gnaw his way through a tough piece of carrot. To his credit, he never complains, just accepts that Delia and I are on different planets. I have every single one of her books. I use them to stand on to clean the windows.

I am just about to clear away when Levy crashes through the patio doors, caked in mud and wet twigs.

"What's that dog got in his mouth?" Jack asks "Looks like a dumpling to me."

"Don't be ridiculous, where would he get a dumpling from at this time of night?"

"Bit big for a dumpling," he says, wandering into the lounge with his coffee. I deny all knowledge and carry on clearing the table. I shall have to find a new hiding place for all my cooking disasters. There's a whole turkey, complete with giblets under that compost heap. And several fruit cakes come to think of it.

CHAPTER EIGHT

Big Ears & Banana Trifle

"The trifle's not even set yet and I've got a million things to do you know." Ma is stressed, it's Sunday, a big day in her social calendar. Not just this Sunday, any Sunday. Ma is a huge Sunday Tea person. Her life would not be complete without a banana trifle and plates of assorted French fancies. It's a family tradition that goes way back to prehistoric times I'm sure. Ever since I can remember, we have been doing Sunday Tea. The dining room table heaving under the weight of plates of tinned salmon finger rolls and bowls of Walkers crisps. It's not that I mind, it's just that she get's so worked up about it all. Like now for instance, she's been on the phone for fifteen minutes ranting about the consistency of her custard.

"Today of all days, he decides to get an exploding ear!" she rants.

"Pardon?

"Your Father, on a Sunday of all things and his ear's the size of an African elephant's."

"God, is he alright?" I ask nervously.

"Course he's alright. You know your Father, he's doing the crossword in the Sunday Mirror."

"Is he in pain?"

"I have no idea, we're not speaking at the moment."

This is par for the course. Ma gets stressed and picks fights. Usually with Pa. He meanwhile, will refuse to be drawn into the fracas and sits quietly pondering over his puzzle. Yet another Sunday tradition.

"Why's that then?" I ask her distractedly.

"It's typical! He knows how hectic Sunday's are and he comes waltzing downstairs with that ear."

"He was fiddling with it last night, during Blind Date," she fumes. I resist the temptation to laugh, knowing it will only incite her to violence.

"Perhaps it was hurting."

"I daresay, but fiddling with it's made it twice as bad." This is a no win situation. Nothing, and I mean nothing, comes between Ma and her trifle. I swear Pa could be lying on the kitchen floor having a heart attack and she'd still be arranging glace cherries in neat little patterns on top of that sodding trifle.

"Can I speak to him?" I ask, exasperated.

"Your daughter's on the line!" she barks, slamming the receiver onto the worktop. I am momentarily deafened and Pa is on the line before I clear the ringing in my ears.

"Is that you Cassie?"

"Pa, are you okay, what's all this about then?"

"Pardon?"

"Your ear! What's wrong with it?"

"Hello, are you there?"

No prizes for guessing he's holding the phone up to his elephant ear. "PA! PUT THE PHONE TO YOUR GOOD EAR!!!"

"That's better, good morning daughter," he giggles.

"What have you gone and done?"

"I have no idea. It was itching and burning last night and now it's huge!"

"Is it painful?"

"A bit, not too bad, it just looks ridiculous."

"I can imagine. Did Ma give you a smack, you can tell me."

"I shall have another one to match if her trifle doesn't set properly," he sighs.

"You should ring the doctor, get him to have a look at it."

"I might do later if the swelling doesn't go down. I can't get my cap on."

"Really?"

"People were staring when I went to get the papers." I can hear Ma chuntering in the background. She obviously doesn't find it amusing.

"Better go, I've got to fetch her another box of sponge fingers."

"Be careful Pa, put your anorak on... the one with the hood."

"Good idea, see you later." The receiver clicks and he is gone. Off to Safeway in search of the perfect trifle filling no doubt.

We finally get a look at the offending ear later as we arrive dutifully for tea, and trifle of course. I am quite shocked when the front door is opened by an enormous, throbbing ear, with Pa following close behind.

"Christ! That looks awful," I cry.

"It's getting worse," he groans "My head will blow off in a minute."

"You should get that looked at," Jack tells him, examining the mutant ear.

"Trifle won't be ready for ages!" Ma yells "I've been held up today." I resist the temptation to plunge her face into the bloody trifle lying on the table, and instead concentrate on the invalid.

"Come on, you must be in agony, let me ring the doctor," I plead.

"But it's Sunday, they don't like being called out on a Sunday."

"Never mind that, this is an emergency," Jack pipes up "I'll ring him."

"Go and sit down Pa… I'll make you a coffee." I head for the kettle, choosing to ignore Ma's indignation that her Sunday tea be disrupted by a medical emergency. She senses I am cross and tries to smooth the waters.

"I told him not to fiddle with it," she moans, whisking a tub of double cream.

"Well he's obviously in pain, we can't let him sit here all night like that."

"The doctor won't like it."

"The doctor can sodding well lump it! It could be something serious," I shout back. She ignores me and concentrates on spearing glace cherries onto a cocktail stick, muttering to herself at the same time.

"Trust him, couldn't get a swelling in a private place, it has to be where everyone can see it."

"Oh, so you'd prefer it if his privates were swollen would you?"

"Cassandra! Don't twist what I say."

She always calls me Cassandra when she's cross. She knows I hate it.

"Look, the man's in pain, and will you stop fiddling with that bloody trifle!" I have crossed the line now. Way beyond the realms of decency and everything that is morally right in society. I have dared to verbally trash the trifle. Life will never be quite the same again. She is stunned into silence, her trembling hand suspended in mid-air over the bowl of cherries. I seize the opportunity and escape into the lounge. Pa is examining the ear in the ornamental mirror on the wall.

"Bit like that bloke in Dr Who," he muses.

"What bloke?"

"The Vegan, with the ears."

"It's Star Trek Pa, and he's a Vulcan."

"That's the one."

"Mr Spock."

"Mm, beam me up Spotty and all that." I had no idea Pa was into science fiction. Show's how little we know about our parent's eh?

"He'll be here soon," Jack says, coming in from the hall "He's doing an impacted bowel."

"I hope he washes his hands before he comes here!" Ma suddenly shouts from the kitchen. What a way to spend your day off! Impacted bowels and elephant ears. I couldn't do that job. Yet another career prospect shattered.

"Drink your coffee Pa, before it goes cold."

"Thanks, I've got a raging thirst today."

"Probably a fever," Jack volunteers "Infection or something."

"No, I couldn't get down to the watering hole, had to go to Safeway for the sponge fingers." We are all laughing, except Ma of course who is sulking and stabbing cherries in the kitchen.

"You could get work with that ear, as a look-alike," Jack says.

"Looking like who?"

"I dunno, Prince Charles."

"Or Noddy, you could do kid's parties!" I cry.

"That would be Big Ears, not Noddy," Pa corrects me. All this frivolity proves too much for Ma and she comes charging into the lounge in a fury.

"I'm glad you lot find this so funny. The doctor will be here any minute and you're all rolling around laughing. How's that going to look?"

"He'll probably be grateful for a few laughs after an impacted bowel," I snigger. She's just about to bite back when the doorbell rings and we all jump to attention. Pa straightens his face and looks suitably morose as Dr Firth sweeps cheerily into the lounge.

"Goodness! That looks painful," he says, plonking himself down on the sofa "Let's have a look shall we?"

The silence is nerve-wracking and we all hold our breath. Even Ma takes an interest and leaves her trifle alone for a second to join us.

"Otitis media," he finally says "Quite a severe case by the look of it."

"Otis who?" Pa asks, he's back on names again, thinking of some 70's soul singer.

"Infection in the ear canal, very nasty."

"That's a relief, I thought it was elephantitis," Pa laughs. The doctor laughs too and we all join in, relieved it's not some deadly flesh-eating disease that will rob Noddy of his assets.

"Can I offer you a cup of tea?" Ma asks, ever the considerate hostess.

"That would be lovely, no sugar thanks."

"Right."

"I'll just give you a quick jab of penicillin, not allergic are you?"

"I'm allergic to cockles, at least I think I am."

"Really?"

"Last time I ate some I was throwing up for days," Pa tells him.

"That was crabmeat, not cockles!" Ma bellows.

"That was it, on a day trip to Scunthorpe."

"Cleethorpes!" she rants, getting more flustered by the second.

He barely flinches as the needle jabs into his arm. Ex-navy you see, take more than an enlarged ear to phase him.

"I'll give you a prescription for some more, make sure you finish the course."

"I will, thanks doctor."

Ma returns with the tea tray, complete with several French fancies and the trifle in all it's glory.

"Trifle doctor, I made it myself?" she gushes.

Dr Firth is nothing if not tactful and takes his time before speaking. He views it with a certain amount of suspicion, which is not surprising considering she's gone completely insane and sprinkled an entire tub of hundreds and thousands on the top. Along with the bananas, cherries and a pint of whipped cream.

"Not for me thanks, I have supper waiting at home," he declines gently. I have a sinking feeling that we will all be needing medical help after eating this one. I knew it would happen one day, she's finally flipped and started producing trifle that's capable of killing people. He finishes his tea and picks up his bag, "That was lovely, thank you."

"I'll see you out," I offer, going towards the door.

"Bye and thanks again," Pa says.

He looks quite flushed now, his face pink and glowing with the beginnings of a temperature. A sharp contrast to the ear, which pulsates darkly on the side of his head.

"How's the car running Finn?" Jack asks him. Finn being his pet name in the family.

"Bit sluggish, I'm having trouble with the indicators as well."

"Just stick your ear out of the window if you need to turn right," Jack suggests.

"I might trade her in later in the year."

"Go for a hatchback Finn, there are some bargains around at the moment."

"I'm talking about Ma, get a newer model, somebody allergic to trifle." She is standing in the doorway listening and I am mortified at the hurt expression on her face.

"Come on Ma, get me a dish, that trifle looks amazing," I lie.

All is forgiven as she bustles around searching for dessert spoons and napkins. Bless her. She can't help being a product of the war years. All that deprivation and rationing. Now that food is plentiful and easy to get, she over compensates and buys enough to feed the Third World. She was fourteen before she saw a banana, or so she's fond of telling us. That, and the fact that the world is a much lesser place since the demise of powdered egg.

"Delicious!" Jack raves "One of your best."

Don't get carried away pal, she'll be making this concoction for ever if you overdo it.

Pa is dozing in his armchair, poor bugger. I bet he's in agony with that ear and never said. Typical. He had a heart scare a few years back and jumped on the number 11 bus to the hospital. Just pitched up in casualty and sat waiting his turn with all the other patients. Never made a fuss, just took his turn as if it was the most normal thing to do. I can just picture him, clutching his chest and doing his crossword at the same time. Different generation see, made of stronger stuff.

"It'll be starting in a minute," Ma informs us.

The Antique Road Show, yet another ritual for Sunday night's. Trifle and teapots. Fine bone china teapots that some old dear thinks are worth millions. Their suicidal expressions when an expert tells them they're worth twenty-pence crack me up. Pa is convinced he has a valuable heirloom in the attic. Some bit of jewellery or pastel print he bought in the Bull Ring years ago. Every Sunday he vows to get up in the loft and sort it out and every Monday he forgets again. Jack is asleep now, he always goes into a prolonged comatose state after eating Ma's trifle. Must be that sudden rush of sugar to his blood. He'll end up with diabetes after this latest one.

"There's a smashing recipe for a chocolate trifle in one of Delia's books," I tell her.

"Bet it's not as good as mine," she sniffs.

"Course not, you could adapt it though… to your own recipe."

She's interested now, visions of several pounds of cooking chocolate bubbling on the stove.

"Bring it round, I'll have a look,"

"I'll drop it in tomorros," I promise.

There is complete silence as the familiar theme tune starts up. Talking is strictly forbidden during this programme and I'm grateful for that. I feel quite nauseous and am struggling to keep my portion of the trifle in my stomach. If I move, it might just end up splattered on the carpet. I stay still and pray my digestive tract can take the strain.

Ma is engrossed, as ever and kicks off her slippers. I bet she's been on her feet all day in that kitchen and all for the sake of a ruddy trifle. She'll never learn. I've tried to encourage her to take the easy route but she's not an easy route type of person.

Things either have to be done properly or not at all. No short cuts, no compromises. I've even pointed out the extensive range of ready-made puddings in Sainsbury's to her. A positive plethora of mouth-watering meringue's and chocolate fudge cakes. She's having none of it. To buy a ready-made dessert in her eyes, is to make a pact with the devil, and I am invariably made to feel like a slut for suggesting such a thing.

This is something on which we will have to agree to differ. She will never alter her opinions and neither will I. I'm all for saving time in the kitchen. She on the other hand, doesn't feel like a real woman unless she's up to her armpits in boiling pots and potato peelings.

"Your Dad looks a bit better," she whispers, peering over the top of her glasses. And indeed he does. His mouth is wide open, his head tilted backwards in a deep sleep. The ear is reclining on a cushion of it's own.

"That'll be my trifle… put a lining on his stomach," she brags. I can't argue with that.

CHAPTER NINE

Leg Stretches for The Living Dead

Tilly's Top Ten Tips For Trifleheads, a fascinating guide to picking yourself up after a bout of depression. That's not the official title of course but I prefer it to the real one, something along the lines of Regaining Your Self Esteem After A Mental Health Problem. Awful isn't it… that mental health thing? The mere mention of those words is guaranteed to send people scurrying indoors, terrified you'll attack them with a machete or bite the head off their hamster.

It encompasses so much you see, mental health. Minor things like a few blue weeks after the death of a loved one or full blown paranoid schizophrenia. As far as the general public are concerned, you're a nutter, full stop. I accept that in my case that's probably very true, but I resent the implication that just because I lost the plot for a while, I must be insane.

If you break a leg or have your appendix out, people will sympathise and buy you a bunch of grapes. Tell them you're having counselling and they cross you off their Christmas card list.

And I'm as guilty as the next person on that one. Or at least I used to be. After spending a year or so in therapy my outlook has changed. If you'd have told me a few years back I was heading for a breakdown, I'd have laughed in your face. Try it now and I'll punch you in the face.

Anyway, this program for getting back on your feet. It's very good. Gives you lots of ideas for rehabilitation and regaining your marbles. I'm working my way through it, albeit at a very slow pace.

Tip number three is to socialise. Get out there and stop hiding away in the attic. I never did to be honest but I feel I'd be letting Tilly down if I didn't at least give it a try. Which is why I'm standing at the window, watching the cars arrive at the village hall across the way. It's Friday and they're holding a 'Fitness For The Over Forties' group. I'm just sussing out the rest of the members before I take the plunge.

I was in Boot's you see, buying a bottle of Sea Kelp, when I saw the poster on the till. It said to ring a woman called Lydia, so I did and here I am. All psyched up in my t-shirt and trainers, ready to go for the burn. I don't own a lycra thong or a headband so these will have to do. Besides, I'm thinking more of a toning up regime. Tighten up the muscles, firm up the floppy tits, that sort of thing. Lydia tells me the exercises are all done to music so I'm wearing a support bra just in case.

I wonder what club Alicia Afterbirth will join? The Stamp Collecting Society probably. Give her something else to lick apart from her own arse.

The deciding factor on joining this particular group is the fact that it's literally right opposite my house. If I hate it, I can always run back home and hide. They hold a lot of different classes in that hall, Tai Chi, Tae Bo, whatever that is. People are always wandering in and out in various states of undress. I just never thought I'd see the day when I became one of them.

I have no desire to lose weight, I've lost almost four stone since I left work. If my skin gets any saggier I shall be forced to seek the services of a taxidermist. I average five miles a day with Levy as well. I know this because Jack bought me a pedometer for Christmas. Marvellous little gadget, just clip it onto your bra and off you go, fascinating.

I have my fifty-pence for the loan of a rubber mat and it's only another two quid for the session so I'll be off. See what Lydia has to offer.

Lots of traffic now. Including two invalid cars and one of those Social Services mini-buses with a hydraulic lift on the back. Oh dear, maybe this wasn't such a good idea after all. The driver's loading a woman onto it in a wheelchair. Can't be for my group surely? Must be something else going on in one of the other rooms. Pull yourself together girl! Go and have a look and see how the land lies. It wouldn't seem fair not to turn up... Lydia was very welcoming on the phone.

I realise I've made a terrible mistake as I climb the steps to the hall door. Lydia's idea of the word 'mature' and mine seem to differ somewhat. I am surrounded by a sea of blue rinses with varicose veins to match. One poor woman is being wheeled in on a hospital trolley, with a nurse in attendance! It's beginning to resemble a scene from a disaster movie with me as an extra.

"Excuse me, is this the fitness group?" I ask the woman sitting behind a table in the lobby.

"Yes dear, follow that lady in the oxygen mask," she shouts above the din. I'm just about to beat a hasty retreat when a voice squeaks, "You must be Cassie, welcome." It's Lydia and I am doomed, my escape route blocked by a woman in leg callipers.

"Lydia! I was just about to go in," I lie.

"Come along then, chop, chop, spit, spot." Chop chop, spit spot? What sort of a stupid expression is that? I'm not a five year old on my way to the girls toilets for a wee-wee. The words "fuck," and "you," spring to mind. I should have known. As soon as I spotted the pink shell suit with a diamante tiger on the back I had my doubts. True to form, I follow her like a lamb to the slaughter, noticing her bright pink socks as I go. The omens are not looking good. She might just as well have walked up and punched me in the face, such is the effect her clothes are having on me.

I try to lose myself at the back in the hope of making a sharp exit but I hadn't bargained for She Of The Shell Suit. She homes in on me with a steely glare and warbles,

"Down here at the front Cassie, I like to keep an eye on my new ladies."

Every eye in the room turns on me, some with cataracts, others myopic. I have no choice but to do as she says and meekly shuffle to the front. Lydia is up for it and removes her shell suit jacket, revealing a pink Perry Como t-shirt with the words Perry Como... 1967 Tour! emblazoned across the front.

"Ladies!" she shrieks, clapping her hands at the same time, "We have a new face with us today." I am mortified and blush down to my roots as the rest of the group turn to eye up the new girl.

"Lovely! Now Cassie, if you'd care to get a chair and slot in somewhere over there," she sings. The chair bit throws me briefly, until I realise that all the women in the group are now seated.

"Take that space next to Rita," Lydia yells.

I sit, as instructed and nod politely to Rita who has bright pink hair. I suspect she's been drawn into Lydia's cult because she's also wearing a pair of pink socks. Maybe Be-Wise are doing a special for pensioners. Rita must weigh roughly twenty stone, most of which is crammed inside a pair of lycra leggings. At the end of the leggings are two gnarled feet and several ingrowing toenails. She suddenly leans forward and whispers in my ear,

"You'll love it, we have such a laugh."

"Really?" I whisper back, unsure as to whether Rita's idea of fun is the same as mine.

"Widow, lost him in seventy-two. Two grandkids and a plastic hip," she continues.

"Husband still alive, no grandchildren yet and my own hips thankfully," I tell her.

She smiles sweetly and turns her attention to Lydia who is warming up at the front. Lydia's idea of warming up is to stretch her arms in the air and pop a Polo into her mouth. I watch, fascinated, as she fiddles with the ancient tape recorder on the table. She is obviously having problems selecting a tape. Considering there are only two on the table I can't see what her problem is. We have Perry Como's Greatest Hits and a Bing Crosby Christmas Collection.

"Be with you in a second ladies," she grins "Talk amongst yourselves." Rita is just about to confide in me again when a latecomer crashes through the doors and flops down next to us. I'm getting a bit scared now as she too has the pink socks. Perhaps it's a secret society of some sort. Like the Masons but for hosiery people.

"Bloody buses, waited nearly an hour for the 23"

"Glad you made it," Rita says "How did you get on at the hospital Maud?"

"They cleaned it out and fitted me with a new tube. Blockage they said." I have no idea and have no intention of asking! I'm not altogether sure that a woman with a blockage and new pipe work should be attending a class like this. What if she gets a burst and several gallons of bodily fluid gush onto the hall floor?

"Right ladies! Sorry about the delay... shall we begin... nice and easy now." With Perry crooning in the background, she begins to show us the first move. It appears to involve raising your left arm above your head and lowering it again... slowly.

"One arm at a time now, don't go mad," she tells us very sternly. I watch in amazement as she repeats this exercise several times, her face a picture of intense concentration and effort.

"That's it... now the other arm... Iris steady!" she barks. I crane my neck to get a glimpse of Iris the athlete, hitting that wall, overcoming the pain barrier. She is sitting to my left and has overdosed on the Sanatogen I think, her arms flailing around like a windmill.

"She used to work on a cruise liner you knos," Rita informs me, nodding over at Lydia. I'm impressed. She must be one of the few remaining survivors of the Titanic.

"Revert to legs now ladies… revert to legs," she tells us, lifting one leg just an inch off the floor. I revert to legs with Rita and Maud swinging along beside me. If Jack could see me now he'd bust a gut laughing. Perry's soothing voice wafts over me and I can feel myself slipping into a coma. This must be what it feels like to be injected with formaldehyde. You want to get up and run but your legs won't move in the right direction.

"Slow down Iris, remember your colostomy!" I like Iris. I don't know her from Adam but the girl's got guts. She's obviously in her eighties and up for it! Go on girl, give it some welly!

"And stop ladies, nice and gently."

What on earth induced me to get involved in this? I was looking for fun and instead I've ended up in the remake of that Michael Jackson 'Thriller' video.

"Easy, let's bring it to a close shall we?"

The tape is coming to an end and so is my patience. Rita and Maud on the other hand are worn out and delve into their respective handbags, searching for wet-wipes.

"She puts you through your paces doesn't she?" says Maud, wiping the sweat from her face. Rita nods excitedly "Wait till the upper body section, after coffee," she raves. I don't think I can face the upper body section. I could keel over from the exertion. Besides which, Maud has been making some extremely unpleasant noises from her nether regions and I suspect her new piping is about to explode.

"Better nip to the ladies," I lie, jumping to my feet.

"Hurry up before the queue starts." I may be crumpled but I could still beat this lot in a race to the loo. Come to think of it, a tortoise with it's toes hacked off could beat this lot.

"You having tea or coffee?" Maud asks Rita as I turn to leave.

"Neither, I've got an Oxo in my bag."

I leave Rita to suck on her Oxo cube and head for the exit. I shall break out if necessary.

"Did you enjoy it dear?" the woman behind the table asks.

"Great!" I lie "Must dash, got an appointment."

"See you next week," she shouts as I make a run for it. What a learning curve that was! I must have misread the poster, it should have read 'Leg Stretches for The Living Dead'. I shall miss Iris, I'd love to be a fly on the wall in that nursing home…

"Iris!!! Stop that! You know Mr Saunder's only got one kidney!" Sadly, Iris and I are destined never to meet again. I feel rotten saying this, but I was seeking something uplifting not drag-me-down depressing.

I'm home and hiding in the pantry before Lydia even realises I've gone. It's at times like this, I realise just exactly how drastically my life has changed in the past few years. Not that long ago, I was running a business and ticking over on pure adrenalin. Now, I'm reduced to gentle leg exercises with Rita and Maud.

When did all that happen then? Sales targets to senility in one foul swoop. Levy is hiding in the pantry with me. He thinks it's another game and is wrestling with the flex off my Dyson. To be fair, it does resemble a rather large snake, so he's only protecting me.

"Get your lead lad." Time we went to check on Gertie and Gilbert. It's been ten days now and still no sign of the goslings. I'm very worried and feel I may have to call in Rolf Harris soon.

This really is a delightful area to live in. As well as the pond, we have our own bowling green, complete with bowlers in straw hats and the unmistakable aroma of TCP as they glide across the green. We have the tennis courts of course, and a skittle alley and even an amateur dramatic society. A dying breed these days what with Sky television and Cable.

Perhaps a geography lesson might help. We live in Oakham, a small suburb on the outskirts of Birmingham. I suppose it's quite affluent really, with it's tree-lined avenues and the odd Porsche parked up.

More and more of the properties are being sold off to the corporate high-flyers. I don't have a problem with that, except when they party at weekends and their braying voices echo across the lanes until three in the morning. Should this happen on a regular basis, I simply let Levy piss up their petunias. They're usually specially imported petunias that they've had flown in from Holland.

Levy is in pursuit of a Cyril and as usual I take off, exceeding speeds of thirty miles an hour along Park Ridge. The Unigate milkman looks quite startled as we overtake him on the bend.

"Morning," I pant as we hurtle past.

"Morning," he waves back, putting his foot down on the accelerator. We beat him to the corner, no problem. There's not a milk float in the land that can keep up with this lad when he's on full throttle.

Standing room only on the pond today. At least a dozen ducks, mallards and even Herbert's popped over for a visit. Herbert, a huge heron, quite magnificent. The first time I saw him, I thought he was a plastic garden ornament that some joker had placed on the island in the middle of the pond. I had quite a shock when he suddenly dipped his head into the water searching for food. This habit of mine of naming everything is getting out of hand. The moorhens are Milly and Malcolm by the way, just in case you happen to be in the area.

"Lie down lad!". Surprisingly enough, he obeys for once. Only because he's found a jam donut lying by the railings. He likes donuts, preferably ones with lots of strawberry jam oozing out of the middle. Gilbert is circling the island, giving out warning signals to anything that dares approach. Gertie is nesting on there and must be due any day now. All I can do, is pray that she has a safe delivery.

Neville will be on the case anyway. Neville from West Gate. RSPB member and fanatical about birds. I think he's retired, either that or he has a very understanding boss as he spends hours hiding in the bushes, watching the wildlife. I assume he's watching the wildlife anyway. He could be a pervert for all I know. Skulking in the undergrowth, fiddling with his privates. No, that's highly unlikely. He carries binoculars and a thermos flask. A flasher wouldn't carry a thermos would he?

Levy's got jam all over his nose now and is getting restless. Sugar rush, always sends him loopy. He makes a beeline for the bushes and disappears inside, snuffling like a truffle pig. Several Kwik Save carrier bags are tossed into the air, along with an old umbrella, as he hunts for treasure.

"Is that you Cassie?" a voice suddenly pipes up. Now, I know I'm inclined to hallucinate but if I'm not mistaken that hawthorn bush is talking to me.

"Sorry?" I whisper, glancing around to check no-one is watching me.

"Neville... down here, I've got my eye on that ginger tom." I'm catching up now, it takes me a while but I get there in the end. The ginger tom in question has been pestering the birds for weeks and Neville is on the case.

"Bastard! I'll be waiting when he comes back," he rants. Levy is also on the case. The case of the talking bush. Before I can reel him in, he's off and heading for Neville at a rate of knots. He's not keen on people who hide in bushes, or ginger toms for that matter.

"Look out Neville, he's heading your way!"

"He's here, he's got my thermos in his mouth."

"Sorry, is it broken?"

"Just the handle," he sighs.

"I'll replace it, sorry."

"Does he like chicken soup?"

"Not sure."

"Only it's punctured."

"Oh sorry, I am really."

"No matter, I have another one at home." He sounds quite resigned to the fact that Levy has just polished off his soup. Poor bloke's probably been there all night as well.

"Big for a Labrador isn't he?"

"Mm, huge."

There are sounds of a scuffle and I fear the worst.

"Got it!" he says triumphantly.

"Oh good."

"He's found something else."

"What is it?" I ask. There is a pause and I hold my breath, praying it's not a duckling or a baby moorhen.

"Looks like a pie... steak and kidney I think."

"Bloody dog's a scavenger honestly."

"Oh dear, sorry Cassie, it's not a pie... it's a tortoise."

"Oh shit! DROP IT NOW!" I bawl at the top of my voice. Yet more scuffling from the undergrowth as poor Neville wrestles with ninety-pounds of black Labrador and his new friend Tommy. I can't look and expect to hear the crunching of shell at any minute.

"Got it!"

I seize the chance and reel him in sharpish. He is quite startled at this sudden exit and looks at me with a puzzled expression. He has dribbles of chicken soup down his chest and a hawthorn branch behind his left ear.

"Is it okay Neville?"

"Think so, it's gone into it's shell. Just a slight crack on his back."

"Thank goodness, better be off before he does any more damage."

"Right, see you later."

"Cheerio."

I head for home, with one extremely disgruntled dog in tow. He's sulking. Just as he was about to crack that shell and eat the contents, I stepped in and spoiled his fun. I'm surprised he didn't swallow it whole. Maybe the legs were sticking out.

The milkman is dropping off two banana yoghurts at number 9 as we waddle past.

"What's that all over his chest?" he asks.

"Chicken soup," I tell him, as if it's the most normal thing in the world. He stops, mid-stride, and peers even closer at the dog.

"And on his nose?"

"Strawberry jam."

Silly man. Obviously never owned a dog.

CHAPTER TEN

Thou Shalt Not Covet Thy Neighbour's Teeth

Pickled Pete's new get-rich quick scheme is driving me mad! He's gone into the lumberjack business and the constant drone of his chainsaw is beginning to grate on my nerves. Jack says if he persists, he'll go round there and show him exactly how dangerous a chainsaw can be, if inserted sideways up your anus. Like all his moneymaking schemes, he throws himself into it with a fervour, regardless of the noise and inconvenience to the rest of us.

Lumberjacks are a rare breed, especially in central Birmingham, but Pete's not one to be put off easily. He's got it into his fuddled head that come winter, people around here will be queuing up to buy delete logs for their fires. The fact that this is a smoke-free zone appears to have escaped him.

This latest career move came about simply because a local forestry firm are working in the neighbourhood, lopping branches off some of the older trees. Pete's been following them around with his wobbly wheelbarrow, collecting up the debris and stockpiling it in his shed. I have no idea what the going rate is for firewood but suspect it's already cost him more than he'll ever make in electricity and bandages. Add to that, the cost of the red lumberjack shirt he got from Oxfam and he's in debt already.

Then there's the inevitable fire risk of course. A pisshead and a chain smoker. He falls over a lot as you know and can remain comatose for days. Mix that with several tons of dry tinder and whoosh! I am keeping my garden hose on standby just in case.

See, the problem with Pete is, he's not just an alcoholic. He's an articulate alcoholic. A man with a brain, well, a pickled one I know, but a brain that still rationalises and functions quite well when he's sober. Dopey drunks are harmless, they just get hammered and sleep it off. Pete meanwhile, has periods of intense lucidity and it's during these periods that he dreams up these daft schemes. It's early and I'm in the middle of Deric Longden's latest book but the words keep drifting off with the constant buzz of the chainsaw.

"Pete! Can you give it a rest? I'm trying to read," I shout over the hedge.

"Ouch!"

"Have you cut yourself again?" I ask, without the slightest trace of sympathy in my voice.

"Just a nick," he groans.

"Come here, let's have a look."

He appears from inside the shed, a disaster on legs. Completely covered from head to foot in sawdust and wood shavings. His Oxfam shirt shredded at the sleeves and his hands covered in cuts and an assortment of grubby plasters. To complete the picture, he has what looks like the remains of an empty birds nest on his head. It's either that or a very badly made toupee. I resist the temptation to burst out laughing and concentrate on his outstretched hand.

"You should bathe that in antiseptic."

"The one on my foot's worse, it's gone a funny colour," he tells me dejectedly.

"Oh Pete! Is it worth it? All this noise and those cuts."

"You'll see, I'll be rolling in it come November," he beams. Ever the optimist eh? I suppose all that hope and expectation comes from looking at life through the bottom of a whisky glass. Being sober might mean he has to face up to life. I know better than to disagree with him. Instead, I grab the first-aid kit from the kitchen.

"How many logs have you got to sell then?" I ask, wiping his hand with some Savlon.

"About five hundred so far."

"Should make a tidy profit then."

"Thought I'd do them in bundles of ten. Ask a pound a bundle."

"Will they burn do you think?"

He looks aghast at the very suggestion.

"Course! Top quality timber this lot," he insists. He's quite indignant and I refrain from pointing out that he is stacking them in his shed. The same shed that has no roof to speak of. And the fact that it's been raining on and off for days.

"How's Budd?" I ask, changing the subject.

"Upstairs on the bed, he doesn't like the noise."

"I know how he feels, it does make your head ache after a while."

"Sorry, would you like one of my painkillers?" he offers.

"No thanks, I'm fine."

I finish dressing his hand and say a silent prayer that the next cut won't sever a main artery.

"Anyway, if the wood doesn't sell, there's always the guinea pigs," he smiles.

"Pardon?"

"Didn't I tell you? Some guy in the pub was saying, they pay a fortune for guinea pigs in pet shops. I got two from Bearwood on Friday. Should have a litter soon." I'm not sure whether to laugh or cry. The prospect of several hundred guinea pigs roaming around his house is just too bizarre to contemplate. What with Budd and the newspapers and the logs. The mind boggles!

"Is that a good idea do you think? What about the mess?"

"What mess? I let them run round the garden."

It get's better! His garden bears a striking resemblance to the jungles of Borneo and now he's got Percy and Pamela running amok.

"Pete, what if they escape?"

He looks at me as if I'm retarded and laughs,

"Escape? Why would they want to do that?" he asks incredulously.

Like I say, a lost cause. A lifetime of soaking your senses in scotch tends to warp your outlook. Arguing with him would be futile, you just have to let him learn by his own mistakes.

"Thanks for that," he says, examining his newly bandaged hand.

"No problem."

"Better be off, they'll be open in ten minutes."

"Right."

"Would you like one, when they breed?" he asks, heading indoors.

"I don't think so."

"Well the offers there if you change your mind."

I can hear him, clattering around in the porch. Probably searching for his shoes. I noticed while we were talking he was wearing odd slippers, and just the one sock.

When he first moved in, I thought he was slightly eccentric, but now I know it's because he can't focus enough to dress himself properly. His peculiar dress sense is a source of great amusement to everyone locally. Not least yours truly, who always was fascinated by the bizarre. His best combination to date being a pair of tartan plus fours and a Metallica t-shirt. I swear the volunteers in Oxfam just sell him all the crap nobody else will buy.

In August last year, he emerged in a pair of tiny Speedo swimming trunks and green wellies! That little number kept me giggling for days. I'm sorry, I know you shouldn't mock the afflicted but it is funny.

He's off now. The front door just slammed, which is unusual in itself because he never usually locks any of his doors. Only so he can get back in when he staggers home at closing time and can't find his keys. I used to worry that he'd be burgled but after seeing the inside of his house it would be impossible to tell if it had been ransacked. See, apart from everything else, he robs skips as well. Spends hours wandering around searching through other people's rubbish. He doesn't just grab the stuff as he passes, he actually climbs inside the skips to root around in the bottom. Technically speaking, I don't suppose it's theft as the stuff has been thrown out anyway, but I often wonder what people think when they see their belongings disappear up the road on the back of a staggering drunk.

One day, he keeps telling me, he's going to have a garage sale and clear the lot. At the last count, he had seventeen pop-up toasters so that should be fun. He offered me a Philips Ladyshave last week. I declined of course, I'm particular about sharing my shaving gear with a stranger.

I'm just thankful that the NHS hasn't got round to paying people for donating blood like they do in the States. He'd be bled dry by now. When he came back to England, from America, he was still comparatively wealthy and could afford crates of Chivas Regal. Now, he's reduced to cans of special Brew and bottles of Strongbow.

If I run out of Benson's or Mars Bars, I simply lift a fiver out of Jack's wallet. Pete doesn't have that option so has to resort to these crazy schemes to get by. I can sympathise on that score. Nobody will employ him because he's a pisshead and I sometimes feel nobody will ever employ me because of my brief visit to Trifletown.

Still, look on the bright side, if I were working now I wouldn't be sitting on the patio reading a wonderful book and watching Levy chase what appears to be an Albino guinea pig around the lawn. The guinea pig has the advantage, for the moment, of being small enough to hide in the hedge. Levy has his bucket head wedged in the privet trying to ferret him out.

"Come out of there you pillock!" I bellow, in an attempt to end the chase.

A polite cough can be heard from the garden on the other side. New neighbours, moved in a month ago but as yet we haven't been formally introduced. I'm not one to push myself onto people and they seem a bit aloof, so apart from the odd nod out in the street, we remain strangers.

Which is fine by me. I'm all for having your own space and all that. Besides which, she appears to be the sort of person I would cross the road to avoid. Sorry, I don't normally make assumptions but the minute I heard her nasal voice braying across the garden the other week, I realised we were never going to be bosom buddies. She has that look, you know, the look of someone who went to a finishing school in Switzerland. She coughs again. It's either a case of TB or she's waiting for me to speak. Oh well, here goes.

"Sorry, I was shouting at the dog, he's chasing a guinea pig."

"Raarrrly?" she neighs back. What is that? A new word in the English language? Raarrrly!... never heard anything like it!

"Labrador, chases anything that moves," I tell her.

"Quite! He was chasing our cat yesterday," she drawls "Poor thing was petrified."

I resist the temptation to laugh, as the cat in question is positively huge and probably weighs as much as the dog. We have nicknamed him Bentos, as in Fray Bentos, you know, who ate all the pies. Or just FB as Jack calls him... Fat Bastard.

"Well, dogs chase cats, it's an animal thing," I point out sarcastically.

"Mm.." she says in a disinterested voice, obviously not listening to a word I'm saying. I persevere, not wishing to get into a fist fight on our first meeting.

"Have you settled in?"

"No point, it's only a short lease, just while Henry sets up the new branch," she sneers. I had a feeling he'd be a Henry, you can tell can't you? I wonder what sort of a branch Henry is setting up. Kentucky Fried Chicken probably. I don't really care and am fast losing the will to live as she continues to snort and sigh behind the hedge.

"He's in the city," she persists, dying for me to ask more. A beggar probably, hunched up on the pavement outside the museum.

"Well, we all have to earn a crust. I'm unemployed by the way," I giggle.

"Raarrrly?" There goes that sodding word again! I know for certain that she doesn't give a toss what I do. As long as I don't run naked round the garden and show her up in front of her friends. Ten to one she hasn't heard a word I've said. I'll just put my theory to the test.

"It's terribly quiet around here at night isn't it?" she whinnies.

"I wouldn't know, I'm usually in bed by ten with a cup of cocoa. It's the medication I think."

"Absolutely," she drawls.

"The injections make me drowsy see…" I persist.

"Marvellous."

"Still, I've finished my electric shock treatment."

"Super!" Told you! She hasn't heard a word I've said. Silly mare. One thing guaranteed to wind me up is indifference. Complete and utter indifference to another human being. I imagine her eyes glazed over the minute she heard my Brummie accent and the fact that I'm unemployed. Levy obviously feels the same as he suddenly lets rip with one of his earth shattering farts. A fart that ricochets around the Southern Hemisphere, sending the folk of Peru into a panic, fearing an earthquake. The aforementioned fart has the desired effect and jolts her back to reality.

"Have you lived here long?" she asks.

"1939… just before war broke out."

"Smashing!"

"I was in the Land Army… grew beetroot for the troops."

"Amazing!"

Yes, it would be amazing actually since I wasn't even born until 1955 you tart! Am I so insignificant that you haven't even bothered to look at me? Yet another bimbo who keeps her brain in her Burberry handbag.

"Must dash, I'm meeting Henry for lunch," she brays, shoving her horsy face over the hedge.

"Right."

"By the way, don't be alarmed if you see a strange guy in our garden. It'll be our man from the house in Chelsea, he's popping along to tidy things up."

"Ditto, if you see a strange guy in here… it'll be my husband," I grin back.

"Quite!"

"Toodle-pip!" I trumpet at her, but the witty banter is lost on that one. Silly woman. And the teeth! I have never in my life seen such teeth! Huge great things glinting in the sunlight like dazzling blocks of marble. Where do these women get such teeth I'd like to know? It's not natural. I am in fact older than most of my teeth and it rankles somewhat.

The patio doors slide shut and I can hear her resetting the alarm system. Probably thinks I'll break in and steal her Prada purse while she's out. Amazing, I've just spent the best part of half an hour chatting to a woman who can't be bothered to introduce herself. I shall call her Fiona Fuckwit. That has a nice ring to it.

Pete's back already. Must have been barred from the Kings Arms again. The back door flies open and he lurches headfirst onto the yard.

"You alright Pete?"

"Fine," he mutters, with his face buried in the rockery.

"Been barred again?"

"Yeah."

"Never mind eh?"

"Fell off my bar stool," he sighs.

"Hurt yourself?"

"No, landed on the barman," he slurs, closing his eyes.

I am sympathetic as ever. He's harmless, just hopeless as I say. Experience has taught me to leave him when he falls. He's a giant of a man and quite floppy when drunk and impossible to pick up. I peer through the hole in the hedge and he's flat out with his face nestling serenely in the daisies, his feet dangling over the edge of the rockery. He'll come round in a while. Best not disturb him, let him sleep it off. The guinea pig is chewing on the elastic sticking out of his waistband. I think it's the elastic from his underpants.

Bentos is up there watching us from the shed roof. Hope it can stand the weight. Fat cat. Quite appropriate really considering his owners. Thank God it's only a short lease. I'll introduce them to Pete later, take him round next time they have dinner guests. That would be the neighbourly thing to do. They'll be back in Chelsea in no time.

CHAPTER ELEVEN

A Pale Green Aura & A Pickled Egg

I have a pale green aura apparently, some woman in the queue at the chip-shop told me. I was a bit startled, being deep in thought over whether or not to have a pickled egg with my haddock. I do wish people wouldn't spring these things on you without warning. I never asked her to read my aura, she just went ahead and did it without my permission. Still, I suppose if you have the 'gift' it's hard to ignore when everybody around you is glowing with incandescent colours. My aura is probably green because I used to live next door to a power station.

She's playing the fruit machine now, shovelling in pound coins and praying for a jackpot. You'd think with her psychic powers she'd be able to foresee the lottery numbers wouldn't you? You'd also think her Red Indian Guide would advise her not to wear lycra pedal-pushers with a see-through blouse. What with her being on the ample side and all that. She has the look of someone who dabbles in the supernatural. Hooped earrings and a weathered face.

This queue is moving at a snail's pace. Friday night and the world and his wife want a battered sausage with extra chips. I always have problems ordering in this place. The counter-top is too high and I have to stand on tip-toes to see over it. They invariably mishear what I'm saying and I end up with two cod and a pastie every time I come in.

I think the height of the counter is meant to act as a deterrent to drunks at closing time. Pissed people tend to get aggressive if their chips take too long. Mystic Maureen over there has already ordered, she's waiting on a whole roast chicken with mushy peas. It could take a while.

"It's very strong you knos," a voice suddenly pipes up behind me. She's back and not about to give up easily.

"Yes, so you told me," I snap.

"Quite distinctive, you must be a lucky lady." I really do not want to get into this but the girl serving is obviously doing her community service as the queue gets longer and longer. If I move away, I'll lose my place.

"Look, it's very nice of you but I don't believe…" I start to say.

"You can't escape your aura Missy," she insists, daring me to argue otherwise.

I get the distinct impression Mystic Maureen has been at this game for a while. I suppose it's the modern day equivalent of selling clothes pegs. She's obviously not going to let this go and as if to demonstrate this, she lays a hand on my shoulder, forcefully and with menace.

Now, in a situation like this, you can either go with the flow and let yourself be dragged along with it or you can gently make a stand by being assertive. Tilly taught me that. Assertive not aggressive. With this in mind, I gently remove her hand from my person. She is nothing if not persistent and leans forward to whisper in my ear.

"I can sense energy around you. Your field is unbroken," she smirks.

"If you touch me again, your nose will be broken," I smirk back. I'm not sure that's how Tilly would have handled it but it seems to do the trick. She backs off, deciding not to push her luck.

There's a fat man in front of me and he giggles nervously. I suspect he thinks a fight might break out and the dozen meat pies he's just ordered will be smashed in the fracas. His concerns are unjustified as she turns her attention to another girl at the back of the queue.

She's in her teens and on her way home from work I should think. Still wearing a little metal name badge on her lapel with a Natwest logo on. Bless her. Bet it's her first job and her feet are killing her in those dinky little high-heels.

"You have a strong purple aura," Maureen tells her while grasping her hand. The kid looks embarrassed and her cheeks flush with colour. She's trying to get away but her escape route is blocked by the Pie Man. Come to think of it, if a fire broke out in here right now, we'd all perish. We'd have to eat him to get out the door. I am starving myself and could manage both his legs.

"I see a great deal of money," she drones on "could you spare a little to hear more?"

Here we go! She's going in for the kill and the kid is bound to hand it over. See, I told you, a crisp five pound note just changed hands. I bite my tongue and hold back. None of my business. Ms Natwest will have to look out for herself. Ten out of ten for trying it on with me Maureen but nothing comes between me and my fish supper. I have a thing about people invading my space anyway. Press your face too close to mine and I'm liable to pluck out your nostril hairs. I have no idea why this bothers me so much. Maybe it's a throwback to my days in a pram when complete strangers would shove their faces inside and declare "What an ugly baby!" I'm at the front of the queue now, "Two cod, chips, a battered sausage and a pickled egg please."

Jack just drove past again. There are double yellows all along this section of the High Street so he just keeps driving round in circles. He'll have to stop in a minute, he looks dizzy.

"A boy and a girl, I can see them now," Maureen blabbers in the background to Ms Natwest. Yeah right! Easy money I suppose. Just pick a mug out of the crowd and empty their purse.

He's just gone past again. Fancy putting double yellows outside a chip shop. You have to walk three miles to the nearest car park and your chips are stone cold if you do that. He looks a bit nauseous actually but he's grinning so he must be okay to drive.

"Was it you wanted mussels with your haddock?" the girl behind the counter asks.

"It was cod actually and I don't mind if it's scrawny," I jest.

"Six-fifty then," she snaps, ignoring me. Witty banter is lost on Harriet Haddock as I call her. She seems to have a block of lard in between her ears, probably from dangling her head over the fish-fryer all day. It's a thankless job I know but a cheery smile doesn't cost anything does it?

As I leave the shop, Maureen has some little bloke pinned up against the wall. He looks petrified, yet another punter about to part with their hard earned dosh. Why doesn't she just go out and mug people in alleyways, it's the same principal.

I'm standing on the pavement with my bag of cholesterol ready to go and Jack is nowhere to be seen. He's probably collapsed at the wheel with vertigo. Oh, here he comes with Levy draped around his neck like a scarf. He starts off in the back of the car, but somehow manages to work his way forward to the driving seat. I don't know how Jack manages to drive with those huge paws throttling him. If we ever go on a long journey, he'll have to go on the roof rack. The dog that is. We could stick him to the rear shelf with Blu-Tak, like one of those nodding dogs. That should keep the folks in the car behind amused. Jack pulls over and I leap head first into the passenger seat. Once you stop in this traffic, it's impossible to get going again. He's used to me by now, and carries on driving with my head wedged firmly between his legs.

"Did you get any mushy peas?" he asks, pulling into the main stream of traffic.

"No, I was having my aura read."

"Nothing unusual there then," he sighs.

"Got you a battered sausage though."

"Oh deep joy."

"You're welcome."

I have no idea how he manages to remain calm, living with me. He's either incredibly laid back or on large doses of Diazepam. With my restricted view of his flies, I can see that Levy has started on the chips. Bits of chip paper and batter are flying around the car in his frenzy to get at the food.

"Might as well eat them nos," I suggest "Or what's left of them."

"He's had a bite out of my battered sausage," Jack moans, holding up the shredded paper.

"Well start at the other end then."

Silence as we nibble at the remains of our supper. Levy meanwhile is lying bloated on the backseat.

"How was your aura?"

"Pale green."

"Probably from that power station."

"Quite."

"Your hair will drop out soon… And your fillings."

"Thanks."

They do say love is blind don't they? He hasn't noticed that most of my hair has already dropped out, ditto the fillings.

"That dog's got a nasty lump on the side of his jas," he says, looking in the rear view mirror.

"It's your pickled egg. I forgot it was in with the chips."

"That's a relief, I thought it was a malignant tumour."

"He'll just roll it round then spit it out, he's not fussed on pickled things."

The words have barely left my mouth, when true to form, the egg is catapulted out of his gaping gob and ricochets against the windscreen with the force of an Exocet missile. Thankfully, the side window is open and it exits, sharply, hitting the forehead of a chap cycling past. No serious damage done, he just looks a bit stunned. I don't suppose it's every day you get hit by a pickled egg doing speeds in excess of twenty miles an hour. Jack gestures with his hands as an expression of apology. The cyclist gestures back with two fingers.

"You could do that job," he says, pointing to a board outside the swimming baths. I swivel round and see they are advertising for a lifeguard.

"How do you distinguish though… that waving not drowning thing?" I ask.

"Valid point."

"And the swimsuit, I can't see me in a red lycra thong can you?"

"No, quite."

"Forget that one then."

"It was just a thought," he grins.

Yet another career move thwarted. No wonder the unemployed look gaunt and haggard. Lying awake at night worrying about your future is exhausting. The only job I could do at the moment would be testing Slumberland mattresses.

Pete is on the wall outside the Pig & Whistle. It's almost opening time and he's got his running pumps on. He's looking quite dapper tonight, nice pair of khaki trousers and a matching pair of shoes. Not bad, although the Postman Pat t-shirt does little for the ensemble. Budd is lying loyally at his feet as usual. That dog must know the inside of every pub in this area. He never leaves his side and I suspect he survives on a diet of pork scratchings and pub grub. I can feel the tears pricking at the back of my eyes. It's a sight I have seen a million times yet it still moves me to tears. Jack sums it up in his usual practical way.

"They're both happy, look at 'em."

"I know but it's sad."

"Now there's a job you could do, counselling, you're a good listener."

"God knows I've had enough experience over the years with Pete."

"Precisely."

"Couldn't do drugs counselling though, an 'E' to me is still a vowel, I'd have no idea."

"You'd need training."

"No, I'm out of touch, you need street cred for that job."

"Right, suppose you have a point."

"What do I know, the only powder I've ever ingested is a Beecham's."

"I don't see why you can't just chill out and enjoy the rest."

"You know why."

"Okay, I know you miss the salary but it's not as if you ever earned that much is it?" he laughs. I am indignant and try to react accordingly.

"Don't knock it pal, it may have only been a bit but it helped."

"Yes, I distinctly remember you paid the milkman once... June 1978 it was."

"Pillock!"

"Look, it doesn't matter, we get by don't we?"

"Of course."

"Well then woman, let it go."

As we pull onto the driveway, the phone is ringing. Don't you just hate that? It's bound to stop just as you pick it up. I get to it first, just as the caller rings off. It's bleeping so there's a message.

"Mrs Ryder, Tony here from the bank. I'm a bit concerned about your account so I've pencilled you in for two-o-clock tomorrow. If that's not convenient, can you call and cancel, thanks."

"Shit!"

"Who was it?"

"Tony from the bank, he's pencilled me in for two tomorrow."

"Bit cheeky of him."

"I know! They expect you to drop everything and run down at a minute's notice."

He's laughing at me, knowing the state I get into regarding institutions, so to speak.

"Just tell them it's not convenient Cass, they're there to provide a service, not the other way round."

"It's okay for you, you're solvent, you actually have money in your account."

"So do you, well, sixty-nine pence, what's his problem?" he laughs.

"I shall have to go, he's been pestering me for months."

"I'll put the kettle on."

"Strong, three sugars please."

"For the trauma?" he calls from the kitchen.

"Mm... exactly."

"They know you knos," he suddenly blurts out.

"Know what?"

"When you're afraid. They can smell the fear on you."

"Oh cheers!"

"You have to march in with your head held high... and your sixty-nine pence."

"Any more advice?"

"If all else fails, offer him your body."

"Do you think that might work?"

"No, but it should make him laugh at least."

My bank bears a striking resemblance to a dentist's waiting room and I'm sure it was designed that way intentionally. Lots of chrome furniture and pale blue walls, with the odd dog-eared magazine scattered around. Now and again, you can actually hear people screaming out back, so yes, it does resemble a dentist's. The place gives me the creeps. All the staff dress exactly the same in those naff polyester navy-blue uniforms. A bit like clones, robotic figures shuffling silently past you, on wheels I should think.

"Is anybody waiting to pay in?" an Android asks "I can take money but I can't pay out today." That's novel! She'll grab all your dosh but can't give you any back. Charming! See what I mean? it's all one-sided with this lot. As long as you keep shoving the squids over the counter at them they're happy but woe betide if you ask to withdraw a tenner. Just the one till open today then. That's par for the course. Fifteen windows and only one in use. The other fourteen robots are out back having their castors oiled I bet.

"Paying in?" she asks again, her circuits are overloaded, she may implode at any minute.

I've been waiting for fifteen minutes now and no sign of Tony, or should I say, Toni with an 'i'. So the robot on reception informed me when I arrived. She gave me one of his business cards and it's there in print, Toni with an 'i'. One can only assume he was christened Antoni. Daft bugger.

Are all bank staff anally retentive do you think? So far up themselves that they can't see the funny side of life? I've been with this branch for over thirty years and have yet to see one of them crack their faces. I have this overwhelming urge to breeze in one day wearing a black ski-mask, just to provoke a reaction. I'd be laughing my socks off if I had their perks. Low interest mortgages, credit cards, cheap life insurance and a big fat pension when they retire at thirty. All that, and yet if you or I go overdrawn by three-pence they send in the bailiffs.

"Mrs Ryder, go to the door at the far end," R2D2 bawls at me from behind her desk. Toni, with an 'i', is expecting me and gives me a cheesy grin as I step inside his office. The cheesy observation is mainly because his face resembles a cheese and pepperoni pizza. At a rough guess, I'd say he was about fifteen.

"Please, take a seat," he smarms, not bothering to stand. I sit, and grin back, all my previous fears dispelled at the sight of this pubescent boy. I bet he's still wearing short trousers under that desk.

"Thought I'd better get you in, the old account's looking a bit grim," he sneers. My hackles are up and the gloves are off.

"You're quite right, my account is old, probably older than you I should think." He looks quite shocked, probably not used to a bankrupt with attitude.

"I see you haven't worked for some time," he leers, flicking through my files.

"No, lost the plot a while back. Finding it difficult to get another job."

"Oh I see.."

"Tends to put people off you know, working with the insane… we dribble a lot."

"Er… I" he gasps, loosening his Mickey Mouse tie.

"Although, I always did work… before… you know. Worked all my life actually."

"Really?"

"Mm, until the men in the white coats came for me."

I'm on a roll now and there will be no stopping me.

"Oh dear."

"I'd love to work again, maybe you could find me something here. Any vacancies?" I gabble.

"I don't think so…" he splutters, his voice trailing off.

"Oh well, not to worry, as long as you're aware that I am looking for work."

"I'm sure you are," he winces. We have reached a deadlock, with me glaring at him like a lunatic and him believing I truly am one.

"So, this account then. It's overdrawn, I have no money to rectify that, so what's your answer?"

He swallows hard and is beginning to look very uncomfortable. Probably needs a change of underwear.

"Well, in circumstances such as this, we should be able to give you a bit of leeway," he says "I could extend your overdraft, drop the charges for a while perhaps, would that help?"

"Marvellous, I knew we'd find a solution," I beam.

"I'll do that then, right away, thanks for popping in Mrs Ryder."

"No, thank you Toni."

"You take care nos," he says, rising to his feet and extending his hand.

"Yes, and you mind the road on your paper round," I tell him.

I can almost feel him reaching for the panic button as I leave. He'll think twice before he sends me any more nasty letters. If only these people would stop and think. How do they know what dire circumstances their customers may be in? They are number crunchers basically, without a care for the person behind the account number.

I pause on the way out and punch my number into the cash point machine. Toni with an 'i' has been true to his word and extended my overdraft immediately. I withdraw a tenner just for the hell of it. Chicken fried rice for two tonight, courtesy of Toni with a 'i'.

CHAPTER TWELVE

Don't Count Your Goslings

"Five babies, all safe and well, proud parents showing them off." It's only 5.32am and I'm barely awake, but the message gets through. Jack is leaning over the bed, handing me a cuppa and a slice of wholemeal toast.

"Cass, they're wonderful, get your knickers on and go see," he grins at me. Joy oh joy! They've arrived at last. I was beginning to think Gertie was egg bound.

"No casualties?"

"Not that I can see, they're waddling around on the water," he beams, as if he were the father. This mother Nature thing really is infectious, there'll be crowds down there later when news gets out. Maybe I should put a notice in the Times.

"Mr and Mrs Gilbert Goose are proud to announce the arrival of their five goslings."

I hit the floor running, and am washed and dressed in record time. Levy is startled at my speed and drags himself downstairs, still wearing his pyjamas.

"Come on sleepyhead, Gertie's had her babies," I tell him. The mere mention of her name is enough to spur him on and within minutes, all three of us are down at the pond. The early morning sun glistens through the trees onto the water as we stand in silence, waiting for them to appear. Even the dog stands stock still, as if in awe of the moment.

When they do appear, from behind the island in the middle, I am overcome with emotion. Gilbert striding out in front, followed by the babies, with Gertie bringing up the rear. Five tiny bundles of downy yellow and grey fur, all paddling along furiously behind Dad.

"Impressive eh?" says Jack, handing me a tissue.

"Wonderful!" I sob.

Gilbert knows we pose no threat to his brood and as if to

demonstrate this, he leads them towards us, swimming past with his head held high, his chest puffed out with pride.

"Congratulations Dad!" I whisper in between sniffles, "Well done!"

"Promise me you'll never get a job in a zoo," Jack whispers, wrapping his arms around me. We stand in silence for ages, just watching them, overwhelmed by their sheer softness and beauty.

"I'd better go, I'll be late for work."

"I'll walk back with you, make you a fresh pot of tea."

"I hope they'll be okay."

"Don't worry, I'll keep a close eye on them," a voice whispers from the bushes. Neville! Should have known he'd be out on patrol.

"Morning Nev" Jack whispers back, as if it's perfectly normal to talk to a bush.

"Morning."

"How long have you been there?" I ask him.

"All night. They hatched at 4.39 this morning."

"Amazing eh?"

"I've got it on video if you'd like a copy."

"That would be lovely, thanks."

"I have to go," Jack insists, looking at his watch.

"Bye."

We stroll home with Levy rooting in the undergrowth in search of breakfast. He's hoping for a nice juicy sausage but settles for half a packet of cheese and onion crisps someone has dropped on the verge.

"I can't think of a better way to start the day, can you?" he whispers. It seems as if we are the only people awake for miles around, apart from Neville that is.

"We must get a copy of that video," I whisper back.

"Better not let anyone see us, handing over video tapes from the bushes."

"The Vice Squad might take an interest."

"Neville could be arrested for peddling penguin porn."

I needed an early start anyway. Got a full day today. I've volunteered to help out at a car-boot sale. It's a charity thing, fundraising for our local Guide Dog Unit and you know me, anything with a wet nose and I'm gone. The unit's only a few minutes walk away on Long Lane and every time I walk past, it stuns me at just how devoted and determined the dogs and their owners are. I don't normally do car boots. Mainly because I don't have a car, but also because I hate the thought of a stranger rummaging through the remnants of my life. All those intensely personal items being handled by some geek in an anorak.

I'm doing this one because of the charity involved and also I'm hoping Levy will pick up some tips on behaviour. Fat chance I know but stranger things have happened. Looks like it's going to be a glorious day anyway. We won't be needing our wellies. Nothing worse than standing in a quagmire trying to flog your old 78's.

I thought I was early but the grounds are heaving already. The volunteers must have been here for ages, several stalls are already set up, festooned with balloons and bunting. I make a mental note of the home-made cake stall. You can't beat a bit of home baking. Unless it's mine of course.

I'm touting my stuff from the back of a Transit apparently. My friend, Maggie, who works here organised it for me. Maggie is one of my bestest friends and a delight to be with. She has a smile that can light up a room and a laugh that sends me into fits of giggles whenever we meet.

"Cassie! Over here!" she calls, beckoning me towards a rusty Transit parked by the far wall.

"Thanks for coming."

"My pleasure, is this my pitch?"

"Mm, bit grotty but the caretaker lent it to us for the day. Your stuff's in the back."

"It'll be fine, just give me a minute to set up and I'll be off and running."

"Back later, have to set up the refreshment's," she giggles, disappearing into the crowd.

I'm quite excited by all this. My very own van and a paste table as well. Oh, and a bumbag for the money. Jack dug that out of the loft last night. Neither of us has ever owned a bumbag but it was up there just the same. I have several carrier bags of junk with me to sell. Might as well kill two birds with one stone.

"Up you go lad!" He leaps into the back of the van, delighted to be let loose amongst all that treasure. Within seconds he has an enormous stuffed teddy bear in his jaws and is wrestling it to the floor. That should keep him busy for a bit. The queue outside the gates is growing by the minute. Better get a move on and set up my pitch. There's bound to be a mad rush when the gates open. People are always anxious for a bargain. I understand several pensioners have been killed in the past at church jumble sales, trampled underfoot in the rush. Maggie is waving at me from across the way.

"Everything okay?" she shouts, wrestling with a huge tea-urn at the same time.

"Fine!" I reassure her. She does worry, although with my track record for disasters she has every reason to. She's in charge today and it's a big responsibility I feel. She just takes it all in her stride and breezes through as usual.

"How much for the dog?" a gruff voice suddenly grunts from my left. I'm startled for a second, I haven't even got my paste table up yet.

"Sorry?"

"The dog, how much?" he grunts again. A piggy little man with body odour that could stop you at ten paces. I take a step back, gasping for air.

"The dog's priceless I'm afraid, definitely not for sale."

"Everything's got a price lady," he leers, eyeing up my beloved boy with his piggy eyes.

"Like I say, he's priceless," I tell him in no uncertain terms.

"Please yourself!" he snorts, wandering off.

Damn cheek! As if! Porky Pig was probably eyeing him up for dinner, roast dog and dumplings. I shall have to keep an eye on that one. If he comes back, I'll poke him in the eye with that old fishing rod in the van. Levy is unaware that a bloke has just been bartering for him. He has teddy's head in his mouth and looks about to decapitate it. One of it's eyes is hanging out as well.

I catch sight of Porky Pig being escorted back out of the main gate by Maggie. She has a firm grip on his pudgy shoulder and is having none of his cheek. Bet he crept in one of the side gates to get a sneak preview. Honestly, some people! Let's hope he gets relegated to the back of the queue by the mob. Right! Table set up, bumbag on, let's start arranging the goods eh? Show them what's on offer. I can't sell the teddy, it's lost an arm and a leg and most of it's stuffing. Looks quite scary with one eye popping out of it's socket. I'll make a donation for it. A fiver should do. Here we go, casserole dishes, cracked of course. Couple of flowerpots, oh and that's not bad, sort of a wine rack thingy. Just spread them out, make it look a bit more professional.

"That dog's humping that bear..."

He's back again! Porky Pig, I can tell by the voice. I grip the fishing rod in my hand just in case.

"Excuse me?"

"That dog, he's humping that teddy bear," he smirks. I can just about see Levy out of the corner of my eye, forcing himself onto the bear with relish. This is nothing unusual, but he normally doesn't do it in public.

"Yes, well, is there something in particular you wanted?" I ask him defiantly.

"No, just looking."

"Only, we are here to make money you know. It is for charity."

"Yeah, bit pricey for my liking," he moans.

"Really?"

"Twenty pence for a tea over there," he grunts, pointing to the refreshment stall.

"Jolly reasonable I'd say," I argue, determined not to let this go.

"It's only ten pence at the Scout's do."

"Do a lot of these boot sales do you?" I ask him.

"Fair few."

"Would you be a dealer by any chance?"

"Might be, what's it got to do with you?"

"Nothing, just curious," I say, flexing the fishing rod in anticipation.

Bet he's a dealer! Barging in early and trying to snap up all the good stuff before anybody else get's a look in. He's probably got a little shop somewhere, making a mint out of other people's junk. I watch him closely as he scrutinises everything on the table. His piggy eyes darting back and forth, taking everything in

He's still hovering behind me as I unload the rest of the boxes from the van. I can feel his eyes boring a hole in my back. Some nice stuff here. Box of Dinky Cars, some Beano annuals and a lovely pair of children's wellies with a Kermit head on the front.

"Give you a pound for the cars," he snorts, sorting through the box. Now, I may be daft but I'm not that daft. I raised a son who was fanatical about Dinky cars and even I know they're worth a lot more than that. Must be at least twenty in that box.

"Multiply it by twenty and we'll talk," I tell him.

"You're having a laugh!" he bellows.

"Is this face laughing?"

"Silly cow!" he barks, striding off, leaving a trail of sweat in his wake. He must think I was born yesterday. Listen pal! I ran a charity shop, I know all the tricks.

Maggie is waving again from the hoop-la stall. I bet she knows Porky Pig of old.

"Sold anything yet?" she shouts. I shake my head dejectedly and she laughs. I must look a sight, standing here in my shorts with an assortment of cracked pots on display. Not to worry, business will pick up in a bit. Levy has finished with the bear. He's lying on his back, smoking a Marlboro. Poor bear, lost most of it's stuffing and all of it's self respect by the look of it. The crowds are flooding in now with several interested faces jostling in front of my pitch.

"What size are the wellies?" a young woman asks.

"A three… yes just check… a three."

"They'll do, our Jason's a four but he'll squeeze into 'em."

Our Jason appears to be a little boy with a shock of ginger hair and a trail of green snot dangling from his left nostril. Poor bugger, destined to have foot problems in the future as well I should think.

"Are you sure?" I ask her, not wanting to look as if I'm interfering.

"Yeah, they'll do, how much?"

"Fifty-pence be okay?"

"Bargain! look Jason, Kermit!" Jason is unimpressed. I'd guess he's about four but he has the look of a wise old man about him. Probably seen it all before and is heartily sick of being dragged around these boot sales.

"Ere, grab hold of these," she snaps, shoving the wellies into his arms. My heart goes out to Jason. He'll be crippled for life wearing those. I offer him a Dinky car as consolation and he grabs it greedily.

"Say thanks Jason," his Mother urges, poking him in the back.

"Thanks."

"You're welcome pet."

Better put a donation in for that as well. Must make a note, that's five-fifty I owe already.

It's only just after eleven and I'm sweltering. My pitch is facing South and the sun is glaring down onto my back. I can feel my t-shirt sticking to it. I should have worn a hat. I'll have to have a root round in the van, see if there's one in there.

"Have you got this in a sixteen?" a woman's voice suddenly asks.

"Pardon?"

"Sixteen!" she bawls quite rudely, shoving a gold lurex jumper under my nose. At first, I think she's winding me up but then realisation dawns that she's deadly serious. Silly tart! This is a boot-sale, not John Lewis.

"Sorry, it's the only one," I tell her.

"Typical! Never do the bigger sizes!" she snaps, throwing the jumper onto the floor.

My gob is well and truly smacked! How ridiculous, coming to a boot sale and expecting to find a range of sizes and colours. I'm still giggling hysterically when another voice calls me.

"Could I have a look at that fishing rod please?"

Another small boy, only this time comparatively snot-free. His excited little face glowing with perspiration. I suspect he's been on the bouncy castle. He has the look of a freshly bounced boy.

"Course, here you go," I say, handing him the rod.

"Smashing, just what I need. Grandpa says he'll take me fishing when he's out of hospital."

Oh dear! Here we go again! His Grandpa in hospital, probably never coming out... gulp!

"That's nice, you'll have a great time," I say encouragingly, praying it's nothing terminal.

"How much is it?" he asks, lovingly fingering the rod.

"Fifty-pence?"

His face slumps dramatically, crumples in fact, as if he's about to burst into tears.

"Sorry, I don't have enough," he sighs, putting the rod back. I'm not strong enough for this, you have to be made of stone to be a good business woman.

"No, my mistake, that's ten pence, sorry," I grovel. His eyes light up again and he painstakingly counts out ten pennies from his pocket. I resist the urge to burst into tears and mentally add another forty pence to my debt.

"Thanks," he beams, skipping off with the rod under his arm. I do hope Grandpa makes it to the river. That boy could be damaged for life if he doesn't. I'm making a list on a piece of paper of the takings. I like things to be in order, so, that's... Kermit wellies... fifty pence. Fishing rod... fifty pence. Teddy bear... five pounds. Dinky car... fifty pence. I. O. U... five-pounds ninety so far.

Two elderly ladies are browsing through the magazines on the table. They are both wearing plastic raincoats with matching hats, those dinky little ones you buy at the seaside with umbrellas on. It must be eighty degrees in the shade and I have the burns on the back of my neck to prove it.

"Hello ladies, can I help at all?"

"How much for the magazines?" one asks. The one wearing a yellow rain hat. The other is in blue.

"Shall we say a penny each?" I smile.

"That's very reasonable, are you sure?"

"Yes, they're a bit dog-eared, that's fine," I tell her.

"I say Lil, only a penny each," she tells her friend.

"Bargain Ivy, let's get them shall we?"

"Sold!" I nod enthusiastically. Things are moving along at a fair pace now. I count out the magazines, twenty-five in all, and take the money with a smile. Lil and Ivy shuffle off towards the bouncy castle. Heaven forbid! I hope they're not going to have a go on that. I don't think the insurance will cover them. I add the twenty-five pence to my list and am suddenly besieged by customers. Things are flying off the table and before I know it, practically everything is gone, apart from the cracked pots.

Almost lunchtime and I have a terrible thirst. This sun is really strong. Time I took Levy for a walk to stretch his legs. Get a drink as well while I'm at it. I scan around for Maggie and spot her painting a little girls face. Such talent! Not only an organiser but a face-painter too. I wish I were multi-talented, although my sales technique seems to have improved. She catches my eye and waves to acknowledge me, she can see I have Levy on the lead and reads the signals.

"Carry on, I'll get someone to cover for you," she shouts.

We weave our way through the masses towards the gardens at the back. This is a lovely place, very serene, a perfect setting for the visually impaired. All the shrubs seem to have been especially chosen for their perfume, a veritable assault on the nostrils for anyone wandering through. The back of my neck is quite sore now. I shall probably end up with a thumping migraine at the end of the day. Fancy forgetting to bring a hat.

We find a quiet spot and spread out on the lawn, Levy gnawing at my sandal, while I take a second or two to swig on my bottle of Evian water. I have some ham rolls in my bag but I'm feeling a bit queasy to be honest. I can hear the clock on St Peter's chiming two. Where did this morning go to?

That same clock is suddenly chiming three when I wake up! I've been asleep for an hour without even realising it. Hell! Maggie will be frantic, she'll think I've forgotten what I was doing and gone home. How on earth did that happen? I only meant to sit down for a minute.

Levy has drunk all the Evian water and shredded the plastic bottle into bits. Poor thing, he's been lying here by my side all the time. What a stupid thing to do! Thank goodness we were lying in the shade… he could have fried to death. How careless!

As I stand, my legs appear to take on a life of their own and go off in a different direction. I feel extremely odd, sort of disorientated and dizzy. It takes every ounce of energy I possess to steer myself along the path to the grounds.

A familiar face is waiting anxiously as we get to the van. She takes one look at me and rushes across to us, her face a picture of concern.

"Cassie, are you okay, you look dreadful!" Maggie asks, taking my arm.

"Not sure, I feel a bit odd," I tell her, drooping against the side of the van. She grabs my wrist and seems to be searching for a pulse. God! I hope she finds one.

"It's racing, sit down on here."

"No, I'm fine... really."

"Sit!" she orders and I obey, too weak to argue. Surprisingly, Levy sits too, must be a one-off, he's never done that before.

"Your face is burning, I think you have a fever."

"Hot, yes, I'm very hot," I croak.

"What's that on your neck?" she asks, alarmed.

"Neck, turkey neck, gobble, gobble," I rant in my delirious state.

"Cassie! You're burnt, your neck is all sunburnt."

"Chestnuts roasting on an open fire," I sing at the top of my voice to a crowd of amused onlookers.

"Oh crikey, it's sunstroke," I hear her say to one of the crowd.

"Better get her to hospital," a woman with three heads is saying.

"Bee-baw... bee-baw!" I wail, doing my famous impression of an ambulance. It's at this precise moment that Maggie loses the plot and throwing her head back, she roars with laughter, her entire body convulsed with glee. I join in and we stand there, rocking together.

"I'll get you home," she says, guiding me gently towards her car.

"I'll drive," I suggest.

"No, I'd better," she titters.

With Levy on the back seat, we make our way onto the main road. I am propped up in the front, veering in and out of consciousness while bursting into a raunchy version of Great Balls Of Fire during my lucid moments. I remember getting home. I remember vomiting into Maggie's handbag. And I distinctly remember the wonderful shock of icy cold water as she held my head under the shower. Now, it's 7.03 according to the clock on the bedside table. I was right about the migraine, it's a corker!

"Back in the land of the living are we?"

It's Jack, sitting beside me on the bed. My vision is still a bit blurred but I know it's him.

"What a nightmare!" I groan, sitting up.

"Stroke," he says gently, holding my hand "Sunstroke... you silly tart!"

I am mortified, fancy not realising. And Maggie, what must she think?

"Maggie.." I start to say.

"It's okay, she'll pop round in the morning, when she's cleaned her handbag out."

"Oh no, how awful!"

"She rang me at work. She was very worried."

"What a mess and I didn't make much money," I sigh.

"It's alright, I gave her something, and enough to buy a new handbag."

"Thanks."

"Can I get you anything?" he asks, heading for the stairs.

"Aspirin please and a cold drink."

He pauses at the door and grins...

"What's all this about you impersonating a turkey?"

CHAPTER THIRTEEN

Beware of the Bogeywoman

We are supposed to be on holiday in Shropshire, but I got the dates mixed up. Yet another symptom of Trifledom, a fog inside your head that makes you confuse dates and times. Good job Jack checked the receipts last night, or we'd have pitched up at some holiday cottage thinking it was ours for the week. No real harm done, just the nuisance of having to unpack the cases and wrestle Levy's bucket and spade off him. He does so look forward to his holidays.

The holiday was Tilly's idea. I haven't really been anywhere since I became ill and she suggested a break would do us all good. She was probably including herself in that, give her a break from me for a week. I don't travel well you see, a bit like wine or cheese. Motorways scare the shit out of me and as for flying, well, forget that for the time being. I never used to be this way. She says it's a symptom of my illness. The fear of leaving the security of my own home. I'm happy at home. It's safe and I know where everything is. Tilly says it's time I let go of that security blanket and ventured further afield.

Anyway, I fucked up the dates, which is why I'm sitting here in the Crumple Clinic, watching Alicia pick her nose and wipe it on her tweed skirt. Dirty cow! She's one of those pervert pickers, you know the sort, does it while nobody's looking, slyly poking her little finger up her left nostril and rooting around for a bogey. Yuk! No wonder she's still single, there can't be anything more off putting than a nose-picker surely?

Alan's pretending not to look and is concentrating on the hole in his sock. It's quite a big hole actually, looks as if it's been nibbled by a mouse. I do worry about that lad. He has a boil today as well. Right in the middle of his forehead, big, pulsating red thing. Let's hope there are no cargo ships in these waters or he'll be guiding them into the wrong shipping lanes.

Just the three of us today, and Tilly of course. Good job I turned up or poor Alan would have been on his own with the Bogeywoman. It goes like this with the group. People come and go and miss sessions or just plain forget, something I have done several times in the past. Tilly just smiles bravely and accepts our excuses without any irritation whatsoever. A true professional is our Tilly. Either that or she's taking huge doses of the drugs we are supposed to be on.

"I have a question for you," she says "Pull your chairs closer if you could." We shuffle towards her on our vinyl seats and I notice that Alicia panics and wipes the bogey on her finger underneath the seat of her chair. Disgusting woman!

"Today I want to discuss peace of mind."

We stare at her blankly, as if she's about to give us a lecture on Nuclear Physics.

"Peace of mind, now what does that mean to you?" It's a subject I've never really thought about to be honest. I suppose we all strive to achieve it but never actually think about it. I say none of this out loud, not wanting to go first.

"It's all relative I think," gushes the snot-gobbler "It means something different to all of us."

"Okay, so what does it mean to you Alicia?" Tilly asks her.

"Ah, peace of mind, well to me that would be my savings and making sure my investments are sound." Here we go! I knew she'd have a portfolio. She looks the type. More interested in the FT Index than her fellow man.

"And Alan, what about you?"

Alan wouldn't have a portfolio. A polo neck jumper probably but not a portfolio. From what I gather, he's never had a job, so stock options are unlikely to be high on his list of priorities. Keeping warm in the winter and having enough food in the larder, those would be his priorities.

"Er... sorry," he stammers.

"Take your time Alan, no rush," Tilly coaxes him gently. His cheeks flush a deep crimson colour, the same colour as the boil, and my heart goes out to him. If the Bogeywoman interrupts him now, I shall karate kick her in the crotch I swear.

"The electric meter," he suddenly blurts out "I worry if my tokens run out." We are all slightly startled by this and look to Tilly for inspiration.

"Right, so that upsets you Alan, making it hard for you to find peace of mind?" she whispers.

"No, if the leccy goes off my fish tank goes cold."

"Sorry?"

"My tropical fish, the heater stops and the water goes cold."

"I see."

"You can lose a fish in minutes you know."

"Really?"

"I'm down to five already after the last time."

"Sorry Alan, what was that?"

"July, in that heat wave, I set the thermostat wrong and the water boiled."

"Oh dear."

"Lost four angel fish, jumped right out of the tank while I was at Aldi," he rants.

"Goodness!"

"Found them on the carpet when I got back."

"I'm sorry to hear that Alan, if we could..." Tilly says, trying to cut him off.

"Cat ate one of 'em then sicked it up on the settee."

My life! Where is all this coming from? I have never known Alan string more than three words together and now this! He's unstoppable, the veins in his forehead bulging with the pressure. I hope to God that boil doesn't burst, or we'll all be covered in puss.

"Cassie!" Tilly shouts "What about you?"

Alan stops in mid-rant and I have to say, he looks quite embarrassed. He'll have to go and lie down in a dark room after this.

"Me? It has to be my family, and the dog of course, if they're okay then I'm okay," I tell her.

"Good, I think we're getting the idea nos," she says, smiling at me.

"I don't have any family," the Bogeywoman suddenly pipes up. I suspect she's looking for the sympathy vote but I'm not falling for that one.

"Well, strictly speaking, I do have a father, but we don't speak," she whines. Now there's a surprise, not the fact that they don't speak, but that she has a father!

"He fell out with me when I sold the house and got him a room at the home."

Nice! Sell his house and shove him in a home! No wonder he's not talking to you.

"I never see him now, it's too far away to visit," she whimpers. It get's better! Sell his house and put him in care... in a home that's miles away?

"We seem to be veering away from the point," Tilly says, looking exasperated. We fall silent again, waiting for her to guide us back to the subject in hand.

"I'm going to read you a statement and I'd be interested to know if you can tell me who said it."

The Bogeywoman leans closer in her chair, desperate to score some Brownie points.

"If you haven't got peace of mind, you haven't got nothing," Tilly says, reading from a notebook on her lap. The grammar is slightly obtuse but I know exactly where she's going with this.

"It's obviously one of the Greek philosophers, Plato perhaps?" Bogeywoman butts in. Tilly shakes her head politely and I go in for the kill.

"It's Michael Caine actually... in Alfie," I gloat.

"Excellent Cassie! well done!" Tilly laughs, clapping her hands together with joy. I just knew my vast knowledge of old films would come in handy one day and here we are! A great British classic and it just ran off the tip of my tongue. One-nil, one-nil, one-nil, one-nil! Shove that up your nose and pick it!

"Really, how silly of me," Alicia gulps, cringing with embarrassment.

"The point I'm trying to make, is that peace of mind is vital to us all," Tilly says. We nod in unison, my head expanding to twice it's normal size at my unexpected triumph.

"We all have to look inside ourselves and question what it means to us."

"Was that the one where they all got massacred in the desert?" Alan suddenly asks me.

"That was Zulu," I tell him.

"Her who was married to a Bee Gee?"

"That was Lulu!" I giggle.

"She was in that film with Sydney Poitier," he beams, as if a light just came on in his head. This is getting ridiculous! I can feel my face beginning to crack and know that I'm about to lose it completely. I shall end up in a heap on the floor.

"Perhaps you could think about it a little more at home?" Tilly suggests, closing her notebook, a sign that the session is coming to an end.

"Think about it and we'll pick it up again next time." We stand and place our chairs back against the wall. I make a mental note not to pick up the one with the bogey on next week.

"Take care everyone," she trills, disappearing into the main office. Poor thing, I bet she nips in there and head butts the wall after sessions like that.

As I get outside, Alan catches up with me, quite breathless with the effort of running.

"Was it Please Sir?" he asks as if his life depends on it. I haven't got the heart to tell him that was a television series in the seventies.

"That's it Alan, well done!"

"See ya!" he grins, running for his bus. You see, these sessions do work! Alan is participating at last! We'll probably get him a girlfriend before the year's out. Someone to do his shopping, and lance his boils.

I wish we were in Shropshire now, relaxing in a little cottage miles from anywhere. I wish I were anywhere but here. Standing looking out onto my garden, with a total stranger picking damsons off the tree in the far corner. I have no idea who he is and it's yet another 'fight or flight' moment. If I leg it, that gives him the freedom to break into the house and ransack it. If I go out and challenge him, he'll probably cave my skull in. What do you do in a situation like this? I just got back from the clinic and there he was. Bold as brass, helping himself to my fruit. Cheek!

Levy is straining at the leash to get at him, but there lies another dilemma. If I let him out and he savages the intruder, what then? He could end up in court and get five years.

Under these circumstances, I'd normally ring Jack who would fly home with the aid of his cape and red underpants and see off this geezer. As it is, he's miles away today in Cheltenham and if I ring him he'll only worry.

If I call the police, they'll arrive a week on Thursday, so as you can see, I'm in a bit of a quandary. I shall have to be assertive. Put some of those sessions into practice. I have Levy on the lead, just in case.

"Excuse me, can I ask what you're doing in my garden?" I ask him. He turns, smiling broadly at me, "Morning missus," he says, continuing to pick the damsons.

In the sunshine, a flash of gold blinks out at me from one of his front teeth, dazzling me briefly. He's a big bloke, at least six feet tall with a shock of jet black hair, tied in a ponytail at the back. I'd guess he was about fifty but it's hard to tell. The clothes are quite dated, sort of hippyish, lots of denim and suede with a bright red scarf tied at his neck.

"I said, can I ask what you're doing in my garden?" I repeat quite forcefully.

"Sure, I'm taking a few of these," he laughs, holding up the damsons.

"I know, but they belong to me."

"I thought they were his," he grins, pointing to the sky.

"His?"

"The good Lord," he laughs. There's no answer to that and I'm gobsmacked for a second.

"Yes, well, the tree's in my garden, so if you don't mind."

"You'll not be missing a few, there's plenty," he says, ignoring me.

"Actually, I will, now I'm asking you nicely to get off my property."

"No problem missus, I'm on my way," he sighs, and with that he steps back from the tree, gathers up the damsons on the lawn and leaps over the fence into Pete's garden. I remain frozen to the spot, fascinated yet frightened at the same time.

The fruit felon meanders down Pete's path and into the house. What on earth is going on? Has Pete done a moonlight flit? I could have sworn I heard him fall down the stairs early this morning. Someone's in the kitchen now, I can hear them banging about and whistling. Probably making a fruit pie with my bloody damsons. Honestly, you pop out for an hour and people pick your fruit without even asking! Whatever next?

If I stand on the top step on the patio, I can just about see into Pete's kitchen. There he is, told you, that guy's making a pie or something. I can see the dish and a rolling pin. Well I never!

"Pete, are you there, hello!" I bawl through the hedge.

"Hi Cassie," Pete's voice calls back from the kitchen.

"Can I have a word?"

"Sure, I'll be right out."

He steps out of the back door, wearing a ladies towelling bath robe and a pair of bovver boots. I feel obliged to inform him that there's a strange man baking a pie in his kitchen. He's prone to delusions and probably thinks this guy is a mirage.

"Pete, did you know there's a guy in your kitchen, baking a pie?"

"Damson and apple with honey sauce, delicious!" he grins.

"I suppose the apples came off my trees as well?" I ask exasperated.

"Knew you wouldn't mind. Gabriel's a great cook."

"Gabriel?"

"Mm, my lodger, moved in yesterday."

It's not the first time he's bought a stranger home from the pub. The last one was an incredibly ugly woman called Pearl, who I suspect earned her living hanging around on street corners.

"Is that wise do you think. Taking in another stranger?"

"Gabriel's sound! He's a horse trader, and a Buddhist." Well, that's okay then! This man's logic never ceases to amaze me. He's been on the turps again.

"Not much call for horse traders in Birmingham I shouldn't have thought."

"Silly, he's on his way to a horse fair in Somerset, needed a place to stay for a bit," he laughs.

Fancy me not knowing that? I must try to keep abreast of the latest in donkey dealing.

"Right, I see."

"Besides, it's a bit of extra cash for me," he says apologetically.

"Well, if you could ask him not to climb into my garden unannounced."

"Will do, sorry."

He disappears inside again, his boots flapping against his bare legs. There's nothing else I can do. It's his property and he's quite entitled to invite who he likes to stay, but his house guests are invariably drunks of one description or another and I know this will all end in tears.

When Pearl finally did a flit, after a three week stay, she took a portion of his broken heart and most of the bed linen out of his airing cupboard. Enough said. Jack will be livid! He worries with me being here on my own all day. I have Levy of course, but he knows full well I would throw myself in front of a mad axe man rather than let anything happen to that lad.

What do you do? Like I say, it's his property and none of my business. I just hang around to pick up the pieces. And there will inevitably be pieces. Trust me, I know about these things.

Gabriel! What sort of a name is that? Romany I should think, he has the look of a gypsy about him. The hair and the scarf at the neck, and the solid gold tooth of course. I hope he's not thinking of bringing those horses here to graze. Those poor guinea pigs could get trodden on.

I have to let it go, a valuable lesson in life that Tilly taught me. Walk away and let him get on with it. Besides, I've got loads to do today. A seventy foot beech hedge to trim for a start and the remains of yesterday's supper to bury in the compost heap.

"Take me home again Kathleen," a voice booms out from next door, and it's not Pete. "Across the la-la Irish sea." La-La Irish sea? I'm not sure those are the right words but he's got the gist of it anyway. Sells ponies, bakes pies and sings too. I'm impressed. Next thing you know, he'll be reading my palm and telling me to beware of a tall, dark stranger. I'm already onto that one thank you.

"Would you be having any cinnamon Pete?" he calls.

"Got some coriander somewhere."

"That'll do my friend."

Lovely! Damson and coriander pie, remind me not to rush round for a slice of that.

"That guinea pigs in the fridge Pete."

"He's after the cheese."

"Right enough."

I don't know whether to laugh or cry. The mind boggles at what goes on in that house. No wonder Budd spends his days sleeping in the shed. It's the only place he can get any peace.

"Carling or Carlsberg?"

"One of each I think."

"Wash this pie down nicely my friend."

Pete's fridge is always fully stocked. With booze. He once told me, he'd worked it out that you can fit exactly thirty-six cans of Fosters and four bottles of Bells in it. Never mind food, you have to get your priorities right don't you?

"Smells good!" I hear Pete say.

"Be ready in an hour, enough time to get a couple in eh?"

"Ready."

"I'm right behind you my man."

I can only hope they don't get sidetracked and stay out until the early hours. That pie will be ruined.

CHAPTER FOURTEEN

All Creatures Great and Small

Jack is sitting on the patio, browsing through his copy of Golfers Balls or whatever it is golfers read every month. He has abandoned his Nike golf cap for a change as it's a glorious day and far too hot for a hat. He's trying to catch some rays before it rains again which could be any minute judging by the look of that sky.

"That dog's behaving very oddly," he suddenly says, beckoning me to come and look.

"So what else is new?" I laugh, joining him outside.

"No, honest, he's doing daft things, really."

I watch, fascinated, as Levy circles the lawn, again and again, going round and round in spirals, as if he's stalking something.

"Perhaps he's got rabies," he observes.

"Be serious! I've never seen him do that before."

"He's practising, for the sheepdog trials. Told you he watches too much television."

"Will you stop it! I'm getting worried now."

"Worried about what? That he might be insane, we know that already," he laughs.

"Look, he's flopped down on the grass now." We watch as the dog visibly droops and slumps to the floor.

"Come on lad! What's up?" Jack shouts.

"Levy! Come on, fancy a walk?" I call to him.

Nothing! Absolutely diddly-squat. We both react in a split second and race up the garden towards him. Something is badly wrong, I just know it! Jack is faster than me and reaches the lifeless form on the lawn first. The alarmed expression on his face confirms my fears. He must be dead! I freeze on the spot, too terrified to even contemplate it. My beloved boy, gone!

"Cass! Don't panic, he's collapsed... get the car keys," Jack shouts. Don't panic! What a ridiculous thing to say! My boy, dying in front of me and he says don't panic.

"Cass! Get the keys!" he bawls again, scooping the lifeless dog up into his arms. I'm on my toes now, running as if my life depended on it, with him behind me carrying the dog. I jump into the back seat of the car and he places Levy gently onto my lap, his huge body limp and apparently lifeless.

"Levy!" I scream "Come on lad, wake up please!"

"Just hold onto him, we'll be there in a few minutes."

He shoots off the drive, tyres screeching as he rounds The Cedars doing about sixty miles an hour. I can't believe this is happening and go onto auto-pilot, cradling the dog, sobbing hysterically and making siren noises out of the window to clear the traffic.

"Please don't die! Please God, don't let him die," I wail.

"He'll be alright, trust me." I have convinced myself that he's dead already and mentally prepare myself for his burial in my head.

"Oh God!, oh God!" I keep repeating to myself as we pull up in front of the surgery.

Jack is out of the car and has the dog in his arms before I can even open my door. With a few short strides, he's inside and I follow, still wailing like a banshee.

"Sudden collapse!" he tells Beccy on reception "Just keeled over in the garden."

"This way," she says, racing through to the consulting room.

Mr Orchard, our vet, is in the middle of a very delicate rectal examination on a Siamese cat and I'm not sure who looks more startled, the cat or the vet.

"Levy... sudden collapse," Beccy tells him. He is nothing if not in control, and sensing the urgency of the situation, calmly removes his hand from up the cat's bum and apologises to it's owner...

"Could you wait outside please?" he asks her. The Siamese cat and it's owner look relieved and discreetly disappear into the waiting room. Levy is flat out on the examining table with the rest of us gathered in a circle around him.

"When did he collapse?" the vet asks, running his hand over the dog's belly.

"A few minutes ago, literally, we bought him straight here."

"Has he eaten anything odd?"

Eaten anything odd? How much time have you got mate?

"Poison... anything in the garden... weed killer?"

"No, we never use the stuff," Jack assures him.

"Bones? Anybody left any bones lying around?"

"No, not that I know of," I tell him. He's prodding the belly now, palpating it, gently gliding his hands along, feeling for something.

"There! It's an obstruction of some sort, in his intestines, have to go in and get that out," he barks. It's at this point that I collapse into a heap on the floor and to their credit, the vet and Beccy simply step over me and carry the dying dog through to the operating theatre.

"Wait outside, I'll be with you in a minute," Beccy whispers gently.

Jack is forced to physically lift me, in order to get me to my feet. My legs have turned to jelly and my brain too.

"Come on Cass, he'll be fine, they know what they're doing."

"Waaah!"

I am inconsolable and he gently deposits me onto one of the chairs just as Beccy returns.

"Mr Orchard's about to operate, it could take a while."

"Waaaaaaaaaaaah!"

"Why don't you go home. I'll ring you as soon as it's over."

"Waaaaaaaaaaaaaaaaaaah!"

"He's an expert surgeon, he'll be fine I'm sure," she says, not very convincingly I feel.

"We'll do that, thanks," Jack says, shaking her hand.

"I'll ring you, as soon as..."

I can't speak. I have a lump the size of a grapefruit in my throat and a pain in my chest as if my heart is being ripped out. The woman with the Siamese cat's crying now. I've started everybody off! She nods sympathetically as we leave, her expression one of grief and understanding.

Inside the car, I lose the plot completely, my entire body wracked with sobs. Just a few hours ago he had his humungous head stuck inside a flowerpot and now this! How on earth did it happen?

"It's all my fault," I wail.

"Don't be silly, these things happen."

"I should have been watching him, he must have eaten something in the garden."

"Cass, listen to me, that dog eats disgusting things ALL the time. He loves disgusting things, you know that."

"Yes, but this one's gone and killed him," I sob.

"Listen! He's not dead yet! They're in there fighting for his life, don't write him off yet."

"Do you think?"

"I do think, honest," he whispers, wiping the snot off my nose.

His kindness and assurances only serve to make me cry even more. The prospect of never romping in the woods again with my beloved boy is just too awful to consider. He has been such a huge part of my life for so long I can't imagine life without him.

"Tea... strong... several sugars I think," Jack says, starting the car.

"Mm, please."

"I'll stop at Safeway, get him some of those little beefy biscuits he likes, for when he comes home."

"And some chocolate buttons?"

"Yeah, lots of chocolate buttons."

"He'll be hungry, he didn't eat this morning."

"Well he ate something, we just don't know what," Jack smiles.

"God! I hope it's not something alive."

"Perish the thought."

I sit in the car while he races round Safeway, searching for treats for the baby. I daren't go inside, not with my face like this. All swollen and red from crying. People tend to stare at you and make assumptions when they can see you've been crying. I'm in no state to shop, one look at a box of Bonio's at the moment and I'd break down. I have a word with the Big Guy while I wait, assuring him that if he let's Levy live, I promise never to be rude to a Jehovah's witness again.

It's been five hours now and no news. I have convinced myself that they are too scared to ring and tell me that he died under the anaesthetic. Beccy knows us of old, and Mr Orchard. They've probably decided that the news would be too much for me to take. They'll send us a telegram instead... "DOG DEAD. DID ALL WE COULD. SORRY." END OF MESSAGE. I'm pacing up and down, wearing a hole in the kitchen carpet, while Jack sits by the phone, willing it to ring. When it does, he pounces on the receiver, swooping it up to his ear.

"Hi... really... never!... I see... right... I'll tell her... bye."

"What?!"

"It was a pebble, it's out, he's fine," he sighs, a huge grin washing over his face. I can't speak, instead I just flop onto the sofa and sob like a baby with relief.

"Would you believe it? Vet says it was the size of a small orange."

"No?"

"Yeah, stuck right in his intestines."

"Oh my life!"

"He's coming round, we can pick him up any time after six."

"Thank you God!"

I owe him one, big time, and make a mental note of my promise earlier. I feel as if a huge weight has been lifted from my shoulders and suddenly feel very tired and drained.

"How the hell did he manage to swallow something like that?" he asks me.

"I have no idea, a pebble, where would he get a ruddy pebble from?"

"How do we know what he get's up to in the night. He might have cycled to Skegness."

My head is throbbing and I still feel sick with worry but at least he's come through it.

"What time did he say?"

"After six, when the anaesthetic's worn off properly."

"He'll be all dopey and wobbly on his legs," I tell him.

"That'll be a first then."

Another two hours before we can collect him. I don't think I can wait that long. The thought of him coming round in some strange wired cage upsets me. I should be there, waiting for him to open his eyes, ready with my stethoscope to check on his heartbeat.

I hope he hasn't sustained any brain damage. What if his oxygen supply was cut off when he collapsed? Best not dwell on it. Wait and see when we pick him up.

Beccy and Mr Orchard are waiting for us as we arrive. Both of them wearing wonderful smiles that say, "Told you so, he's fine." I have an overwhelming urge to kiss Mr Orchard but decide against it. He's had enough trauma for one day.

"He's one lucky dog Mrs Ryder, it was a close call," he says, taking my hand in his.

"I don't know how to thank you, I'm lost for words," I tell him gratefully.

"Nonsense! We know how important that boy is to you."

"Can we see him now?"

"I'll go fetch him," Beccy offers, disappearing into the surgery.

"Would you like to keep the pebble?"

And with that he produces a plastic bag, with what looks like a decent sized boulder in it. Great big, shiny grey pebble, like he said, the size of a small orange.

"It was causing an obstruction, had to cut into the intestine to remove it. He'll have to stick to a liquid diet for at least ten days. Give the gut time to heal."

"Oh my life! How on earth did he manage to swallow that?" I cry.

"Jesus!" Jack chips in, examining the bag.

"Like I say, it was a close call. He's got a terrific scar on his belly but that will heal."

"What about stitches?"

"They'll dissolve, no problem."

I can hear Levy's claws skittering on the tiled floor in the consulting room and expect him to drag himself through the door like a wounded soldier. I am wrong. One look at me and he leaps headfirst into my lap, knocking me over in the process. I lie, flat on my back on the floor, while he smothers me in wet kisses and dog snot. That's my boy! Take more than surgery and stitches to keep him down.

"I was about to say, try and keep him quiet for a few days but still, he's on the mend," the vet laughs. Beccy is behind the desk, punching numbers into the computer, while I lie on the floor looking up.

"Did you want the liquid food as well?" she asks Jack.

"Yes, whatever he needs."

"He'll need two tins a day for the next ten days, it's a bit like baby food."

"Fine, whatever you think."

"And we'll need to see him in a week, just to check him over."

I'm on my feet now while Levy decides to take an unhealthy interest in the vet's crotch. I have no idea why Labrador's do that! Every single lab I know makes a beeline for people's crotches as if they have a personal hygiene problem, which is not true of course. I prefer to think of it as their way of making friends.

"I'd better go and finish off. Nice to see you smiling again Mrs Ryder."

"Thanks again Mr Orchard, really."

The computer is on meltdown as it prints out the itemised bill. I have a feeling we are going to have to re-mortgage the house to pay for this one. Thank God for American Express I say.

"Would you like to sit down?" Beccy laughs, handing Jack the bill.

"No, I can take it."

"That's five-hundred and two pounds and seventeen pence please."

To his credit, he doesn't faint, just hands over the plastic and sobs quietly into his hankie.

"There's your receipt."

"Thanks."

"See you in a week."

"Bye."

The patient is straining at the leash and as the fresh air hits his fuddled head he takes off, with me hanging on for grim death. He comes to a halt suddenly and cocks his leg, for what seems like forever, against the wheel of the vet's Audi.

In the car, I smother him with kisses and feel the tears starting again just looking at his scar. It's about ten inches long and running in a neat line right down the centre of his tummy. Jack is watching us in the rear-view mirror.

"That's got to be the most expensive pebble ever," he laughs, shaking his head.

"Sorry, I'll pay you back... when I'm rich and famous."

"When will that be then?"

"Never I should think."

As we hit the rush-hour traffic, Levy shoves his head out of the window and starts to howl at the passing traffic. I have a feeling he's going to be fine.

"Think I'll make a water feature out of it, in the garden," Jack suddenly says.

"Like that woman on telly?"

"The one with no bra and enormous breasts?"

"Mm..."

"Can't say I've ever noticed."

"Liar!"

By the time we reach home, the ordeal has caught up with Levy and he is zonked out on the back seat, his paws paddling in mid-air as if he's having a nightmare. It takes the two of us and several helpful neighbours to carry him indoors. They are most concerned, as he's somewhat of a celebrity in this neighbourhood and Jack delights in showing them all the pebble and the ten inch scar. Oh, and the bill of course.

CHAPTER FIFTEEN

Short Back and Sides Please

S tep four in Tilly's self-help program, be kind to yourself. Treat yourself now and again. Indulge, I think is the expression. I've never been one for self-indulgence. Quick slop with some soap and water in the morning and I'm ready, but maybe she's right. Which is why I've decided to get a haircut. It takes me longer to comb the hair on my face than it does the hair on my head these days, so I can do with all the help I can get. Yet another aspect of growing older I'm afraid. As a child, I had waist length locks that Ma took great pleasure in weaving into plaits. The only plait I could manage now would be a pubic one. If I walked around on my hands nobody would notice.

I kept the waist length hair until I was well into my thirties then decided it looked really naff. Lovely hair, double chin, saggy tits, so I had the lot cut off. Quite a drastic step for someone who's spent a lifetime doing mermaid impressions. It's really short now, not your average "I'm a dyke and my name's Dill," style but not far off. It's Cathy! My hairdresser. Ask her to take an inch off and she takes five and to be honest, I'm far too much of a coward to tell her.

I have seen that woman eat four Shredded Wheat in one go. She has three kids, all bald and works out at the gym five nights a week. We are talking Bruiser Babe here. Standing on her feet all day has given her the added bonus of calf muscles that can crack open a bottle of Budweiser, so I generally keep my opinions to myself. If I ever did upset her, I imagine she'd scalp me and hang my head on the aerial of her Fiat Punto.

It's far easier just to lie back at the basin while she drenches you in freezing cold water while fracturing your skull bones with her enormous hands. If you dare to dither over the latest copy of Woman's Weekly, she'll throw you physically into the chair and ignore your cries for help as your head cracks open on the sink. Sometimes, she applies so much pressure during the rinse, the circulation in your neck gets cut off and you can actually faint. Like I say, not a woman to be messed with.

Protesting is pointless, she wears her Sony walkman on full volume all day. She cares not a jot and it shows. Call me warped if you like, but for some reason I find all this incredibly amusing. I actually look forward to my sessions at the sink with Cathy strong-arming some pensioner in the next chair. I never said I was a well balanced individual did I?

I quite like the Sony aspect as well. Every hairdresser should wear one. It would avoid all those terribly tedious chats you feel obliged to have about your holidays and their aching feet. It's a bit of a nightmare when she slices through your earlobe with the scissors, but you have to expect a few battle scars when you're striving to keep what's left of your looks.

I once made the mistake of taking a photograph with me, cut out of a magazine. Just to give her a rough idea of the style I was aiming for. She tore it up in front of my eyes and ate the pieces. Cathy's not one for photo's, she prefers the "Sit still and I'll cut it how I want to cut it," approach. This generally involves you leaving three hours later, completely bald, minus one ear.

Anyway, I'm here now. I told Tilly I'd do it and I will. As I open the door, a fog of perming solution and cheap hairspray assaults my lungs. No wonder so many retired hairdressers end up with emphysema! You need breathing apparatus in here. Looks like one of Cathy's client's paying at the desk.

"Nice Mohican!" I venture to an elderly woman with a walking stick, waiting to pay.

"She's left her walkman at home," she warns me in a hushed voice.

This does not bode well. I've never seen Cathy without her walkman. Does this mean I'll have to make conversation with her! Before I can turn tail and run, she grabs me by the scruff of my neck and hurls me into a chair.

"Morning Cathy, how are things with you?" I gulp.

"Crap!" she roars, bouncing off into the rest room.

Several knowing looks are exchanged in the mirrors as those of us waiting to be done listen to her crashing around out the back.

"She's lost her best scissors," a young girl sitting behind me whispers. I have a feeling someone has hidden them, considering the foul mood she's in. Might be a good idea to remove all sharp objects from the shop until she gets her walkman back. Oh God, here she comes!

"Thought I'd go a bit blonder today," I suggest. The expression on her face says it all, a sort of mixture of contempt and sheer boredom.

"Suppose it works for some women of your age," she snarls, sharpening her old scissors on the sink. I think I know where I stand now and decide to opt for the jokey approach.

"Perhaps not then, how about one of those nice blue rinses?"

"Is that meant to be funny?" she roars "I don't do funny!"

All eyes in the salon are focused on me now. This could turn nasty at any minute.

"I'll leave it to you then eh, perhaps best?" I grovel like a complete coward.

"Cut and blow then!" she barks back. It's a compromise of sorts so I settle back and resign myself to an early death.

"Sit up then!" she bawls, and I do indeed sit up, quickly and without moving a muscle in my face, in case she thinks I'm taking the piss and decides to head butt me for good measure.

Even without the walkman, I can see there's not going to be much chance of any pleasantries. Her face is set like stone as she hacks away at my head with a vengeance. I let her get on with it and concentrate on the woman behind me. I can see her in the mirror and find it hard to stop staring. She's having a shampoo and set. With just the three rollers. Probably because she has just the three hairs on the top of her head. She looks about sixty but could be younger. It's hard to tell. The hairs are a sort of smoky silver colour. At current prices, that works out at about five quid a roller.

"I've got a do on next month," she tells Annie, the manageress.

"That's nice, anything special?"

"Ruby wedding, our Joanie."

"Lovely."

"Thought I'd try something different with my hair."

"What did you have in mind?" Annie gulps, her face a picture of shocked horror.

"One of those French pleats would be nice, go with my new suit."

I hold my breath and my heart goes out to Annie. I've seen her perform some miracles in this salon but even Annie's not that gifted.

"Remind me nearer the time, I'll have a go," she says diplomatically.

"Thanks Annie."

Is this vanity taken to the extreme or just sad? When my time comes,

I shall comb the hair on my chin in an upward sweep and do it that way. Be a lot cheaper for her to just wear a hat. I'm sorry, but if that were Ma I'd have to tell her...

"Look you old bat, you're bald, live with it!" I hope to God Cathy never get's her hands on those three hairs. She'd have them out in a jiffy. She's doing a damn good job of shearing my head as we speak.

I think she's an ex Ozzie who grew up on a sheep farm in Canberra. That would explain the calf muscles, all that wrestling with rams and having to walk fifty miles to school every day. If she attempts to brand my buttocks after she's finished I shall have conclusive proof that my theory is correct.

"Floss, are you alright?"

Annie is standing over an extremely elderly woman sitting under one of the driers. She's either asleep or dead. It's difficult to tell. She looks quite peaceful, so if she's snuffed it I can only assume it was a gentle passing.

"Floss! wake up, Floss!" There's an urgency in her voice now and I look away. I don't want to be intruding on somebody's final moments. It's not nice.

"FLOSS!!!!!"

Floss, bless her, suddenly returns to the land of the living. Her eyes wide open and staring as if she's just been woken from a deep sleep.

"Crikey Floss, I thought you were a gonner!" Annie laughs.

"Sorry love, it's Stanley, I've been up all night washing his pants," she sighs.

"Oh dear," Annie says walking away, obviously not wanting to elaborate on Stanley's pant problem.

"Five pairs he got through last night." Floss continues "Five bloody pairs!"

Oh dear. Stanley really does have a pant problem and poor Floss is knackered from all that extra laundry. I bet she looks forward to coming here for a rest. I'd like to offer her my sympathies regarding Stan's pant problem but feel it would be inappropriate. None of my business really. I know for a fact that Jack wouldn't want me discussing his pant problems with strangers... should he ever develop any in the future that is.

"That do?" Cathy bawls, bringing me back to reality with a jolt.

"Mm, lovely," I lie... looking at the GI haircut she's given me in the mirror. Bit severe I feel but it will grow back. It reminds me of somebody, who the hell is it? Oh yes, Vanessa Redgrave in that film about the Holocaust. Dead ringer.

"Pay at the desk," she snaps, pulling my chair our from under me.

"Right, thanks."

I smile at Floss on my way to the till. She's wide awake now and sucking on a fruit drop. Not that long ago, I'd have taken her home for tea and offered to wash Stan's pants but I've learnt not to get involved. Something else Tilly has taught me.

Wendy, the woman on the till has seen it all before. She's an odd one. Only in her thirties but with a face that was born bored. You know that expression that tells you she's tired of life and this job in particular. Wendy has a little girl and chronic acne. It can't be easy can it? She doesn't even bother to look up as I hover in front of her with my cheque book.

"Cut and blow?" she yawns, exposing a mouthful of yellow teeth.

"Yes."

"Any conditioner?"

"Yes."

"Tea or coffee?"

"No." It's certainly not the scintillating conversation that keeps me coming back here.

"Another appointment?" she asks, blowing a large bubble of gum out of her gob.

"Not for a while thanks."

"Twenty-four fifty."

"Thanks."

I get the feeling I'm bothering her as she continues to clip her toenails as I write the cheque. The big toe she is wrestling with is very badly gnarled and discoloured. That toe's the result of wearing Cuban heels. She totters around on them all day, in a job like this. It could be worse I suppose, she could be squeezing her spots. Although, I don't think the acne is helped by the make-up. A three inch crust of panstick, plastered across her pimples. A good scrub with soap and hot water might be the answer. Carbolic preferably.

Not very charitable I know but true. You know how some people have that freshly-scrubbed look, all glowing and sparkly, well, that's not Wendy. Wendy has more of a just crawled out of bed look, with the faintest trace of three-week old mascara on her eyes. It's hard to describe but I suspect she's the sort of woman who only changes her knickers when there's an 'r' in the month.

"Bye everybody!" I shout, squeezing my way through the door.

A chorus of voices bid me farewell as I walk out into the fresh air. Extremely fresh actually, it's blowing a gale and starting to rain as well. I don't have a hood on my jacket or an umbrella so I'll have to walk home naked from the neck up.

Pete's outside the Flapper & Firkin, must be nearly opening time. Nice cravat, shame about the blue overall's he's teamed it with. Spoils the effect somewhat. I keep my head down, hoping to get past without him recognising me but no such luck.

"That you Cassie?" he asks as I shuffle past.

"Oh hi Pete!"

"Have you got nits?" he frowns, looking aghast at my new hair cut.

"Cheek! It's a new style."

"Be easy to look after," he concedes, trying to make amends. He's looking at his watch, counting the seconds until the door opens. I suppose to an alcoholic, every second seems like an hour when you're dying for a drink.

"Must be nearly opening time," I say encouragingly.

"Any second nos," he twitches, getting jumpy at the thought.

"You working for the Council now?" I ask, spotting the logo on his overalls.

"Got them in Oxfam, only fifty-pence."

"Bargain."

"Found a toothbrush in the pocket as well," he beams. Overalls and a used toothbrush for fifty-pence! That is a bargain. I smile and refrain from pointing out the hazards of using a strangers toothbrush. He uses Bells whisky as a mouthwash so I don't suppose he can come to much harm. The lock on the pub door clanks and he's on his feet and moving at a rate of knots in a scramble to get to the bar.

"See you," I shout into the blackness of the bar.

"Later!" he shouts back, already ordering his first round...

"Seventeen pints of Carlsberg and a whisky chaser please."

At least Budd's not with him today. Must be at home babysitting the guinea pigs. They still haven't produced any babies so I can only assume that Pamela is frigid. Either that or Percy is impotent. Who knows? I heard him playing his Mantovani tapes late last night. Perhaps he was trying to create the right atmosphere for pig production. A candlelight dinner for two, soft lighting and some Belgian chocolates. It works for me anyway.

Old Angel Gabriel's still around. I saw him nicking a pint of semi-skimmed off the Co-Op milk float last Sunday.

It's pouring now and what's left of my hair is plastered against my bruised scalp. I catch sight of myself in the window of Walter Smith's and it's not a pretty sight. My waterproof mascara is a lie and is cascading down my cheeks. People will think I'm a battered wife.

"Sue!" That sounded quite urgent, who is it? I swing round searching for whoever's calling out.

"Sue!" There it goes again... silly bugger's got me mixed up with somebody else.

"Sue!"

Oh fuck it! Whoever you are, make yourself known. This is starting to annoy me now.

"Sue!"

I can just make out a figure coming towards me but with the rain and my eyesight it's hard to make out a face. He's getting closer... don't think it's anybody I know.

"Big Issue!... Big Issue!" Would prat be an appropriate word?

"You alright there love?" he asks, breezing past with a sack full of magazines.

"Fine thanks."

He probably thinks I'm homeless. I must look destitute or he'd have asked me to buy a copy. My feet are soaked too. I appear to have sprung a leak on top of everything else. Mind you, I've clocked up about thirty-thousand miles in these trusty old things, so I can't complain. It's amazing how many miles Levy and I cover in a day. My record to date is thirty-seven but that was the day we took a wrong turning and ended up on the Malvern Hills.

The car's on the drive so Jack must be home. That's one of the benefits of being on call. He can flit about and find time to pop in for a cuppa.

"Cathy on a period?" he asks, opening the door.

"Forgot her walkman," I tell him, standing dripping in the hall.

"It's different anyway."

"How different?" I ask suspiciously.

"Well... sort of... lesbianish."

"Oh great!"

"You know, that cropped look."

"Mm..."

"Suits you actually."

"What, the hair or the lesbian thing?"

"The hair, although you can be a lesbian if you want… as long as I can watch," he laughs.

"What is it with men and lesbians!?"

"It's a man thing," he smiles, ruffling my hair as he passes.

I'm making a puddle in the hall so ignore his sarcasm and run upstairs to fetch a dry towel. Levy is asleep in the bath and lazily opens one eye as I root around in the airing cupboard. I'm not sure he recognises me at first, then he rolls onto his back and starts snoring. He likes lying in an empty bath. It's spacious and cool and he can play with the rubber ducks.

"Was it busy?" he asks, pouring the tea.

"Not really, just Floss and a few others."

"Floss?"

"Mm, Stanley's having a problem with his pants. She fell asleep under the dryer."

"Right."

He rubs my head roughly with the towel and when he's finished, my hair is all spiky.

"Looks even more like a lesbian nos," he laughs.

"Cheers!"

"No, leave it, it looks cute."

"Cute? I don't want to resemble a cute lesbian thanks."

"Why not?" he chuckles.

"Some woman might take a fancy to me in Tesco. I could end up as her bitch."

He buries his face in a cushion on the sofa and laughs like a drain.

"She'd probably scratch her name on my arm with a rusty safety-pin and expect me to clean her Dr Marten's," I tell him, alarmed at the very thought.

"Have you been at the cooking sherry?" he asks, looking up.

"I think Cathy's ruptured an artery in my brain."

"Why do you keep going back there?"

"Cos it makes me laugh, the people are funny."

"That haircut's not funny."

"It'll grow back."

I can see my reflection in the glass on the wall unit. He's right, I do look like a lesbian.

"You could wear a hat."

"Thanks."

"Or one of those Afro wigs they advertise in the Sunday magazine."

"I'm not black," I point out to him.

"But you're a lesbian, you could get a grant off the council, start up a woman's group."

"Have you had a bang on the head Jack?"

"Sorry."

There's a pause while he thinks of something else witty to throw at me.

"I could buy you an inflatable woman for your birthday if you like," he roars.

"No thanks, they don't have any feet."

"What?"

"Feet! I read it somewhere, it's the mould or something, they don't have feet."

"And where on earth did you read that?"

"I dunno, stop hassling me... go get some digestives."

"Yes dear."

CHAPTER SIXTEEN

Ma & Pa at the Pink Palace

"Hello, is that you dear?"

"Ma, how's things?"

"Lovely thanks."

"Where's Pa?"

"He's in the Jacuzzi."

"Pardon?"

Now, to my knowledge, when I popped in yesterday, they didn't have a Jacuzzi. Either she's finally given in to Alzheimer's or they've won the Lottery.

"Have you won the lottery?"

"Silly, we're in Blackpool, at the Pink Palace."

"Blackpool?"

"Yes, that's right dear, Blackpool," she says loudly.

"But I spoke to you this morning, you were going to B&Q to get some bedding plants."

"Ah well, your Father fancied a drive, so here we are."

That explains it then. Pa and his wanderlust. We never know where he'll end up next.

"You'd love it here, the people are smashing," she gushes.

"Did you say the Pink Palace?"

"Yes, it was the only place with vacancies. There's a conference on... Labour I think."

"Oh right."

"Anyway, I'm only calling to let you know where we are. I know how you worry."

"Too right."

"I'd better go and fetch your father, he's been in there an hour already."

"Okay Ma, give him my love and have a great time."

"We will, there's a competition on later in the ballroom, we're dressing up," she giggles.

"Dressing up?"

"Yes dear, it's one of those looky-likey things, Shirley Bassey I think."

"Er, right."

"You know I'm her biggest fan."

"Quite."

This gets more bizarre by the second. My parents are staying at a dubious hotel in Blackpool and Pa is about to transform himself into a transvestite version of Shirley Bassey.

"Lucky I bought my gold sandals with me," she laughs.

"What about Pa?"

"He's only got his brown brogues. I told him to pack something smart."

"He packed his trunks," I tell her springing to his defence.

"No, he didn't, Morris on reception lent him a pair."

"Morris?"

"Lovely lad, runs this place with his friend."

"I see."

Let's get this straight then. It's a gay hotel in Blackpool. Pa is in the Jacuzzi wearing Morris's trunks and my mother is seventy-three and dressing up as Shirley Bassey.

"Must dash dear, you know how crinkled he get's in water."

"Right."

"I'll ring you again later."

"Please take care Ma."

"Bye dear."

"Bye."

Yet another surreal conversation with my Mother. No wonder I worry! At eight o clock this morning they were on their way to B&Q and now they're doing all sorts of strange things on the seafront at Blackpool. This is exactly why I worry. They have no conception of the real world and it scares me. They take everyone at face value and find it hard to believe that anyone would want to harm them in any way. I hope Pa will be alright. The prospect of him sharing a Jacuzzi with Morris and his trunks is too frightening to dwell on. Let's hope Morris is in a secure relationship or Pa might end up punching his lights out.

Shirley Bassey! Only Ma would pick a hotel with a looky-likey contest. Pa will be the only man in a suit I bet. He's always going on these little jaunts. Completely out of the blue he'll grab his car keys and flat cap and shoot off to some obscure little place he's found on the map. I worry because his legs are not what they used to be and have been known to seize up completely after a long drive.

Ma just trots along with him, sitting in the passenger seat, sucking on a Polo and guiding him along the motorway system. I have lost count of the number of places they have visited over the years. From Yorkshire to Yarmouth, and always travelling at speeds of no more than thirty miles an hour. Pa is the person you were stuck behind on the M6, tootling along listening to Radio 4. All I can say in his defence is that he's a very careful driver with no endorsements.

I shall be a nervous wreck now until they're safely back home. Now I know how they must have felt when I was younger and dashing around the country on a whim. If only they were a bit more streetwise. Pa had his pocket picked last Christmas and was visibly stunned that anyone would want to rob him. I was livid but he just accepted that he'd become a statistic and let it go. Here we go again… ruddy phone hasn't stopped all morning.

"Hello, Cassie?"

"Pa! How the devil are you?"

"Great, Ma said she rang you."

"How was the Jacuzzi?"

"Smashing! Did my legs the world of good."

Thank goodness! He survived the Jacuzzi without any problems from Morris or his trunks.

"What are you like? Turning up in Blackpool?"

"Fancied a ride out, beats sitting watching Countdown with your Mother," he laughs.

"Where is she?"

"In the bedroom, trying on her gold sandals."

"She told me about the Shirley Bassey thing, you're not dressing up are you Pa?"

"Course I am, I've got my brown sports jacket and my brogues." Bless him! Told you he has no concept of what goes on out there!

"There's a prize for the winner, a bottle of pink champagne."

"Good luck with that then!"

"Don't suppose we'll win. The last thing we won was a tin of salmon at the Legion."

"You never know Pa."

"Better go, your mother needs some corn plasters."

"Take care, remember your phlebitis."

"I will, see you soon."

Funny how life comes full circle isn't it? It used to be them warning me to be careful when I was out on the town. Now it's my turn to fret. It's as if the roles have been reversed and they are the children and I'm the parent. Pa has phlebitis, arthritis in his knees and an ongoing problem with his eyes. Ma has a dickey ticker and diabetes. No wonder I worry!

Not that they do. Far from it, they just accept that the clock is ticking and their bodies will continue to become more and more frail. In the meantime, they live life to the full and keep on taking the tablets. It's the only realistic way to deal with old age I suppose. Pa's philosophy is, if you wake up in the morning it's a bonus. Ruddy phone... I shall unplug it in a minute.

"Hello, me again dear."

"Everything okay Ma?"

"Fine, it's just that I forgot about Fred."

"Oh dear."

"Sorry, I didn't think, your Father was rushing me to get into the car."

"Not to worry, I'll pop round and pick him up."

"Would you? That would be lovely."

"No problem, I'll go and get him now."

"Oh by the way, his sock's in the shed."

"See you Ma."

I'm not surprised they forgot about Fred. He's so tiny you need a magnifying glass to find him. Fred is a miniature Yorkshire Terrier, with no teeth and an attitude. If ever they had burglars, Fred would have to suck them to death. He's a typical lapdog, exercise being a foreign language to him, unless you count jumping onto Ma's lap for a cuddle and a custard cream. Pa tolerates him, just as long as he doesn't crap in his slippers then he's prepared to put up with him.

Now, I have the difficult task of breaking the bad news to Levy that Fred is coming to stay. He doesn't dislike him as such, just seems infuriated by him, a dwarf dog with gums and no conception of the word 'fun'. Fred doesn't do fun. It's beyond his capabilities. No romping in the woods with him or rolling in fox-shit. His idea of a ball is stretching out on a cushion in front of the central heating.

"Listen lad, you're not going to like this, but Fred's coming to stay," I tell him.

The mere mention of the name Fred is enough to send him into a sulk. He demonstrates his disgust by raising his ass in the air and farting loudly. He's not impressed and stalks off into the garden in a sulk. Having Fred as a houseguest is his idea of a nightmare. Better ring Jack and enlist his help on this one.

"Hi, only me, could you do me a favour?"

"Sure, what is it?"

"Ma and Pa are in Blackpool, can you pop in and pick up Fred?"

"Do I have to?" he groans.

"Don't be cruel, he's on his own in that big house."

"Suppose he could get lost, fall down a crack in the floorboards," he laughs.

"Please?"

"Okay, I'm on my way home so I'll go there first."

"Thanks."

"See you in a bit."

"Oh, can you get his sock from the shed?"

"If I really have to," he moans.

The sock thing is an ongoing joke in the family. Pa bless him, in his initial attempts to encourage Fred to play, made him a sort of soft toy out of an old sock. That was twelve years ago and Fred and the sock are never apart. I think he thinks it's his friend or something. He snuggles up to it at night, takes it out in the garden with him and humps it at every opportunity. Jock The Sock is a legend in the Finnemore household.

Sulky Sid is glaring at me through the patio doors. His face says it all. A picture of resignation and contempt. If only Ma had a frisky retriever bitch he could play with. Instead of a mutt the size of your average gerbil. Don't get me wrong, I love Fred and would be mortified if anything happened to him but Fun Time Fred he 'aint.

Fred was born to snooze and sip luke-warm tea from a saucer, not romp in the woods chasing Cyril's. Your average squirrel could eat Fred whole.

"Come on lad, I have buttons!" I call, trying to console him. Fred is forgotten as the magic word reaches his ears. He is at my side in an instant, all thoughts of Fred forgotten. Fred doesn't do buttons either. Fred does fresh chicken breasts braised to perfection in a slow oven with just a hint of gravy and seasoning.

I blame Ma. Dog's are extremely biddable and will generally eat what they are given, but she started him on these expensive cuts and now he flatly refuses to eat anything else. Open Levy a tin of pilchards and he's happy. Show Fred a fish head and he'd probably faint.

Talk of the devil, here he comes now. At least I think he's here, Jack has just pulled up on the drive. Fred could be anywhere in that car. Probably in the glove compartment, hiding.

"Did you bring his sock?" I ask as he carries Fred into the lounge.

"He crapped in my golf shoe," he moans, depositing Fred onto the floor.

"Sorry, I'll clean it for you."

"For a little bugger he certainly produces a pile."

"Too much information thank you!" I grimace, picking Fred up.

I leave him to clean up his shoe and take Fred out into the garden. If he were my dog he'd have been properly housetrained. As it is, he can't be bothered to go outside in the cold, so he just sneaks off and craps at random. This is something Ma and I will never agree on. She follows him round with a pooper scooper and a bottle of Dettox, whereas I would follow him round with a foghorn and frighten the crap out of him, literally! All my dogs have been trained in weeks using this method and it works. You lay a trail of paper to the back door, let them spend on it once or twice, then lead them outdoors. They get the message and you don't spend the rest of your life treading in crap. Simple!

"What was it you said about Blackpool?" he asks, scrubbing the shoe in the sink.

"They're staying in the Pink Palace."

"Sounds nice."

"Probably is, but I think it's a hotel for gay men."

"Excuse me?"

"Gays! Pa's going to a Shirley Bassey looky-likey contest tonight."

"What about Ma, who's she going as?"

"Freddie Mercury probably."

He stands over the sink, roaring with laughter. The mental image of Ma in a white vest and Mexican moustache does conjure up a vivid picture.

"Why Blackpool?"

"No idea, they started out for B&Q... what do I know?"

"Perhaps he took a wrong turning again," he laughs.

"More than likely with his eyesight."

I glance out of the window, hoping to see Fred doing his business. Levy is obviously taking an active part in this training as he appears to have dug a hole and buried Fred in it.

"He's buried Fred," I tell him.

"Thinks he's a bone."

"Better go and dig him up."

"Spoilsport."

Not too much damage done, just mud caked around his ears and nose. He'll survive. I carry him indoors under my armpit with Levy leaping up, trying to retrieve his new toy. It's necessary to carry Fred because if you wait for him to walk anywhere, you'll keel over and die first. Yet another legacy of Ma's school of dog training. I asked her once if she'd do the same if he were a Rottweiller but she ignored me.

"Put him in here, out of the way," Jack says, pointing to the microwave.

"Stop it!"

"It was only a suggestion."

Levy circles the kitchen, waiting for a chance to grab the indignant Yorkie. Fred eyes him with disgust from his safe haven on top of the work surface.

"Funny little thing isn't he?" I giggle, looking at his filthy face.

"Can't really call it a dog can you, that's an insult to dogs."

"What would you call him then?" I ask.

"Sort of a hairy hamster, with a collar."

"That's horrible!"

"So is this shit on my shoe."

Fred is oblivious to the insults being banded about. He's heard them all before and more. Why should he care? He lives a life of luxury and gets carried everywhere under the safety of Ma's left armpit. He should worry.

"When will they be back?"

"Tomorrow I think, it's bingo at the Legion on Friday."

"Blackpool's freezing at this time of year."

"Mm.."

Now I shall spend the whole night fretting over them getting frostbite. Hope Ma's got her Damart vest on.

"Has it got central heating?" he asks, still scrubbing away at the shoe.

"I should think so, it's got a Jacuzzi."

"Really?"

"Pa was in it... Morris borrowed him some trunks."

"I won't ask."

"Best not to."

Fred is trembling at the sight of the running water. He doesn't do wet either. Not like Levy, who is only truly happy when he's sploshing about in a lake or a puddle. Pa tried to take Fred out in the rain once and he panicked and ran up his trouser leg. Good job Pa was wearing his longjohns. I can think of better ways to start the day than having a Yorkshire Terrier clinging to your genitals.

"I should wash his face, it's caked in mud."

"I wouldn't if I were you, the shock could kill him," Jack laughs.

"I'll wait till it dries and comb it off."

"Whatever would we do if he popped his clogs while she was away."

"Stick him in the freezer till she got back."

"What, then thaw him out?"

"Yeah, she'd never know, prop him up on a cushion, say he died in his sleep," I laugh.

"You are one sick cookie Cass!"

"Not really, just practical. If we buried him, Levy would only dig him up again." It doesn't really bear thinking about. Ma would be devastated.

"Anyway, that bugger will probably outlive us all."

"Do you think she'll have him stuffed?" he suddenly asks.

"Sorry?"

"Fred, when he dies, will she have him stuffed, some people do."

"Heaven forbid!"

"Wouldn't take much, half a packet of Paxo, then have him mounted on the wall," he laughs.

"This is grotesque!"

"I was only thinking out loud, she is devoted to him."

"Yes, well, she's devoted to Pa but I can't see him mounted and hanging on the wall."

Levy has Jock The Sock in his gaping gob and stands defiantly at the sink, daring Fred to come and take it off him. The expression on Fred's face says it all. Claiming back his favourite toy would involve a bungee-jump off the sink top and he's never been into extreme sports. I step in and take Jock and hide him in the breadbin. Best for all concerned if he stay's out of the way.

"Come on hairy hamster, go rest for a bit while I prepare supper."

I lift him down gently and scoot them both towards the lounge, hoping Fred will settle by the fire. At home he has the luxury of central heating with hot-air blowers all around the house. He lies in front of them all day, blow-drying his hair. He'll have to rough it for a bit while he's with us. I suppose if I were feeling charitable I could give him a quick blast with the hairdryer but I'm not, so I won't. Levy is nudging him up the bum, taunting him because he thinks I can't see.

"Leave him, he's old and has no social skills," I warn him.

Surprisingly, things remain very quiet and as we finish supper, I breathe a sigh of relief that the two dogs appear to finally be getting along.

"More ice cream?"

"No, I'm full thanks," Jack yawns, taking his coffee into the lounge.

I love this time of day. That warm glow you get after a meal and a bottle of Merlot. Time to relax and chat before you trot off to bed and the whole process starts all over again. By the time I finish clearing away, Jack is flat out on the sofa, his eyes drooping as tiredness overcomes him. Either that or he's slipping into a coma after that fish pie I just gave him. The peace is shattered yet again by the ringing of the phone.

"Hello dear, me again."

"Hello Ma."

"Just ringing to tell you your Father won a bottle of Cinzano."

"Really?"

"On the karaoke," she says proudly.

"Oh right."

"He got a standing ovation," she giggles "Morris was in tears."

My Pa, the karaoke king, who'd have thought it. I had no idea he knew what a karaoke machine was.

"What on earth did he sing?"

"One of Shirley's... My Life I think it's called."

Just about sums it up really... My Life! God only knows what they'll get up to next.

"Be back tomorrow, bye dear."

"Bye."

I wonder if Jack and I will spend our twilight years in Blackpool? Belting out karaoke hits and strolling along the front. Unlikely, but with my genes you never know. I'll ask him what he thinks when he wakes up.

Fred is peering out at me from inside the waste-paper basket. Levy must have hidden him in there. I think that says it all really.

CHAPTER SEVENTEEN

Elvis Has Been Spotted in Edgbaston

I don't think Alan has quite grasped the concept of role play. Tilly warned us last week that we would be doing some role play exercises today and he's just arrived. Dressed as Elvis. Bless! It must have taken a lot of courage, especially for someone like him, to come dressed like that. Especially as he travels by bus. Bet that caused a stir on the number 29. Considering Alan has spent the past twelve months muttering into his anorak at every session, I feel the boy should be congratulated for his efforts.

Alicia looks horrified, her gob is hanging open and she hasn't said a word yet. That has to be a first. Tilly looks stunned as well. Ever since he swaggered in a few minutes ago, none of us have said a word. It takes a bit of adjusting to, Alan as Elvis. Fair play to the lad, he's put a lot of thought into his outfit. Dazzling white flares and a shirt with the collar turned up. And an enormous gold belt straddling his midriff. I'm impressed. He's even slicked his hair back Elvis style although judging by the look of it, he's used Spry Crisp and Dry and not gel.

I suppose to someone like Alan, role play would be an unknown entity. He's never worked, so has no idea of the modern techniques used by corporate companies to train their staff. I'm an old hand at this I'm afraid and have been dreading today. I spent four years working in a hotel and they were very big on role play. Role play and obscure training courses that most of the staff avoided like the plague. Not me though, I relished the challenge of learning something new. And skiving off work for a few hours of course.

I took a crash course in Japanese once. To this day, I have no idea why. At the end of the course the best I could manage was ordering a beer in the bar, but the chances of me encountering a Japanese barman in our local is highly unlikely, so I've yet to put my skills to the test.

I wonder where he got that gold pendant from? Massive thing it is, dangling down his scrawny chest like an Olympic medal. Looks like one of those chocolate coins you buy in a bag at Christmas. My life, this boy is coming out of his shell!

He looks mortified poor lad. I think he's sussed that this is not fancy dress and now he's wishing the floor would open up and swallow him. I can't bear to watch. If Alicia dares to laugh I shall grab her by the rucksack and throw her out of the window.

"Nice outfit Alan, you've made a real effort," I tell him, hoping to ease his embarrassment.

"I thought we was all dressing up," he mumbles into his massive collar. Tilly is dying to laugh but her professionalism shines through and she holds it back.

"Well done Alan, it's good that you put so much thought into it," she reassures him. This seems to do the trick and he stops sulking and sits up straight in his chair.

"Just the three of you again today, so we'll have to improvise," she whispers.

She must get very disheartened at times like this. All the time and effort she puts into setting up these sessions and half the group have been absent for weeks. I'm glad I made the effort today. I wouldn't have missed this for the world.

"Alicia and Cassie, would you care to go first?"

I'm not normally one for going first but the prospect of wrestling with Alicia is just too good to resist. I've been dying to lock horns with that one since the first session so here goes. We both nod in agreement and push our chairs back.

"Alicia, I'd like you to play the part of a university lecturer and Cassie, you'll be the student being interviewed for a graduate course."

"I take it that would be a mature student?" Alicia sneers, having a dig.

"I take it you'd like your nose to remain on that part of your face?" I bite back quite viciously.

We're off to a good start I see. Cheeky cow! Don't fuck with me Alicia or you'll find out exactly what it's like to wake up with tubes coming out of your nose. I can't believe she said that!

"Now ladies, let's move on shall we?" Tilly butts in, looking quite startled. I take a deep breath and smile sweetly at old Fucksuck. One-nil to her but that will soon change.

"If you'd care to sit at the desk, as if you're in a proper interview."

Fucksuck grabs the comfy chair leaving me to crouch down on one of the vinyl ones. She's probably thinking that gives her some sort of psychological advantage but I'm way out in front. I'm not falling for that one.

"Alicia you can ask anything you like, just improvise as if Cassie were a candidate for a post on a course, I'll leave it with you," she says, sitting back down. Alicia looks stumped for a second, I don't imagine role play is one of her forte's either. The woman wears pop-socks for God's sake! Can't see her living out her fantasies at home. No crotchless knickers and whipped cream for that one.

"So… what would you expect to gain from being accepted on this Psychology course," she suddenly blurts out, a condescending smirk plastered across her fat face. Psychology eh? Good choice, but don't think you can throw me with that one.

"Well, Professor Parmesan, I'd hope it would give me an insight into people's minds," I grin.

"Can she call me that?" she snaps, looking at Tilly.

"I'm improvising! Tilly said to improvise!" I cry innocently.

"Carry on ladies, just say whatever comes into your head," Tilly urges. Her back's up now. One-all I think!

"Right, well," she stammers. I've got her rattled now. "Let's do some word association shall we?"

Yes! My favourite! Come on girl, bring it on! Just throw whatever you like at me. I'm ready.

"I'm going to say a word and I want you to say the first thing that comes into your head."

"Okay Prof, got that!" I laugh.

"Let me see, er… madness," she stutters, looking at me with a certain amount of fear in her eyes.

"Baggy trousers!" I yell, daring her to challenge me.

"Oh this is farcical! Tilly, she's not taking me seriously."

"What's your problem, you said madness, I said baggy trousers, you know… the song?"

"You're just being silly."

"Look, I'm doing what Tilly told us to do," I protest.

"It's okay Alicia, just go with the flos," Tilly pipes up, with a mischievous glint in her eyes.

"Right, let me see," she dithers "Crackers… that's your next word, crackers."

I have a feeling I know where this is going and go in for the kill. Our eyes lock as if in combat. Like gladiators in the arena, circling each other at the death. Bit like that Gladiator show on TV. If it were, she would be Pansy and I... the Mighty Quarter Pounder of course!

"Did you not hear me?" she snaps "I said crackers."

"Bernard Matthews!" I roar, punching the air with my fist.

"Oh for Christ's sake! Tilly, tell her will you?"

"What? There's nothing wrong with that. Crackers, Christmas, turkey, Bernard Matthews."

Tilly is about to crack. Her shoulders are shaking and I know she's dying to laugh.

"Well done ladies, that was most interesting," Tilly splutters, covering her face with her hands. Mistress Mozzarella glares at me across the desk. Silly tart! That'll teach you to play mind games with an expert. Jesus! I feel much better after that. This therapy really does work.

"Alan, if you'd like to change places with Cassie, it's your turn nos," Tilly tells him.

Oh no! Poor Alan's got to face her wrath now. She'd better be gentle with him or I really will batter her with my pugil stick. He droops visibly and shuffles into my chair. His face a picture of sheer horror and panic. Don't worry son, I'm on your side.

"Now Alan, I'd like you to pretend to be the manager of a shop and Alicia is applying for a job."

"What sort of a shop?" he asks, sweat forming on his upper lip.

"Any sort, I'll leave that to you," she smiles encouragingly. He sits for what seems like ages, staring into the carpet, his brain going into meltdown. Alicia is still reeling from her confrontation with me and looks visibly shaken.

"Can you work Saturday's?" he suddenly asks her.

"Pardon?"

"Saturday's... can you work Saturday's?" he repeats. She's flustered and it takes her a second to reply "Yes, that's not a problem."

"Good, 'cos I go down the Villa on Saturday's."

"Alan! What sort of a shop is this!" she rants, losing her cool. Now, now girl! Get a grip. The lad's trying his best, I think to myself, dying to laugh out loud.

"Butcher's... it's a butcher's," he throws back at her, quite forcefully for him.

"Right! As long as I know."

"So then, er... what about pork scratchings?" he asks. I'm losing it now. This truly is a joy to watch. Thank you God!

"Excuse me?"

"Pork scratchings."

"What about them?" she barks.

"Do you sell 'em?" he asks in all innocence.

"For God's sake! Tilly, he's supposed to be the shop manager!" she pleads, close to tears.

"It's alright Alicia, just bear with him," Tilly says "Let him get into it," Alicia will blow in a minute. I can see it coming. Her face is purple and the veins in her neck are bulging with the strain.

"Sorry, I got mixed up," he sighs, obviously genuinely full of remorse for his mistake.

"Can we continue?" Alicia snaps and I can see the tic in Alan's eye begin to twitch.

"Have you got a hairnet?" he suddenly squeaks.

"Oh for goodness…"

"You have to! The woman in Walter Smith's wears one!"

"Alan! Can't you think of anything sensible to say?" He crumples visibly and I have to sit on my hands in order to stop myself from slapping her.

"Tilly said to make it up!" he protests, looking to Tilly for support.

"Yes, to improvise you idiot… not act out a scene from the Teletubbies!" Hark at her! Watch it Alan or La-La will hit you with her handbag.

"Okay everyone, let's calm down shall we?"

"Well, I never heard anything so ridiculous in my life."

"I said let's calm down shall we?" Tilly tells her sharply.

I can't look at any of them. If I lose it now, I'm liable to pee my pants.

"Let's take a minute to get our breath back shall we?" Tilly says, closing her eyes. She'll probably be on the phone to the Samaritan's after this poor girl. I close just one eye and watch as Alicia 's face returns to it's normal colour. Alan is busy picking melted chocolate off his chest. His medallion is falling apart in the heat.

"Okay, is everybody calm now?" Tilly whispers, opening her eyes. We nod in unison and I feel sorry for her, having to put up with this. I started it and now I'm feeling a bit guilty. Just a bit. I'll get over it though. This has been priceless. I didn't expect it to get any better after Elvis marched in, but it has.

"Now, perhaps next week we can concentrate on our relaxation techniques," she sighs.

"I'm on holiday next week Tilly," I remind her.

"Of course Cassie, you did mention it, have a lovely time."

"Thanks."

"Where are you going to?" Alicia asks, looking down her nose at me.

"Shropshire, we've rented a cottage."

"Are you flying?" Alan suddenly asks me.

"Sorry?"

"Flying? On your holidays?"

Alicia rolls her eyes and I can see her cheeks flushing with annoyance again.

"No, going by car," I tell him.

"Well you enjoy it Cassie," Tilly smiles.

"Don't you like flying?" Alan asks again.

"Pardon?"

"Is that why you're going by car?"

"Er, no, it's only an hour away," I tell him, trying to escape.

"It's safe now, they've got an x-ray machine that looks up yer bum."

"Yes quite," Tilly stops him before he goes into graphic detail.

"I seen it on the news, one bloke had a battery up his ar…" he continues in full flow.

"Oh for God's sake!" Alicia snaps.

"Yes Alan, thank you," Tilly butts in again.

I am speechless and get to my feet before I lose it altogether. Alan knows when to shut up and decides against elaborating on the subject. I have a feeling Alicia won't bother to come next week. The prospect of spending an hour alone with Elvis and his bum battery stories will be too much for her. She is delicate after all.

"Well thanks everyone, that was most interesting," Tilly giggles, heading for the door.

I follow, with Elvis close behind. Alicia remains seated, still shaking from the ordeal, and to think I was dead set against coming to these sessions when Dr Green first suggested it. Misconceptions you see, like everybody else, I always assumed therapy of any kind was for people who dribble a lot and howl at the moon.

Alan is still behind me as I get to the main drive. I'm trying to keep ahead in case anyone I know spots me chatting to Elvis outside a Mental Health Unit. He catches up with me, his collar flapping in the breeze.

"It was Casualty," he wheezes, gasping for breath.

"What was that Alan?"

"Casualty. The x-ray machine. Not the news."

"Oh right," I smile, trying not to laugh.

"See ya!"

"Bye Alan."

I shall watch Central News tonight. Just in case a passing film crew have captured Elvis, roaming the streets of Edgbaston with a chocolate medallion round his neck.

CHAPTER EIGHTEEN

Drop the Dead Donkey

Only two days left and I don't want to go home. I'm considering barricading myself in and declaring squatter's rights. We haven't seen a police car since we arrived, so the local plod probably cycles around on a bike. What would our chances be against one bobby on a bike do you think? I would imagine he doesn't have much knowledge of squatter's rights anyway. Trout tickling and game poaching but not squatters.

Of course we shall have to, somebody in this family has to behave like an adult and go out and earn some money. That's not me at the moment, so I concede defeat and accept that in just forty- eight hours we'll be back in Birmingham. I shall sulk of course, just long enough for Jack to cave in and book another week later in the year. October would be nice, just as the seasons are changing.

And to think we nearly chose Yorkshire instead. It was a toss up between the two and we chose Shropshire. Mainly because Levy doesn't travel very well and the prospect of a ninety-pound dog hurling himself around the interior of our knackered Cavalier was too horrendous to consider. We got here in just over an hour and he was already hanging out of the window, howling, so I think we made the right choice.

We stopped on the way, in one of those little picnic areas, and do you know he flatly refused to get out of the car. Jack said he probably thought we were going to tie him to the litter bin and drive off.

This has been a major step for me too. It's the furthest I've been away from home since I jumped on the tram to Trifletown. Home is where I feel safe and the prospect of this holiday has kept me awake for ages I can tell you. It was Tilly who finally talked me into it. She pointed out, and quite rightly too, that it's been a while since Jack had a decent break.

It always works with me, the guilt trip. No sooner had she said it than I was on the phone asking for brochures to be sent.

I'm so glad I did. We're staying in the Oast House. One of four cottages situated in a cobbled courtyard, miles from anywhere. I feel as if I'm in a time warp. The week has flown by and we've woken up to yet another gloriously sunny morning, with dozens of baby rabbits skittering around in the meadow across the way.

I'm still in bed, half awake and luxuriating in the softness of the duvet. Jack is up and watching the dawn break yet again. I thought he might get tired of it after a few days but I was wrong. He's over by the bedroom window with a silly grin on his face.

"What are you doing?" I ask, rubbing the sleep from my eyes.

"Trying to count the rabbits. I got to four million then I had to start again."

"Silly sod."

"Three million and thirty-three..."

"Scrumptious aren't they?" I yawn.

"Delicious served with potatoes and gravy." He flexes his muscles and stretches, displaying an impressive suntan across his back.

"Get back into bed, it's still the middle of the night."

"Rubbish woman! This is the country, people start work in the middle of the night," he laughs.

"Yes, well that farmer over the way is probably in his field now... wondering why you're standing at the window flashing your dangly bits... put your pants on."

"We country folk don't wear pant's. Just an old potato sack tied with string."

"All that fresh air's gone to your head, get back into bed."

"Can't," he insists "I've got pigs to milk and cows to shear."

"Enough!"

"And eggs to collect..."

"Yes, I'll have a couple please, lightly boiled with soldiers."

This country air certainly does give you an appetite. I reckon I've put that four stone back on in the last week. Every time I've opened my mouth it was to shovel food in. Jack says it's nice to see me eating properly again. He won't be saying that when I'm thirty stone and can't fit into my clothes.

"I'll take the dog out while it's quiet," he says, slipping on his jogging bottoms.

"It's always quiet!"

"You know what I mean, I'll introduce him to the rabbits."

"Be careful, I couldn't face a dead bunny at this time in the morning."

"You underestimate us. He's gun dog stock remember."

"Mm, I forgot."

"Go back to sleep."

I can hear him clicking across the quarry tiles in the kitchen, calling to the dog, who has taken to sleeping up in the loft since we arrived. I caught him last night, gazing out at the stars. He's in love you see. Her name's Milly, a delightful golden Labrador with huge brown eyes. I'm not surprised he fell for her, we all did. When we arrived, she came lolloping out of the main house to greet us as we pulled into the courtyard. Levy was out of the car before us and after the initial sniffing of bums they ran off into the paddock and we've hardly seen them since.

I was a bit worried, knowing his tendency to hump anything that moves, but Mrs Wareham, the owner, wasn't phased at all. She must have read my thoughts.

"They'll be fine! Milly knows her way around, let them have a romp," she grinned.

"Is she, er..." I dithered, not quite knowing how to put it.

"Spayed! Yes of course, now come on in and I'll show you round."

We followed and struggled to contain our excitement as she unlocked the door to the Oast House. It was everything the brochure promised and more. Spacious and sparkling clean with heavy oak beams and furniture. The French windows in the lounge, opening out onto an orchard crammed with damson and plum trees. "This be alright for you?" she asked, going towards the door.

"Marvellous!" we chorused, unable to believe our luck. You never quite know what you're going to find do you when you book these places over the phone?

And marvellous it has been too. For all of us. Levy has spent the week rolling around in the paddock with Milly, while we have strolled the lanes and riverbanks, eating picnics in the fields. At night, we generally sit out in the courtyard sipping Jack Daniel's, and drinking in the silence. Silence punctuated now and then by Levy snoring. I have never known him to sleep or even sit still for more than ten minutes and now, after days of frolicking with Milly, he collapses every night into a heap. Jack commented that he'd be exhausted too if he were frolicking with a young lady all day in the paddock. Dream on pal!

It's only 5.42am according to the clock, but I feel amazingly refreshed. Fresh air and lots of exercise. Invigorating. It must be the prospect of another day relaxing by the river, instead of your everyday slog at home. I'm lucky, at least I don't have to clock watch anymore or trudge along with all the other commuters like Jack. This week has worked wonders for all of us and the thoughts of becoming a squatter appear even more tempting.

My daydreams are shattered by the sound of the door latch clanking followed by Levy pounding up the oak stairs. He hurls himself onto the bed before I can hide in the wardrobe.

"Hello lad! Look at you, all frisky and grinning at this time in the morning."

"Just bumped into Milly in the yard. He's got it bad that boy." I can tell, he has that glorious glint in his eye and a permanent erection. Dead giveaway. Which reminds me, I need a new lipstick, must see if I can get one in the village. It's unlikely they'll stock lipgloss at the village stores though. The woman behind the counter looked at me as if I were mad when I asked for some Ryvita yesterday. Don't think they're big on Ryvita around here. Rye bread cut like doorsteps but not wafer thin crispbreads.

It's a smashing little shop. Crammed full to the rafters with things that I thought were obsolete years ago. Rainbow coloured sherbet in glass jars, and that Camp coffee, the liquid stuff with a soldier on the bottle. It's like stepping back in time. And hairnets! Those brown and black ones in little cellophane packets stuck on a card. Do people still wear hairnets I wonder?

"I'm popping to the shop for the paper's, can I get you anything?"

"A hairnet and a quarter of rainbow sherbet please."

"Okay, back soon."

These early morning strolls have become a ritual. Jack spends so much of his life working and sitting in traffic, this must seem like heaven to him. He's a country boy at heart and I feel he'd do well as a gamekeeper, patrolling the banks of some Scottish river, with Levy at his side. Problem is, how would one go about getting a job as a gamekeeper? It's not as if they're likely to advertise on the board at the Jobcentre is it? Men are born into it I suppose. Generations passing their knowledge on to the next son. His Dad was a painter and decorator so that rules that out.

This bed is so comfortable, must be the mattress. Probably stuffed with straw from the fields. I have slept like the proverbial baby since we arrived, which is another first for me. At home, I hit the floor running just before six every day. Here, I've been lying in until at least ten past. Sloth is indeed a terrible thing.

Just give it five more minutes. Get those sausages sizzling for when he get's back. Something else about staying here, you feel almost obliged to tuck into a Full English every morning. The full monty, with bacon and beans and eggs and mushrooms and anything else lying in the fridge. My arteries are furring up just thinking about it. At home, we generally grab a glass of juice and a slice of toast while listening to the traffic reports on BRMB.

I must have dozed off again! Oh hell! I can hear him clanking around preparing breakfast. That unmistakable aroma of fried bacon is wafting up the stairs.

"Sorry!" I shout down the stairs "I dozed off."

"No problem, almost ready."

"Did you get the papers."

"Mm.."

By the time I get down, the table is laid and breakfast is on it. Steam rising from the mound of tinned tomatoes he's piled onto my plate. What a wonderful way to start the day! My hairnet and rainbow sherbet are resting by the teapot. Bless him. He's a terrific shopper that man, send him on an errand and he always comes back with exactly what you asked for, even if it was a joke. Never mind, Ma will find a use for it, probably hang her sprouts in it ready for Christmas.

Last day tomorrow and I'm putting off packing our stuff away. Trying to drag out every last second until we have to go. Jack has gone for a walk round the trout lake while I prepare supper. It's a beautiful evening, still hot with a warm breeze wafting across the courtyard. The Labrador lovers are lying in the shade on the cobbles, panting after a day of frolics in the field. It's a pity Milly has been spayed. What delightful babies they could make together.

Mrs Wareham just drove off in her four-wheel drive. Lovely lady! Very down to earth, no nonsense kind of person. Obviously loaded what with all this land and property but not snooty in the least. She owns all the land for miles around but you wouldn't think it to look at her. Muddy jeans, scuffed boots and a sensible waxed jacket. Just my type of person. Since we arrived, she has discreetly kept her distance, allowing us the pleasure of roaming around in peace, which is very considerate I feel.

I could sit out in this courtyard all night, just watching the world go by. Not that much of the world actually does go by. We've only seen

about two cars and as many people in a week. Now and again, the bell
will ring on the stable block and she'll come dashing across the yard to
answer the phone, but that's about it. Maybe this is what Tilly meant
when she talked about peace of mind.

I can hear something clip-clopping down the lane. It must be a
horse. You see, I've only been here a week and I'm already a country
bumpkin. I was right, an enormous chestnut coloured beast is turning
into the courtyard. There's a guy riding him who bears a striking
resemblance to Terry Wogan. Big smiley face and rosy cheeks.

"Evening!" he booms, spotting me sitting on the cottage steps.

"Evening."

"Hils about?" he calls, steering the horse towards me.

"Sorry?"

"Hilary... Mrs Wareham?"

"No sorry, you just missed her."

"Bollocks!" he roars, climbing down off the horse.

Now I love animals but have to admit that I am absolutely petrified
of horses. It's the teeth. I have no idea why they bring me out into a cold
sweat but they do and as the horse edges closer to me I start to panic.

"Ruddy donkey's just keeled over," he booms again "She'll be upset."

"Oh, I'm sorry," I squeak, while keeping an eye on those bloody
teeth.

"Have to bury the bugger, before it get's dark."

"I see."

"Rats will have a go otherwise, Hils would be mortified."

This is where my extensive knowledge of the countryside falls flat.
The only donkey's I have ever seen were on Blackpool beach and I have
no idea on the logistics involved in actually burying one. Surely you'd
need planning permission or something? I'm reluctant to show my
ignorance on the subject and try to bluff my way through it.

"Is there anything I can do to help?"

"Jolly decent of you but I need somebody with muscle," he laughs.

"My husband will be back soon. He's very strong," I boast.

"Excellent! Just put Charlie in the stables and we'll get started."

Charlie Chestnut is led away towards the stable block and I breathe
a sigh of relief. I got quite a graphic view of the inside of his mouth
when he was standing close by and the teeth are worse than I imagined.
I have just volunteered Jack's services as a donkey funeral director
apparently and I'm hoping he'll be up for it. He won't mind, he'll help
anyone out in a crisis. Although where they'll get a mechanical digger

from at this time of night, I have no idea. At the very least I'd imagine you'd need a vet's certificate or something before you go burying a donkey. People would be burying donkey's willy-nilly surely if you don't need permission of some sort. Maybe he's not dead, just tired. Oh what do I know? I'm a city girl and not exactly au fait with donkey death rites. All this rubbish is racing through my head as Wogan strides back across the courtyard.

"Back soon you say?" he asks, lighting up a cigar from his jacket pocket.

"Any minute I should think. I could call him on his mobile if you like."

"Splendid!" he beams. I dash into the cottage and pray that Jack's got his mobile switched on.

"Hello, only me."

"Hello, are you okay?"

"Listen, this is very bizarre but could you make your way back. Sharpish?"

"What's up?" he asks, his voice full of concern.

"This guy just turned up, on a horse… he needs your help to bury a donkey."

"Ha-ha, very funny."

"No honestly! He's here in the courtyard, the donkey died and the rats will chew it," I tell him.

"Have you been inhaling the fumes from that fertiliser in the barn?" he laughs.

"I know it's weird but I swear it's true, please come back now!" He's still laughing on the other end of the line. You'd think he'd be used to me by now eh?

"Shall I bring a doctor with me, a psychiatrist perhaps?"

"Stop it! Just get here as quickly as you can," I yell, just as the signal goes dead. Wogan is watching me from the doorway and probably thinks I'm insane, city folk see, no idea.

"He's on his way," I tell him "Can I get you a drink?"

"Lovely thanks!"

"Tea… coffee… Jack Daniel's?"

"JD! excellent… lots of ice please," he grins. I can see that Wogan and I are going to get along just fine. I have an affinity with anyone who appreciates the unique flavour of Jack Daniel's. I pour him a large one and join him on the bench in the courtyard.

"This is very decent of you," he smiles, taking a swig of his drink.

"Not at all, glad to help."

"Hils loved that crusty old bugger. She'll be dreadfully upset."

"The donkey?"

"Mm, Dylan."

Now I'm in a dilemma. Was it Bob Dylan, Dylan Thomas or Dillon out of the Magic roundabout? I hate loose ends! Dylan Thomas I should think, she doesn't look like a folk music fan. Then again, if she has children, it could be the character out of the Magic Roundabout. Oh hell! I shall have to ask him later, when I've got to know him better.

"Had he been ill?" I ask him.

"Off his legs a while back but apart from that he's been fine."

"Good job you found him," I say sympathetically.

"Just trotting past with Charlie and down he went like a ton of bricks!"

"Oh dear!"

"Ah well, best way to go," he grins, draining his glass.

"Another?"

"Lovely, thanks."

I slip indoors again, and while Wogan waits for his drink, I call Jack.

"Me again, can you call at the shop and get another litre of Jack Daniel's," I whisper.

"Aha! I knew it, you're hammered!"

"No really, it's Wogan, he's drinking us dry!" I protest, knowing he doesn't believe a word of it.

"Yeah right!"

"You'll see when you get back, just hurry!" He's laughing again! He'll feel very silly when he does get back!

"Not long now, he's on his way," I smile, passing Wogan his drink.

"Splendid!"

His cheeks are even rosier now and he grins at me as the amber liquid slides down his throat. There's something about Jack Daniel's that inspires calm and a sense of well-being to a body.

"I'm so sorry dear, how rude of me, I'm David Lambert... just call me Lambert," he smiles.

"Cassie," I grin, returning his handshake.

"Got about two hours light left I'd say."

"Right, whereabouts is the... er... Dylan," I ask.

"Over there on High Top, won't take us long."

I follow his gaze and see he's referring to one of the fields just across the lane. Poor old Dylan, dead and lying all alone in that field.

"What about Mrs Wareham, should we try and contact her?" I ask.

"Not much point, she'll be at her whist drive, Friday see, won't be back till midnight."

"Oh I see."

"Best get it over and done with. I'll wait up for her, break the news," he says softly.

"That's kind of you."

"Nonsense! She'd do the same for me. Known each other for years."

"I see."

"We can take the tractor, shove some spades in the back and some plastic sheets."

"I'd like to help if I can, I'll come with you," I offer.

"Are you sure my dear, bit gruesome you know, burying an animal."

"That's okay, I'm not very strong but I could hold a torch or something."

"Splendid!"

We sit in silence, watching the sun disappear down behind the trees. Thankfully it's still warm so we won't be needing jumpers or anything. I would imagine you'd work up quite a sweat digging a hole for a donkey anyway.

"Here he comes!" I giggle at the sight of Jack hurrying along the lane towards us.

"Marvellous! I'll go and start up the tractor," Lambert roars jumping up.

He is half way across the courtyard as Jack turns into the drive. A litre of Jack Daniel's in one hand and a six pack of Walker's crisps in the other. Silly sod thinks it's a party. Lambert waves to him excitedly and he waves back, with difficulty.

"So, where have you hidden the donkey?" he grins, flopping down onto the bench beside me.

"Long story, that's Lambert... the donkey's Dylan... dead in that field over there."

"Right, got that. I'd better change into my wellies."

"Bring mine as well will you?"

"Sure."

"And the bottle. We might need a drink."

"Crisps?" he asks, shaking the bag under my nose.

"No, that would be disrespectful to Dylan."

The tractor chugs into view as he locks the door to the cottage. Levy is snuggled up inside with Milly, best not take them along, probably be a bit traumatic for a dog, a donkey funeral.

"Room for two on the back!" Lambert booms, heading towards us.

I'm not sure he should be driving a tractor after guzzling down two very large glasses of Jack Daniel's. My measures are usually the equivalent of a triple in a pub. Let's hope we don't bump into that plod on his bike.

"Hold on tight!" he yells, as we cling onto the back by our fingernails. I always thought tractor's went at a snail's pace, but this one seems to have a reconditioned engine. As he pulls out of the courtyard, we veer dangerously to one side and Jack is forced to grab onto my left breast to stop me somersaulting over the side and to a certain death.

It's at this point, I get the giggles and begin to collapse into a heap of helpless laughter. This has to be THE most bizarre situation I've ever been in and I've been in a few I can tell you. It's seven-o-clock on a sunny evening in Shropshire, and I'm on the back of a tractor, on my way to bury a dead donkey! Pa will love this one.

"Nearly there!" he shouts above the noise of the diesel engine "Nearly there!" The words are barely out of his mouth as we shudder to a halt next to a wooden gate. Lambert leaps out of the driver's seat and bounds across to help us down.

"This is very good of you," he beams, lifting me down off the box at the back. I grab the bottle and a roll of plastic sheeting and we follow as Lambert leads the way towards the deceased. Both men appear to be deep in conversation but I'm too far behind to hear what's being said. I'm concentrating so hard on staying upright in the furrows, I almost miss the corpse as we stumble upon it. Dylan, stiff as a board, on his back, with his legs in the air. Rigour Mortis must have set in already! Perhaps donkey's have a different metabolism to us. Goodness me, with this heat he'll be decomposing soon! Better get a move on.

"Well old chap, let's give you a decent send off," Lambert sighs, stroking Dylan's head. A simple gesture, but one that starts me off. The floodgates open and I am left sobbing at the mere sight of Dylan. Dead… with his hooves in the air.

"Now, now dear, the old chap's had a good life," Lambert whispers.

"She's like this with anything that dies, frogs, dogs, donkeys," Jack informs him.

"You softie," he smiles gently "Let's get on shall we?"

They start digging with a fervour, while I crack open the bottle and take a swig to fortify myself. I plonk myself down in the dirt and watch fascinated as a bluebottle crawls up Dylan's nostril.

"Are you sure he's dead?" I ask them.

"Well if he's not, he's doing a bloody good impression," Jack laughs out loud.

"Daft bugger!" Lambert chuckles, wiping the sweat off his forehead.

They continue with their gruesome task, beads of sweat trickling down their faces and onto their necks. I feel totally useless not having a shovel to help. Lambert gave me a torch but it's not dark enough for that yet. I unroll one of the plastic sheets and sit on it, watching the earth fly sideways as the trench becomes bigger.

"How deep?" Jack gasps, wiping the sweat off his face.

"Another foot should do it. Deep enough to keep the foxes off."

"You work on that side and I'll do this."

"Excellent!"

I watch, mesmerised, as the hole gets deeper by the second, both men standing inside now, shovelling out the damp soil from within. Lambert is about a foot shorter than Jack and seems to be disappearing completely. Dylan meanwhile is becoming stiffer by the second.

"That should do it," Lambert wheezes, throwing his shovel onto the pile of soil. They crawl out of the hole and stand beside it, both breathing heavily with the exertion.

"Now we have to roll him onto that sheet. We can drag him into the hole then," Lambert gasps.

"Right... Cassie get off the plastic," Jack tells me.

"Can't... I'm pissed," I slur.

"Oh my life!" he laughs, glancing at the almost empty bottle. At this precise moment, Lambert loses it and throwing his head back, roars with laughter. His ample belly wobbling with mirth.

"Love it!" he booms into the night "Love it!"

"She get's like this at funerals," Jack tells him.

"Drink anyone?" I offer, extending the bottle.

"Why not!"

"Let's toast Dylan shall we?"

"To Dylan, a fine old friend."

"I think I'm going to be sick," is all I can manage.

They are still laughing at me, as Dylan is unceremoniously rolled onto the plastic sheet, his hooves jutting skywards as if he's freefalling into space. Within minutes he's gone. Just a heap of hooves and ears, lying at the bottom of a hole.

"Should we close his eyes do you think?" Jack asks in a hushed voice.
"Good idea."
He clambers back into the hole, disappearing out of sight again.
"They won't close," his voice calls from the pit.
"Oh dear."
"Have you got any Blu-Tak?"
"No sorry."
"Best leave them then."
"Quiet right."
"Just looks odd, sort of creepy."
"Accusing almost," Lambert agrees, peering into the hole.
"What about that carrier bag over there in the hedge?"
"Over his head you mean?" Lambert asks.
"Mm…"
"People might think we suffocated him," Jack says in all seriousness.
"Oh blimey."
"Here, put these stones on them."
"Nice touch."
"Thanks."
"You're welcome."

I am slipping in and out of a drunken stupor, but am still moved by their kindness. Two grown men debating the niceties of a dead donkey. Strangers almost, thrown together in a crisis and working together to see that old Dylan has a decent send off.

It's at times like this that you feel proud to be British! If this were Spain or Turkey, Dylan would be discarded at the roadside. A feast for the flies and the foxes. This is what a civilised society is all about. I am just about to burst into a chorus of Rule Britannia when Lambert pipes up.

"Just cover him over, then we can get off."
"Be quicker filling it in, shouldn't take long."

And true to his word, Jack has the hole filled in and levelled off neatly in no time at all.

"Well done lads, you did him proud," I slur, falling onto my back.
"She get's emotional, nothing to worry about," Jack laughs.
"I've been known to get extremely emotional myself," Lambert chuckles. I know they are discussing me but my head has landed in a cow pat and my hearing's somewhat muffled. I think it's a cow pat, could be a donkey pat. Who knows? Who cares? Certainly not me, I'm past caring.

"I'll carry her to the tractor," I hear Jack say.

"Can you manage?"

"Course, I just lifted a dead donkey."

And with that compliment ringing in my ears, I am hauled up onto his back and carried like a sack of turnips to the tractor. The rest is all a bit of a blur to be honest. I distinctly remember kissing Lambert goodnight and congratulating him on his Radio 2 show. Most of all, I remember Jack, helpless with laughter as he struggled to get me to bed. Then nothing. Until now.

"Anadin?"

"Please."

"Orange juice or Jack Daniel's?"

"Hilarious."

"It was actually... us burying a donkey and you drunk, lying in a cowpat!" he roars.

"I was overcome... with grief."

"Absolutely darling."

I close my eyes and wait for Michael Flatley to finish his finale inside my head. The Anadin should kick in soon and I can get moving.

"Better start packing soon," I groan.

"It's all done, cars loaded, just waiting for you to move your arse."

I really have no idea what I would do without this man. Statistically, he should have left me years ago but he's still here, hanging in there and keeping me upright.

"Where's the dog?"

"Saying goodbye to Milly, could be tears before the days out."

"I'll be down in a minute, just grab a cold shower."

"See you outside."

He disappears downstairs, leaving me to sober up. What a night! Poor Dylan, and Lambert. He must be in his seventies and it's no easy task digging a trench for a donkey. Good job he didn't keel over in that field. Try explaining that one to the police. Two city folk, a dead donkey, a stiff pensioner, and two shovels! I can hear voices in the courtyard and recognise the other one as Mrs Wareham. I'll go down and give her my sympathies regarding Dylan. I'd get her a card but I'm not sure they do bereavement cards suitable for donkey owners. They do them for dogs, I've seen them in Birthday's.

"Our thoughts are with you on the death of your donkey." Doesn't sound quite right does it?

Hilary is leaning against the cottage wall as I finally appear, looking the worst for wear. She tactfully ignores my mud splattered jeans and crumpled jumper.

"Morning!" she trills, her face glowing with perspiration. Probably been mucking out the stables.

"Morning, sorry about Dylan."

"Well, the old boy had a good innings, thanks for helping out."

"No problem."

"Lambert filled me in on all the gory details," she laughs, "He's taken quite a shine to you!" I blush right down to my boots, remembering my drunken antics of the previous night. Whatever must she think of me?

"You must come and stay with us again, join us for dinner one night perhaps?" she grins.

"That would be lovely, thanks," Jack tells her "We were going to book another week."

"Come through to the house, I'll check the diary," she says, leading the way.

My depression at having to leave is lifted by the prospect of coming back soon. Levy is sitting in the back of the car, his head lolling out of the window gazing longingly at Milly. Poor bugger, imagine having to wait three months for your next hump. Jack would no doubt empathise with him on that point.

"Ready?" he asks, coming out of the house. We climb into the car and wave dejectedly at Hilary, who is standing at the bay window, waving.

"October 4th, it's all booked," he smiles, looking at our sad faces.

"Lovely, thanks."

As we pull off the courtyard, Milly trots alongside the car, almost as if she's desperate for one last look at her boyfriend.

"Bye Milly, see you in October!" I shout, craning my neck for one last look at her.

At the bottom of the lane, just before we hit the M6, I am surprised to see Lambert, making his way towards the field where Dylan is buried. Maybe he's going back to measure up for a headstone.

"Nice man," I say out loud as he disappears out of sight.

"Cracking radio show too," Jack laughs.

"Well he does, he's a dead ringer for Wogan."

"Except he's not Irish!"

"Granted."

"And he's bald."

"You're being picky now."

Within minutes, we are on the motorway, carried along on a tidal way of traffic all heading back to Birmingham. I close my eyes, trying to blot out the enormous transporter in front which seems to be on a death wish, jumping lanes and driving like a maniac.

"It was her late husband," he suddenly pipes up.

"Sorry?"

"Dylan, the donkey was named after her late husband," he tells me.

"How do you know?"

"Lambert told me last night."

"Oh."

"We were chatting while you drank the entire contents of that bottle."

"Sorry."

"So you can stop fretting about the name."

"Unusual name Dylan, was he Welsh?" I ask.

"No idea… but he had enormous genitals apparently."

He's probably winding me up but I refuse to be drawn into this. I have a hangover and half a cow pat on my boot. I shall ask her when we go back in October.

CHAPTER NINETEEN

Winston Churchill & His Black Dog

It's a subject I've never really discussed with Ma. She's of the opinion that you just grit your teeth and get on with your life. I come from a long line of incredibly strong women and she must be terribly disappointed in yours truly. She's never said. Like I say, it's a subject we never discuss. To Ma, and a lot of women of her generation, a breakdown is something you call the RAC out for. It's yet another generation thing. Her generation put up with things and would never dream of discussing their most private thoughts with a stranger. The fact that I have been in therapy for over a year is yet another subject we don't dwell on. When I first became ill, she arrived with her duster and a box of cream horns, and set about polishing my house to perfection. It was her way of dealing with it I suppose.

I'm not knocking her. Just telling it like it is. I suppose if you've lived through a World War and witnessed the horrors of unemployment, rationing and shell-shock, you get tough. This could be one of the reasons why I still, after all this time, feel incredibly guilty about succumbing to this 'crisis' as they call it. To Ma, a crisis is having your custard go soggy on a Sunday.

Call it what you like, breakdown, crisis, whatever, it basically means that your head is fucked up and you need help. I know that now.

It's not that Ma doesn't care. Not at all. It's just that she doesn't understand. The entire concept of the word 'stress' is totally alien to her so she refuses to accept that it exists.

I blame Uncle Albert. I think I must have inherited some of his genes. He was one of Pa's elder brothers and regularly succumbed to depression. A serious, chronic depression, that sent him into the depths of despair, and a ward in the local Mental Hospital. I truly believe that my ingrained fear of anything to do with mental illness stems from our Sunday afternoon visits to see him.

The ward was Victorian and staffed by several surly male nurses who hovered in the background, menacingly, while we tried to jolly Albert along. He would sit there, chain-smoking Park Drive and staring into space as the result of some serious medication. His best friend, Napoleon, lying on the next bed in leg restraints. Is it any wonder people are petrified of anything remotely connected to the mind?

As a child, the thing that stuck in my head about those visits, was the clothes. Patients weren't allowed to wear their own because of the laundry problems, so Uncle Albert would appear in an assortment of odd outfits. Flared trousers and kipper ties being the order of the day. I found out later, may years later actually, that there was a reason for this.

Apparently, during the day, they would all be frogmarched, crocodile fashion, to the workshops, where they churned out plastic coat hangers on a simple production line. In exchange for this slave labour, a major chain store would keep the hospital supplied with outdated stock that was surplus to requirements. I suppose it was a step up from basket weaving. I don't know. I'm only contemplating all this because I can't get to sleep. Funny how your brain goes into overdrive at night.

The flares were always Crimplene. Can you think of anything more off putting that Crimplene flares? I can't! The government should issue them to all men between the ages of sixteen to sixty as a contraceptive. Most men over sixty wear them anyway don't they? The population explosion would take a nose dive I'm sure.

Uncle Albert is dead now and I can only hope he's up there swanning around in a decent pair of Versace.

So, that's my theory regarding my genes and his jeans if you get my drift. Nobody else in the family seems to have been cursed with this bloody problem anyway, thank goodness. My son is comparatively normal, considering he has me as a mother.

I may be mental but at least I don't have a horses mouth like Fiona, she of the Fuckwit face, next door. She's out in the garden now. It's dark but there's no mistaking those teeth, glinting in the shadows. I was just about to shut the bedroom window when I noticed the glare. She wants to be careful, we are on a direct flight path to Birmingham airport and some Russian pilot might mistake them for a landing strip.

I haven't really seen much of her since our meeting weeks ago. Nor Henry. I expect he's still in the city, doing whatever it is people in the city do. Knobbing his secretary probably. Sometimes, we hear the odd tinkle of wine glasses or him revving up his BMW on the drive, which suits me fine. Fiona and I are destined never to share a pot of Typhoo. No doubt she drinks Earl Grey or Lapsung Chung Dung, or whatever they call it.

Those teeth are never normal. Normal teeth are slightly worn and used. Hers are absolutely perfect, sparkling white and symmetrical. They'll be Harley Street teeth, specially imported from Nepal… crafted from the tusks of some poor bloody elephant.

"One of our tea roses is missing Henry," I hear her call down the garden

"Not to worry darling, I'll get Charles to bring another one down."

"Yes, but it was from the house in Chelsea, one of my favourites," she whines.

Henry! At last a voice to go with the face and I have to say, it fits. Henry is very tall and very thin and also extremely ugly. Sorry, but I speak as I find and there's no other word to describe him. His face is accentuated by the hair, jet black and slicked back in that ridiculous Brylcreem style, sort of Wall Street, circa late eighties. He'd probably look at me and think, "Look at that midget with huge tits and cropped hair,", which is fair enough. I never said I was perfect.

"There's a hole here, by the trellis," she calls again.

"Perhaps the cat dug it up dear," he sighs, trying to pacify her.

"Don't be ridiculous, Crawford would never do that!" Did I hear that right? Crawford? What sort of name is that for a cat? A butler yes, not a cat.

"Leave it Fiona, come inside!" Henry bawls, losing his temper.

The teeth head towards the house pretty smartish I have to say. Old Henry obviously wears the trousers in that one, designer ones of course, nothing less than Armani or Gautier I bet. Amazing what you overhear through an open window. Admittedly, I'm hanging right out of the window, clinging to the ledge with my fingernails but nevertheless, it gives you an insight into people's lives. God only knows what folk think when we are out in the garden. Me bawling at the dog and Jack practising his golf swing.

"What are you nosing at?"

"Fiona, one of her roses is missing."

"You didn't, did you?" he asks suspiciously.

"No, I did not!"

"Come away from the window, it's cold in this bed."

I fail to see how he can possibly be cold. Aside from the Nike golf cap, he's taken to wearing a Nike shirt in bed now.

"Not keen on old Fiona are you?" he asks.

"No, can't say I am."

"Any particular reason? Apart from the fact that she's filthy rich and drives an Audi convertible?"

"That's not it. It's just the whole 'IT' girl thing," I moan.

"What do you mean?"

"The teeth, and that accent, and calling a cat Crawford, for God's sake!"

He looks puzzled and I can't say I blame him. There is no definitive reason, it just is.

"So, what's the opposite to an 'IT' girl then?" he laughs.

"I dunno, a 'SHIT' girl I suppose." He laughs, his head rolling backwards and smacking against the light-fitting over the bed.

"What the hell's a 'SHIT' girl?"

"Everything an 'IT' girl isn't," I shout, emphasising my point.

"Tell me, come on, I can't wait for this."

"Well, a 'SHIT' girl would live in a council flat in Wapping, and buy her bras at Woolworth's."

More guffaws from his side of the bed as he tries to grasp this concept.

"And?"

"Her teeth would be full of cavities 'cos of her poor diet." He'll have a cardiac in a minute. I wish he wouldn't ask for my theories if he can't be serious.

"You've got an extremely warped view of the world," he chuckles.

"Tilly says I should vent my anger, not suppress it."

"Absolutely!"

"You have been warned," I threaten him, climbing into bed.

"So, where do you figure in this equation, what category are you?" he asks.

"I'm definitely a 'TIT' girl, you look at me and see tits... end of story."

"Can't argue with that."

He switches off the bedside lamp and we lie in silence. Me contemplating the class system, while he is on the eighteenth hole with Tiger again. It's the Ryder Cup and he's in the lead.

"The dog's quiet, where is he?" I ask, uneasy at the silence.

"Downstairs."

"What's he doing?"

"Playing with something in the porch."

"Night then."

Minutes later, Levy appears at the bedroom door, his face framed in the moonlight streaming through the window. He always patrols the house at night, stalking moths and anyone wearing a stripy jumper and carrying a crowbar. I pretend to be asleep but he's having none of it and shoves his wet nose violently into my face, glaring at me in the blackness, daring me to move. I open one eye, very slowly, praying he won't notice. He has a Thornton's toffee stuck to his ear and a label of some sort on his slobbery chin. I can just about make out the wording,

'Pink Lady... Tea Rose'.

"Are you awake?"

"No, I always hold conversations in my sleep."

"He's eaten their rose bush."

"Hope it doesn't make him ill."

"Should I tell them do you think?"

"What for, he's eaten the evidence, it would never stand up in a court of law."

"Night then."

"Night."

He hasn't vomited yet so I can only assume the Pink Lady wasn't poisonous. I must have been awake until after two this morning. I have nights like that when I can't switch off. Which could explain why I'm like a Zombie most days. Like I say, I can do without the medication. Alicia takes hers, keeps them in a little box with compartments in, specially designed for the job no doubt. She's fond of getting it out during our sessions and popping a pill in her mouth, as if to demonstrate to Tilly that she's a good girl. I know Alan takes his because I've seen him queuing up in Boots with a wad of prescriptions in his hand.

I gave them a try, when I first got sick. Took about three I think then flushed them down the loo. I know this is an awful thing to do, but I've never been one for prescribed medication. Whatever it was they prescribed for me just made me feel stoned to be honest. I was floating on the ceiling and didn't like it one little bit. Took me about a week to come down. I realised I'd got to stop taking them when I opened the washing-machine door in mid cycle and flooded the porch. And for some reason, which I can't explain, I found the whole thing hysterically funny. Rolling about on the floor I was, totally incapable. I've been like that on numerous occasions but usually after ingesting vast quantities of Jack Daniels. A much better option.

Tilly told us, at one of our first meetings, that Winston Churchill suffered from depression. Fancy! A brilliant mind like that clouded by trifle. He called it his 'Black Dog' apparently... shadowing him and hanging on his every move. I have one like that, only he's called Levy.

I'm supposed to be doing my homework for tomorrow's session but it's not coming easy. She sets us these little tasks to do every now and again and I quite enjoy them. Even if it's just a means of scoring points over Alicia.

We have to write down three situations in our life that have caused us pain or embarrassment. Don't think there's enough paper in the world for me to write all my embarrassing moments down. I'm struggling here. I shall have to enlist the help of Jack.

"Having problems?" he asks, as if reading my thoughts.

"Mm... I'm supposed to write down three embarrassing moments in my life."

"Blimey! Difficult to know where to start really," he laughs.

"I know."

"What's all that about then?"

"I think the general idea is, you write them down, read them out, then consign them to the past, you know, let go of them for good."

"Oh right, let's get started then."

We both sit in silence, racking our brains to choose just three.

"How about your Burp?" he suddenly asks.

"Don't!"

"Well, it was embarrassing, one of your finer moments I feel," he chuckles.

"Thanks."

My Burp, as he so politely puts it, happened years ago, in The Angel. It used to be our local but I haven't dared set foot in the place since. I believe the aforementioned Burp has gone down in pub folklore around these parts.

"Go on, put it on your list!" he urges. I'm not sure I want to share that with Alicia. She already thinks I'm a peasant. Still, these tasks are meant to challenge us. Poke around in the past and get rid of some of the baggage. I don't really have any painful memories. Nothing drastic anyway, so it will have to be the embarrassing sort.

And that was a corker I have to say. It was August, and I was dying of thirst, so when my drink arrived, a large glass of Coke with ice, I gulped it down in three seconds flat without stopping to take a breath.

As I placed the glass back on the bar, a friend of ours, well he used to be a friend of ours, came over to speak to us. I opened my mouth to say hello and the most disgusting, gargantuan burp erupted from within. An earth shattering burp that ricocheted around the room, bouncing off the walls and shattering several glasses in the process. I was mortified. So was Simon who took the full force of it in his face.

"That's number one, any more?" I ask him.

"How much time have you got?" he grins, taking the piece of paper out of my hand.

"Oh I know, Ted and the Trump!" I cry, suddenly remembering yet another disaster. He laughs, throwing his head back and dropping the paper onto the carpet.

"Good one, go on put it down!"

"Shall I?"

"Yes, go on, do as Tilly tells you!" he orders.

"Unexpected fart in front of a friend," I scribble.

"You really are priceless!" he laughs.

Ted is a good friend of ours, a master carpenter, very useful to know when you need a job doing. He turned up unexpectedly to do some work on the lounge floor while I was in the middle of one of my Yoga sessions. Ted said he didn't mind, and to carry on as if he wasn't there. So there I was, in the middle of a tricky Python Pose and wallop, as I pushed my contorted body to the max, a disgusting explosion of wind erupted from my ample arse, which was directly in line with Ted's nose at the time. Yoga can do that for you, it expels all the air from your intestines. Which is fine. If you're on your own at the time. Not if you have company.

"Got it, all done!"

"Is this therapy an American thing?" he asks.

"No idea, why?"

"Sounds like something Jerry Springer would discuss."

"No, you have to be a transsexual and engaged to a duck to get on that show."

"Right."

"Come on, I need another one."

"I know!" he roars "What about when you fell off the bus outside McDonalds?"

"Oh don't, that was horrendous!"

"Go on, put it down!" he insists.

The falling bit wasn't the problem. I'm always tripping over and cartwheeling into space. Just clumsy I think. But this fall involved several pensioners, two of whom had to be taken into McDonald's for a strong cup of tea to recover.

"Do I have to, Alicia will love that one?"

"Just do it!"

It was a freak fall anyway. Not your normal, oops-a-daisy type of fall. I was getting off the number 3 and the heel on my shoe got caught in the hem on my calf-length skirt. As I stepped off I just went into freefall, taking an entire queue of pensioners with me. Awful! Shopping trolley's were scattered everywhere. It looked like the scene of a road-traffic accident.

"There, all done!"

"Wasn't so bad was it?" he smiles.

"No, I quite like these tasks. It's never dull with Alan in the group."

"Shame. How is Alan?"

"Fine. He's on in Las Vegas next month."

CHAPTER TWENTY

An Inspector Calls

Mary's in hospital. Yet another fall, only this time she couldn't sustain herself by gnawing on the carpet. She was in a bad way when the milkman found her. Two broken ribs and dehydration. I expect she'll be in for a while, until they get her mobile again, or shuffling at least. She has a family, quite a large one in fact, but they're scattered across the country and she's a stubborn old stick. Determined to see out her days on her own in that big, rambling house. On her own apart from Bilbo of course, her cat.

Bilbo is roughly a hundred and seven in cat years and has the scars to prove it. One eye, no teeth and an attitude. Mary has given him all the creature comforts a cat could ask for yet he still refuses to sleep indoors. Preferring to prowl the lanes at night, stalking his prey and humping any passing female moggy who crosses his path.

Bilbo has street cred and woe betide any newcomer who dares to stray onto his turf. Instead of curling up by the fire at night, he sleeps under the lilac bush in the front garden. That way, he can spot the sassy cats as they come out to play. I went to visit her last week and as per usual, ended up promising to look after him while she's away. It's not that I mind, it's just such a responsibility. What if he pegs it and I'm left with the job of telling her? His hearing's gone as well, so it wouldn't surprise me at all if he walked out in front of the dustbin lorry one day.

"Hi Mary, how are you... by the way Bilbo's dead... he's in this envelope."

I couldn't do it. The shock would probably finish her off. So in the meantime, I keep a close eye on him and pray a lot. Caring for Bilbo involves lots of nocturnal visits to his lilac bush just to check he's still breathing. And two dishes of mashed cat food and milk a day.

He was fast asleep this morning when I checked. He got a bit miffed actually when I prodded him to see if he was still alive. He opened his good eye and hissed at me. I asked Mary once how he'd lost the eye. "Daft bugger's always losing things," she said. Dementia, it must be.

She had a cat-flap installed years ago but he's never used it. The milkman shoves her semi-skimmed through it to save her coming to the door. That's how he found her on Wednesday, lying on the kitchen floor with her head wedged up against the cat flap.

I've stocked up on cat food and I have to say, it's a testimony to our friendship that I will actually handle cat food. Lord knows what they put in that stuff but it reminds me of monkey sick. He'll only eat Whiskas, the tuna variety, so that's simple enough. He's not into treats either.

She bought him a rubber mouse for Christmas and the look of sheer disgust on his face was priceless. Bilbo prefers the real thing. I watched him a while back, stalking a mouse along the Valley Site. I know Mother Nature is cruel but it was fascinating to watch. He played it like a violin, darting backwards and forwards, cutting off it's escape route until the poor thing gave up and resigned itself to it's fate.

I didn't intervene. I'm not over keen on mice, or anything else with yellow teeth and scaly tails. Now, if he'd have been tormenting Gertie and her babies I'd have chased him with a stick. Not that he'd be bothered by a stick. He took on Levy once and it was a close call. Sheer bulk and strength on the dog's part won the day.

I was just about to take his food over but there's somebody coming up the drive, looks like the gas man, he's wearing one of those naff navy uniforms.

"Morning, can I help you?"

"Miss Ryder?" he asks, looking me up and down in quite a patronising manner.

"Mrs actually, yes?"

"Hardwick... Inspector with the RSPCA"

"Sorry?"

"RSPCA, could I step inside?"

"What's all this about then?" I ask, fascinated.

"Be best if we discuss it in private Miss," he insists.

"It's Mrs by the way... As in married with child. Could you elaborate?"

At this point, he clears his throat and I swear if he had a moustache, he'd twirl it.

"I've received a report Miss, a very serious report, regarding the neglect of a cat."

"Excuse me, what cat?"

"Could we go in Miss, these things are best discussed in private," he insists quite rudely.

Against my better judgement, I let him in, if only to get to the bottom of all this. I have a feeling he may live to regret it, as Levy joins him on the sofa... sitting on his lap.

"Labrador?" he groans, buckling under the weight.

"Mm, now what's all this about. I don't even own a cat?"

"Ah, now Miss, the cat in question belongs to a... let me see... Mrs Morgan."

"Oh Bilbo, yes she's in hospital!" He consults his notebook yet again and stares at me suspiciously.

"And you are supposed to be looking after the cat Miss?" he sneers.

He's starting to piss me off now, firstly because of his manner and secondly because of his refusal to believe that I'm married.

"It's Mrs! And what exactly are you implying, supposed to be looking after the cat?"

"The complaint states that the cat in question is being left to sleep outdoors Miss."

"Look pal, would you care to see my wedding photo's? I don't have a clue what you're talking about... Bilbo always sleeps outside!"

"No need to adopt that tone, I have to follow up these complaints," he snaps.

I have an extremely short fuse where pillocks are concerned. A fact he is about to discover.

"I'll adopt whatever tone I like in my own house and as for neglect, it's laughable," I shout,

"Bilbo is ancient, one eye, no teeth, he's a street cat!" His eyebrows twitch as if he's cracked the case, "And how did these injuries occur?" he asks.

"For God's sake! He's been prowling the streets for a century, cat's fight, it's a fact!" I yell. He looks quite startled at my outburst and loosens the knot on his tie.

"And how does he manage to eat without any teeth?" he crows.

"Oh get real! He sucks things I suppose, how would I know?"

"Well, it's my duty to look at the cat," he gulps "If you could lead the way."

"You'll be lucky! You'll have to find him first, then get close enough to examine him!" I laugh.

Levy is extremely sensitive to bad vibes and senses that this geezer is not a friend. To demonstrate this, he wraps himself around the guy's leg and proceeds to hump him. Violently and with feeling.

"He likes you!" I giggle, heading for the front door with him dragging the dog along on his leg.

"Lie down lad!" I tell him, escorting the startled inspector off the premises.

I am livid and it shows as I stomp off down the drive with him trailing behind me.

"Come on, I haven't got all day!" I bark at him.

"I've got varicose veins," he simpers, but frankly I don't give a shit.

Barging into my house and accusing me of neglecting an animal! How ridiculous! Why don't these people check their facts first? If he'd just taken the time to check with one of Mary's neighbours, they'd have told him Bilbo has always slept outdoors.

"Here! He normally curls up under there," I tell him, pointing to the lilac bush.

"I see."

"There's a little wooden shelter there by the porch, his food and milk are inside."

He gets down on all fours and disappears into the bush, his feet sticking out at an odd angle.

"Anything else you'd like me to do for him? Nice piece of fresh salmon with basil?"

"I'm only doing my job Miss," he sighs from within the lilac. If I were a compassionate human being, I'd warn him that approaching Bilbo like that is not wise but I'm not, so I don't.

"Bastard!" he suddenly screams, leaping back out of the bush.

"Found him did you?" I laugh. He has a nasty bite on his hand and what looks like a dead slug on his peaked cap. The expression serves you right, springs to mind.

"Seems okay to me," he groans, examining the bite.

"Quite! Well, if you don't mind, I have better things to do," I tell him, walking away.

I watch, fascinated, as he limps off towards his van. Varicose veins and a cat bite. Not a good day. Then something strikes me, who the hell made the complaint?

"Wait!" I bawl, running towards the van "Who made this complaint?"

"Sorry Miss, it's more than my jobs worth," he sneers, climbing into the driver's seat.

"Tosser!" I shout, as he drives off.

Bloody cheek! How dare anyone imply that I would neglect an animal! It's too absurd for words. What a rude little man! I hope his varicose veins grow to the size of grapes and have to be operated on. I stand in the middle of the road, fuming, just as Pete staggers past.

"Alright there Cassie?" he slurs.

"No, I'm not actually, some idiot's lodged a complaint about me with the RSPCA!"

"What you?" he asks incredulously.

"Yes, me of all people! They think I've been neglecting Mary's cat."

"One eye, no teeth?" he asks.

"That's the one."

"Take no notice Cass, some sad bastard being vindictive," he laughs.

He's quite right of course. Some sad person with no life and nothing better to do.

"Forget it," he advises me, before falling head first into the privet.

"Bye Pete."

"Bye."

The stupidity of the whole thing is bought home to me as I go back indoors. Levy is stretched out on the sofa in the dining room. The sofa with the duck-down duvet on, bought especially for him. His box of squeaky toys tucked against the far wall, along with several crates of Bonio's. Neglecting an animal, I ask you! Wait until I tell Jack… I'll ring him now.

"Hi, it's me."

"Hello pet, what's up?" he asks, reading the tone in my voice.

"You won't believe this, but an RSPCA inspector just called."

"Whatever for?"

"Some plank's lodged a complaint that I've been neglecting Bilbo!" I say indignantly.

"You! Neglect an animal, how ridiculous!" he laughs.

"I'm livid!"

I can hear him chuckling at the other end of the line. He always laughs when I get mad.

"Glad you find it funny!" I shout.

"Come on Cass, it's ridiculous, you know that."

"Yes well, it's not nice."

"Exactly, some nasty individual obviously."

"Mm.."

"Now go and make a pot of tea and let it go," he laughs.

"Okay."

"See you later."

It is ridiculous, best not dwell on it. There are some nasty individuals in the world. He keeps telling me to wake up to that fact. It bugs me though. Who on earth would be spiteful enough to even consider doing such a thing?

The thought is barely out of my head, when it hit's me. Bolak! It has to be. She's the only person around here who would even consider doing such a thing. Bitch!

I should have known. As soon as that creep turned up on the doorstep I should have realised! It wouldn't be the first time she's made false accusations against people. The NSPCC were around last year, checking up on some poor innocent girl in West Walk. Something to do with her being a childminder if I remember rightly. Honestly, that woman is a menace!

I'd bet my life it was her. Wait till I see the old witch, I'll snap the wheels off her shopping trolley. Emotions tend to run high when people find themselves on the wrong end of one of her malicious outbursts. There was talk of burning her at the stake in the Post Office recently. Perhaps we as a neighbourhood are too polite. If she lived in some dog rough area of Glasgow, they'd have planted her in the park by now, feet first!

It has to be Bolak. She's Russian I think. Not that that has any bearing on the subject. I'm sure most Russian people are charming but she's the exception. Bloody woman! What makes a person like that tick? Her husband topped himself years ago, sad I know but understandable. Imagine waking up to that every morning.

Picture a gnarled old woman with long, greasy hair and fingernails that could plough a field. Oh, and the filthy feet of course. Let's not forget the feet. And the eyes, cold and piercing without the slightest trace of emotion. I have a theory about Bolak, one which I have explained to Jack on numerous occasions. She's a vampire. Has to be. Probably at home now, resting in her coffin until it get's dark. I shall have to ring him back and tell him I've sussed it.

"Me again."

"Hello, any more grief from the authorities?"

"No listen, it's Bolak, it has to be."

"Makes sense, you know what a weirdo she is," he laughs.

"Exactly."

"I'll wave some garlic at her next time she slithers past," he giggles.

"A spade over the bonce would be better."

"Let it go Cass, remember what Tilly told you."

"Quite."

"Now goodbye, I have work to do," he chuckles.

"That'll be a first."

"Goodbye."

Tilly would say that actually. Let it go. Life's too short to waste fretting over that evil old cow. A year in therapy has taught me to walk away. I refuse to accept responsibility for her dreadful behaviour. That's something she'll have to discuss with God when she reaches the Pearly Gates. I'd like to be there when she does knock on those gates.

"Name?"

"Bolak."

"You're not on my list. Go to hell!"

Or words to that effect.

Talk of the devil, here she comes, slithering along the road, trolley in tow. A cloud of mist swirling at her feet. Probably been to the cemetery, digging up a corpse. I shall wave sweetly as she flies past on her broomstick. There you go, nice little wave... just the two fingers.

CHAPTER TWENTY-ONE

Come on Over Here
If You Think You're Hard Enough

This is so difficult to put into words, I'm having real problems. I know exactly what I want to say but the words are all jumbled up. Nothing new there then. Tilly, patient as ever, is sitting opposite me. One to one session today. We get them every month, just the two of us which is nice. Saves me from being distracted by thoughts of booting Alicia up the bum.

What I'm trying to tell her, is that my perceptions of people have changed drastically since I became ill. The me that was then, no longer exists and I'm not altogether sure that's a good thing. I've been a People Pleaser all my life and that's gone out of the window. I please myself now and it's a concept I'm finding hard to adjust to.

"This is tricky, but what I'm trying to say is, in the past when people have pissed me off I've just smiled sweetly and gritted my teeth. Now, chances are I'd smack them in the teeth."

She smiles and makes a note in her book. Probably writing 'Section this woman immediately!'. I can't say I blame her. She's seen me with old Alicia, I bet she thinks I'm deranged. She must have seen the changes in me. At my first session, I sat and cried like a baby, for the entire hour. She actually ran out of Kleenex. I don't go there any more.

"Cassie, you've had a rough ride, now you're fighting back, it's quite normal," she tells me.

"I know, but sometimes I frighten myself."

"That's only to be expected, it's a whole new ball game for you," she smiles.

I know where she's coming from. My ticket to Trifletown was purchased by all those 'takers' who drained me dry and sucked all the strength out of me. She taught me the defence mechanisms to protect myself. Only trouble is, I now bear a striking resemblance to Mike Tyson with toothache. This is what I want to get across. How do I find a happy medium?

"Where do you draw the line?" I ask her "Before I get arrested for punching someone's lights out." She laughs again, throwing her head back against the chair.

"You'd never go that far," she giggles.

"Oh but I would! I swear, I have no idea where all this anger is coming from, it's not like me."

"Exactly! Think about what you just said, you're a new person."

"But not necessarily a better one," I protest. She shakes her head and writes something else in her book. 'Schizophrenia' probably.

"Would you like to go back to how you were before, exhausted and drowning in other people's problems?" she whispers.

"Hell no!"

"Well then, accept that you have moved on and this is the new you."

"Okay, point taken."

"Good."

"Bit like a makeover?" I ask her.

"Yes quite."

"Only a mental makeover."

"Mm.."

I'm grasping the concept now but I'm still not sure I'll ever get used to the new me. The old me was gentle and compassionate and caring. This new model is up for a rumble at the slightest provocation.

"You're learning to say no, and to mean it," she says "That's the hard part."

"What... the 'NO' is a complete sentence thing?"

"Absolutely."

I wish I'd met Tilly years ago. It would have saved me a lifetime of grief. Now if someone dares to push me into something I really don't want to do, I fight back. I no longer have the word 'Victim' painted on my forehead.

"It's been proven in America you know."

"Sorry, what?" she asks puzzled.

"This victim theory. If you behave like a victim, people will treat you as one."

"Quite right."

"So in the unlikely event that I should find myself lost in the Bronx, I'm supposed to walk tall and look people right in the eye?" I laugh.

"Something like that."

"I think I'd rather lie in the gutter and pretend to be dead," I tell her.

"Then you would get robbed," she smiles.

Her bleeper suddenly goes off and the noise makes us both jump momentarily.

"Excuse me, I have to go and deal with an emergency. Sit for a while and think about what we've been discussing. No rush," she tells me, making her way out of the door.

Odd how that tiny word 'NO' has changed my entire life. A dinky little word like that and it carries so much weight. Stress is a killer see. We all know that but we seem to think it will never happen to us. You never actually read of anyone dying of stress do you.

'JOHN JONES... BELOVED HUSBAND AND FATHER... DIED OF STRESS SUDDENLY AT THE WEEKEND... WILL BE SADLY MISSED BY HIS WIFE AND FAMILY.

Of course they'll say it was a heart attack or something but odds on it was bought on by stress. We all need a certain amount of stress and adrenalin to survive of course but I had got to the point where I couldn't function properly. When you reach a point where you can't tie your own shoelaces it's time to take stock. Or switch to wearing slippers.

I'd better make a move. I feel a bit silly sitting here on my own. I wonder what the emergency is? First time I've known Tilly to dash off somewhere during a session.

As I reach reception, there appears to be a full scale war going on. I can hear lots of raised voices coming from the recreation room and the air is ripe with expletives. Some of the visitors here are long-term psychiatric patients, which is why I carry a pepper spray and a truncheon concealed in my trousers.

"Fucking did!" one voice shouts angrily.

"Fucking did not you bastard!" If this get's heavy, I might be called upon to head butt somebody. Tilly's only a little slip of a thing. Better hang around and see what happens.

"Come on now, cool it!" she says, her voice firm but not aggressive.

"Tell that bastard to give it back then!"

"Fuck you!" comes the charming reply.

I should really leave, this is not a place for voyeurs, but I'm strangely drawn to the fracas, curious yet scared at the same time. What if it all kicks off and I end up grappling with one of them. Both male by the sound of it. I couldn't stand by and see Tilly get hurt.

"Enough now! Whoever has it, give it to me, at once!" she yells at the top of her voice.

I need to get a look, and slowly poke my head around the edge of the open door. Tilly is standing defiantly in between two enormous men, both at least six feet tall and built for bother. She's got some balls that girl, I have to say.

One guy is a Rastafarian, dreadlocks cascading down across his back. He's enormous and has a scar of some description, etched into the skin on his cheek. Blimey Tilly, careful girl, even I'd have second thoughts about taking him on.

The other one's not tiny either. Same height but a bit leaner. The fact that he has the word 'SKIN' tattooed on his neck doesn't appear to bother her in the least. Nor the swear words etched in ink on his knuckles.

Well, I'm here now. Can't do a runner just because they're bigger then me. Tilly seems to be fronting it out.

"Now!" she bawls again, only this time with feeling. They must know she means business because they back off. The skinhead reaches into his trouser pocket and for a minute I expect him to produce a knife. Instead, he pulls out a tiny little playing card and hands it sheepishly to Tilly.

"There! Now, you can have Mr Bun The Baker back and stop being so silly!" she snaps, handing the card to the Rastafarian.

You have to laugh don't you? Two grown men about to murder each other over a game of Happy Families. Makes my problems look incidental really. I'll leave her to it. She can obviously look after herself.

I tiptoe past the doorway and into reception. The Gatekeeper is watching me and pretending she hasn't seen that I'm waiting to leave. That's cool. Two can play at that game. After a good few minutes, she finally deigns to unlock the main door, but as she does, I pretend to change my mind and amble over to the noticeboard instead. I can feel her eyes burning holes in my back as I linger deliberately by the board, pretending to read the leaflets on display.

"Are you coming or going?" she finally snaps, after a few minutes.

"Good question," I laugh, wafting past and out into the fresh air.

CHAPTER TWENTY-TWO

Give us a Clue

"Rice pudding?"

"No."

"Tinned potatoes?"

"Er... no."

"Powdered milk?"

"Silly!"

Yet another round of guess the shopping with Mary. She's been home for a week and seems even more vague since her spell in hospital. I'm not sure if it's the bang on the head she received from the fall, or the onset of Alzheimer's. She's always been vague, for as long as I can remember, but lately seems incapable of recalling the names of things. Everyday things that should trip off the tongue completely evade her. Writing a shopping list invariably ends up with us playing this exhausting guessing game. Whatever it is that she wants, it's white and comes in a tin. The possibilities are endless and I'm running out of ideas.

"Tinned pears?"

"Yuk!"

I can't help but smile at the expression of disgust on her face. Mary's not a tinned pears sort of person. I should know that by now. Fresh is best. It's a generation thing, people like Mary never take the easy option. None of that open a tin and slap it in a dish. Ma's the same. If it doesn't involve lot's of preparation and sweat, it's not worth eating.

"Chicken soup!" I cry, thinking I've finally hit the jackpot.

"Cat piddle!" she snorts in disgust.

How stupid of me! To Mary, chicken soup is a ritual involving a chicken carcass, lots of fresh vegetables, and three days simmering on the stove. She really does remind me of my Gran, on Pa's side. Thirteen kids she raised on the princely sum of roughly 7s/11d a week in old money.

My Gran could make a lamb bone last for a week, and still have enough left for the dog. Now that's Girl Power!

"Got it!" she yells, a light finally coming on inside her fuddled head, "Dulux Emulsion!"

"Pardon?"

"Emulsion, a large tin please, I want to freshen up the downstairs loo," she grins. Problem solved then. It will mean a detour to B&Q but there you go.

"Got that, anything else?"

"Just the usual," she smiles, delighted that her brain has finally kicked into gear.

The usual being five one-pound bags of jelly babies and sixteen bags of sugar I suppose. Yet another aspect of having lived through the war. An overwhelming need to stockpile things in case the Germans invade Birmingham during the night. Mary's larder is cracking under the weight of her supplies. I have never seen so many bags of sugar and packets of Andrex. If war does break out, I shall know where to come for a cup of tea and a wee.

"You look tired Mary, sure you're feeling okay?"

"Fine love, glad to be home," she sighs.

"Did they look after you in hospital?"

"Bugger's woke me up at six every morning with a cup of cold tea," she snorts in disgust.

"Oh dear."

"Call that a cup of tea! Bet they used one tea bag for the whole ward," she moans.

"Never mind, you're home now."

I can see that she really is tired. Her eyes are drooping as she sits in the chair by the fire, an unopened bag of jelly babies on her lap.

"I'll go Mary, let you have a nap," I whisper.

"No, stay and have a natter. I've missed our little chats," she yawns.

"Nothing much has been happening while you've been away. Pete's still pissed."

"Daft bugger!"

"And Bolak's as batty as ever."

"Her walls collapsed you knos," she suddenly pipes up.

"Who, Bolak?"

"No silly, that woman in the bed next to me, at the hospital."

She's obviously confused. Maybe I should ring the district nurse and have a word.

"Collapsed, bang, just like that, she was in the theatre for hours," she tells me. This is getting more bizarre by the minute. Somebody's wall collapsed and they took her to the theatre? Perhaps it's the tablets she's on.

"Sorry Mary I'm not with you."

"That woman, ginger hair, lipstick. Her vagina walls collapsed!" she shouts, as if I'm thick.

Realisation dawns that she's talking about some poor soul on the ward. I remember now, she did have ginger hair and shocking red lipstick. Bingo!

"Wouldn't credit it would you, your vagina collapsing," she giggles.

"No quite."

"Should have called in the builders!" she roars, rocking with laughter.

This is one of the reasons why Mary and I get along so well. We both share the same sick sense of humour. She may be old and fuddled but the spark's still there.

"Mary! That's awful!" I laugh.

"I know, so was that red hair."

"Enough!" She's chuckling to herself, her face pink and blotchy with the effort.

"And that bloke who came to visit her every night, bit rough that one!" she laughs.

"Mary!"

"He was... All dentures and dandruff... kept fiddling with his privates!"

"No wonder her vagina collapsed," I shriek. She roars at this one and leans back in her chair, her head shaking with glee.

"Now stop it, you'll have a cardiac!" I warn her. The effort seems to have exhausted her, so I grab the list and make my excuses.

"Gotta go Mary, I'll drop this back later."

"Thanks love."

As I get to the lounge door, she's already asleep, her mouth wide open, teeth slipping forward in freefall. No doubt she's dreaming about walls collapsing and men fiddling with their private's. She once confided in me that she and her late husband, Joe, only ever had sex on a Sunday. Came right out with it over a Mr Kipling Country Slice! I was gobsmacked and roared with laughter. It's the way she said it. As if it was the most natural thing in the world to say to a visitor.

"Never in the week," she said "Sunday night... before the London Palladium started."

I was at a loss as to how to respond, but she hit me with another cracker before I could speak.

"He was never much good in that department, one cough and it was all over," she informed me. Poor Joe! Considering she gave birth to seven children, I can only imagine he suffered from severe bronchitis.

I blame daytime television. She was watching one of those awful chat shows at the time. Something about having sex with your cousins, and your pet chicken, or another equally ridiculous topic.

Chat shows or cookery. That seems to be the limit of television schedules during the day. Scandal or scones? Can't Cook Won't Cook, who gives a fuck? Certainly not me. I could quite easily put my boot through the set when they start spouting that rubbish.

"Take a large jar of saffron and four quails eggs."

What bollocks! Saffron's about a hundred squid an ounce and as for the quails eggs, well really! I have a much better idea. Take a pound coin, go to the chippy, get a pig's portion, few rounds of bread and butter, delicious?

I have my own idea for a fabulous new television show. Take that posh totty, the one with a pound of plums in her gob, you know, off that wine show. Well, take her... drop her off at a bar in Glasgow and see how long it takes before somebody head butts her.

"And you kind sir, what do you think of this cheeky little Chardonnay?"

I'd pay good money to watch that. But then again, I'm not a well balanced individual am I?

"Penny for them?"

"Sorry, I was just thinking about Mary and Joe, you know... the London Palladium."

"I'd rather not go there if you don't mind," Jack grimaces.

""I've got her shopping list, it's a bit bizarre."

"So what else is new?"

"No cellulite batteries today."

"That's a relief."

Our weekly trips to the supermarket are becoming more and more chaotic. Apart from our own groceries, we shop for Mary, Pete if he's incapable, and Jack's mother. People must think we're incredibly greedy with two trolleys and a hand-basket. What used to be a half hour task has now turned into an entire evening, with both of us dodging down different aisles, searching for various items.

"Thought you were making a list of your plus points," he laughs.

"I was, but I didn't get very far."

"Why not?"

"I had the paper and the pen but…"

"Yes?"

"I made an Admiral Nelson hat and some paper dollies."

"Fair enough," he laughs.

He should laugh! Standing in the kitchen in his new golf shoes and just a pair of Calvin Klein underpants. He's just stepped out of the shower. Some ding bat at the club told him the best way to break in new shoes is to walk around in them when your feet are wet.

"That look should create a stir on the driving range."

"Might start a new trend, get away from the plus fours and Pringle jumpers," he grins.

"Bit cold in the winter."

"This is the summer collection silly, in winter I shall wear gloves as well."

This obsession with little white balls and a bag full of sticks fascinates me. Was it Oscar Wilde who said golf is a good walk ruined or something? Could have been Nelson Mandela, what do I know? Probably because I'm not into sports. I have tried, but I've got no co-ordination. And no desire whatsoever to become a team-player.

"Are you going shopping dressed like that?"

"And why not?"

"I can think of three reasons, your legs and your lunchbox."

"That's five."

"Idiot!"

"I'll have you know these pants are specially reinforced to carry the bulk," he laughs.

"In your dreams."

He cares not a jot, and continues to squelch around in his new Nike shoes. The stud things on the bottom making indentations in the carpet as he walks.

"What time do you want to go?" he asks, practising his swing with the mop.

"Later, I've got that list to do."

Better start again, and no paper hats this time. Might as well look as if I mean business, even if I don't. Yet another task set by Tilly. A list of all my positive points. This could take a while. He can see I'm struggling and grins at me encouragingly.

"Can I ask why you feel you need to do this?" he asks, swiping an imaginary ball into the air.

"What?"

"This relentless quest for work, there's no need, I keep telling you."

"It's supposed to make me feel better about myself. Channel my energy into finding a job."

"Why?"

"Because, I see you getting poorer by the second, and it bothers me."

"We can go to the workhouse together," he laughs.

"They closed them all, years ago."

"Alright then, the bankruptcy court." Silly sod! It's impossible to have a serious conversation with him when he's half naked.

"You worry too much woman, you can pay me back in kind," he leers.

"That'd take me a million years at fifty-pence a go."

"That's a bit excessive. I was thinking more along the lines of ten-pence."

"Am I that good?"

"Let's just say cross hooker off your list of prospective jobs."

He always does this. Manages to make me giggle when I'm trying to be serious. I really do worry though, about his diminishing savings. Every month when his bank statement plops onto the mat, I seriously fear for his blood pressure.

"Besides, who'll do all the jobs around the house if you go back to work?" he asks.

"What jobs?"

"Well, you made a nice job of digging up that patch at the bottom of the garden."

"The dog did that."

"Oh," he's thinking now, trying to boost my confidence by pointing out the good things I've done.

"Okay, what about all those lovely decorations you made last Christmas."

"They caught fire," I remind him.

"It was only a small fire."

Bless him. He's doing his best.

"You haven't burnt a shirt in ages," he says encouragingly.

"Cos I haven't done any ironing in ages."

It's at times like this, I am eternally grateful for his unwavering support. He lives with a total loon but never complains. Well, not to me anyway. He probably rings the Samaritans on a daily basis for all I know.

"Forget the list, let's hit the supermarket," he grins.

"Only if you put your trousers on."

"Do I have to?"

"Yes."

"Okay."

CHAPTER TWENTY-THREE

Laughter is the Best Medicine

Alicia's looking particularly smart today. Must be on a promise. She's discarded her tweed skirt and Hush Puppies for a sassy little suit. Marks and Spencer's by the look of it. Navy with gold embossed buttons on the jacket. The sort of suit you'd wear to a Bar Mitzvah. Classy but safe. Be pointless me investing in a suit like that. I don't know any Jewish people.

Alan's late. God, I hope he turns up or it's just me and the suit. Tilly may be forced to intervene and break up a fist-fight if she starts again with me. She's got a bag to match as well. Navy leather with a gold clasp. I don't do handbags. The only essentials I ever need to carry on me are my fags and a lighter. Come to think of it, I don't do frocks either. Classy or otherwise. My legs haven't seen fresh air since we went to Feurteventura three years ago.

"We'll give Alan another few minutes, then get started," Tilly says, flicking through her notes. Alicia's obviously taken this co-ordination thing too far. The varicose veins on her legs are the exact same colour as the outfit. I wonder if she suffers with piles? Well, it's the same thing, veins, only in a more delicate area. I shouldn't think so, not with all that organic food she eats. Pulses and lentils and rye bread.

She's a vegetarian. Made a point of telling us all at the first session. Which is fine, as long as you don't try to ram your theories down other people's throats. I think she said it to wind me up 'cos I was eating a Big Mac at the time.

"Have you ladies done your tasks?" Tilly asks. We nod in agreement with Alicia rooting around in her handbag for her notebook. I'd love to get a look inside that book. She jots down all her thoughts for the day in it apparently. Something else she told us at the first session. Her journal she calls it. Bet that would make for a good read. Although I doubt if Jackie Collins has much to worry about. Monday: Went to the library. Had banana for lunch. Tuesday. Finished crossword in Guardian. Had nut loaf for dinner. Wednesday. Smoked a spliff and shagged the vicar.

"Sorry I'm late, I was in the launderette and the spin-dryer broke." Alan! Thank goodness, for a minute I thought it was going to be just me and Clara Carrotcake.

"Not to worry, take a seat," Tilly smiles.

"Me pants are still soaking," he moans, flopping down onto a chair.

He has one of those stripy, laundry bags with him and drops it clumsily at Alicia's feet. The prospect of coming into close contact with Alan's damp pants rattles her, and she moves her chair back in horror. She has the look of a woman who's never had to wash a man's pants. You can always tell.

"Now, let's make a start shall we? Any thoughts on last week's task?" The task in question was to try something new. Something none of us had ever experienced before. Quite tricky when you think about it. I suppose when you're middle-aged you've seen and done most things. Alan's a bit younger, mid thirties I should think. Difficult to tell.

"Who'd like to go first?" Tilly asks, scanning our faces for a response. I adopt my usual technique of avoiding eye contact and anyway, Clara will start spouting at any second. That's a sure fire bet if ever I heard one.

"I will!" she yelps, shoving her hand into the air as if we were in school.

"Lovely Alicia, tell us what you've experienced then."

"Well, it's something I wouldn't normally dream of doing," she gushes excitedly "… on Tuesday I tried one of those Magnum ice-creams." Do what? You fuckwit! If that's your idea of a new experience, you're sadder than I thought.

"Oh," is all Tilly can manage, looking quite dumbfounded.

"I usually try to avoid over indulgence, but it was an experiment after all," she beams. Over indulgence? Which planet are you living on woman! If you'd said you ate a whole box of Magnum's while running round the park naked, that would have been an experience. Silly tart!

"Bit pricey but it was well worth it," she waffles. Yes, I bet that knocked a hole in your savings account. Have to turn the central heating down a notch to make up for that one. Must be all of ninety-nine pence.

"Good, so it was an experience you tried and enjoyed?" Tilly asks, getting back to the point.

"Yes, definitely."

I am completely lost for words and my face says it all. I can tell by the way Tilly is looking at me. A sort of a bemused yet amused expression.

"And you Cassie, how about you?" she asks, turning to me.

"I went to a CBSO concert, at the Symphony Hall. Jack took me. It was excellent."

"Lovely!" Tilly beams excitedly, nodding her head.

"Wouldn't have thought you were into classical music," Alicia pipes up sarcastically.

I should have known. She looks at me and sees the blonde hair and the tits and thinks, half a pint of lager and Abba. She thinks wrong. I adore classical music and probably know more about Mozart than she ever will.

"Thought wrong then didn't you?" I smile back, daring her to pursue it. She doesn't. Which is a good sign really. She's finally learning that I will not be intimidated by her plummy accent and patronising looks. Pity it's taken so long for the penny to drop.

"So Cassie, it was an experience you'd repeat?" Tilly asks.

"Absolutely!"

"Good, you see, there's no need to be afraid of new things. We have to experiment in order to learn about ourselves," she smiles. Absolutely! Alicia has learnt that a Magnum costs nearly a quid. Bet that came as a shock.

"And Alan, how about you?" He's fiddling with the flies on his crimplene trousers. I think they're broke and he's trying to hide the fact by tucking his jumper in. Poor lad. I do wish somebody would take him in hand.

"I had sex, with Tracey," he suddenly blurts out, as if glad to get it off his chest. Blimey! Somebody has taken him in hand. Tracey by the sound of it.

We are all gobsmacked by his confession and the silence is audible as we struggle to come to terms with what he's just said. Alicia looks horrified and I have a feeling she may vomit at any minute. Tilly is visibly stunned and just stares at him as if he's grown another head. Me, I'm dying to laugh but I daren't. Laughter at this crucial moment could make him impotent for life.

"Er... right Alan... I er..." Tilly splutters.

"It was bostin!" he grins "first time for me."

Alicia is about to lose the contents of her stomach and I have to bite on my lower lip to remain in control. Whoever said it was quite right, laughter is the best medicine.

"So Alan... it was..." Tilly butts in.

"Round the back of Kwik-Save... she collects the trolleys," he cuts in. Tilly is floundering which is a first I have to say. I've never seen her so aghast, but then again it's not every day you get to hear all about some bloke popping his cherry round the back of Kwik-Save is it?

"Thank you Alan!" she finally shouts, stopping him in mid-flow.

It takes a minute or two before she regains control enough to carry on. When she does, her face is blotchy and pink with embarrassment.

"Okay then, so you've all tried something new and enjoyed the experience?" she quivers.

"That oral's a bit naff though..." Alan butts in again.

"Alan!" she bawls at the top of her voice, losing control.

I have lost the plot completely now and am hanging on by a thread. One more detail and I shall go over the edge I swear.

"Well really!" Alicia sighs indignantly, wiping a bead of sweat off her forehead. Probably jealous. I suspect her cherry is still intact, and will remain that way for ever. Who'd want to shag a trout-face with sensible shoes?

"Okay everyone, let's take a few deep breaths shall we, find our inner space," Tilly urges.

I am glad of the excuse to close my eyes and blank out the mental image of Alan humping Tracey in the trolley park. Bless that boy! You have to admit though, he does take these tasks seriously. We remain in total silence for a good few minutes, waiting for Tilly to begin again.

"I have a new exercise for you. I think you'll enjoy this," she suddenly tells us. It will have to be a cracker to beat the last one, I think to myself.

"Imagine you could invite someone to dinner, absolutely anyone," she trills "Past or present... dead or alive... who would you invite?" Nice one Tilly! I like tasks like this. Get's the old grey matter ticking over a bit for a change.

"Any thoughts?" she asks, looking to me for inspiration.

I am just about to open my mouth to speak when Clara Cheesecake butts in,

"Margaret Thatcher!" she booms at the top of her voice, "I'd invite Margaret Thatcher!" Oh quelle surprise! A trout face and a Tory. I should have known.

"What a wonderful opportunity that would be!" she gushes, getting far too excited for my liking.

"Interesting choice Alicia," Tilly smiles, making notes in her book. Probably writing 'Twat' if she's got any sense. "And you Cassie, any idea's?"

"Charles Dickens," I tell her without any hesitation, "That would be my choice."

"That's good, any particular reason?

"Mm, I adore his work and I'd love the chance to chat to him."

"Excellent."

Alan is still fiddling with his flies and has pulled a corner of the jumper through the zip now.

"Alan?"

"Jason Philips," he suddenly pipes up, smiling at Tilly.

"Sorry who?"

"Jason Philips, he lives in the flat downstairs."

"Oh for God's sake!" Alicia snaps, shuffling about in her chair with rage.

"Tilly said we could ask anybody!" he protests.

"She means someone famous you idiot!"

"She never said famous, did you Tilly?" he asks, hoping for some support under this barrage of abuse from Alicia.

"Quite Alan, perhaps I should have made myself more clear," Tilly whispers.

"Anybody she said, dead or alive," he mumbles, looking embarrassed.

"Yes Alan, it's okay, if that's your choice then fine," she reassures him.

It's on days like this that I feel glad to be alive. And eternally grateful for these sessions. Now I know what the director was aiming for in 'One Flew Over The Cuckoo's Nest'.

"Why would you invite Jason?" she asks him gently.

"Cos he's got a microwave, I could do one of them Findus Fish Pies."

"God save us all!" Alicia rants, losing the plot completely.

"Alicia please!" Tilly shouts, pulling her back into line. Alicia closes her gaping gob pretty smartish It's most unusual for Tilly to snap like that. To be perfectly honest, I'm amazed she keeps her cool so well with us lot babbling on.

"So that's Margaret Thatcher… Charles Dickens and Jason… er…"

"Philips," Alan reminds her.

"Yes, Jason Philips, of course."

"I wonder what's in a fish pie?" he suddenly pipes up.

"Fish you moron!" Alicia snaps, far too rudely for my liking.

"Alicia!" Tilly tells her again, exasperated by it all.

"I think it's a mixture of different fish Alan," I tell him, trying to regain order on her behalf.

"Oh right."

"Different cuts you know, cod and haddock."

"No fish fingers then?" he asks in all innocence.

"I don't think so," I giggle.

Oh Lord please don't let me die before I get chance to relate all this to Jack. Please?

"Well, I think that's enough for today, thanks everyone," Tilly sighs, heading for a breakdown.

"Any tasks for next week?" Alicia snaps, desperate to get away.

"Oh sorry, yes, I'd like you to bring along something that's important to you."

"Eh?" Alan asks, looking perplexed.

"Something that means a lot to you Alan," she tells him

"Oh right," he mumbles, picking up his laundry bag.

"Bye everyone!"

We file out in silence, with Alan dragging his damp pants along the floor behind him. I have to say, on my part, I'm thrilled that he's finally coming out of his shell at last. This is a very different Alan to the one who shuffled into that first session over a year ago. The therapy's working for him and I'm glad. I'm glad and I'm excited about the prospect of what next week's session will bring. I just know he's going to bring Tracey along.

Alicia's got a new car I see. Probably bought it out of the interest on her shares. Nippy little number, one of those Citroen things with a Save The Whale sticker in the back window. She'll be familiar with Greenpeace. Bet they picked her up last time she was swimming off the Welsh coast. Easy mistake to make. Alicia and a hump-back.

She zooms past me at speed, almost causing me to dive into the bushes for cover. That's cool. Tilly says she's been seeing some of her patients for years. Plenty of time for me to get Alicia back. And trust me... I will.

Pete and Gabriel are having a party. The music's been blaring for a while now and it's getting late. Not that we mind, Jack and I have spent the last hour sitting on the patio, roaring at their antics. It's a very select party. Just the two of them and several hundred cans of Special Brew. At this very moment, they're jigging around on the lawn to the Darren Hayes CD, Insatiable. The Radio Edit mix. I know it well, Pete borrowed it off me earlier. Catchy beat. The sort of music kids would dance to at Manumission in Ibiza. Pete obviously believes he is in Ibiza. He's wearing a pair of Lycra cycling shorts in electric blue and a knitted bobble hat. Gabriel is accompanying him on the banjo. And I'm the one in therapy!